Undercover Love

ANNETTE MORI

ALSO BY ANNETTE MORI

SINGLE STORIES
Compound Interest
Georgetown Glen
Artist Free Zone
Disconnected
The Others
Sculpting Her Heart
One Shot at Love
The Panty Thief
Pleasure Workers
A Window to Love
The Book Witch
The Book Addict
The Dream Catcher
Unconventional Lovers
Captivated
The Termination
The Review
The Thanksgiving Baby Caper
The Ultimate Betrayal
Locked Inside
Out of This World
Asset Management
The Incredibly True Adventure of Two Elves in Love
(Affinity 2014 Christmas Collection)
Love Forever, Live Forever
The True Story of Valentine's Day
Vampire Pussy...Cat
Nicky's Christmas Miracle X3
(It's in Her Kiss, Affinity's Charity Anthology)
Donner Junior Saves the Day

Co-authored
The Organization with Erin O'Reilly

Co-authored with Ali Spooner
Heart Strings Attached
Free to Love
Trouble in Paradise

UNDERCOVER LOVE

ANNETTE MORI

Affinity
Rainbow Publications

2023

Undercover Love
© 2023 by Annette Mori

Affinity E-Book Press NZ LTD
Canterbury, New Zealand

1st Edition

ISBN: 978-1-99-104008-4 (paperback)

Editor: Angela Koenig
Proof Editor: Alexis Smith
Cover Design: Irish Dragon Design
Production Design: Affinity Publication Services

ACKNOWLEDGMENTS

A huge thank you to all of my beta readers who made brilliant suggestions to improve the initial draft: Ali Spooner, Carrie Camp, Dana Holmes, and Danna Micoletti. I would also like to express my gratitude to Affinity Rainbow Publications—JM Dragon and Nancy Kaufman—who continue to provide feedback to tighten up manuscripts that need help and publish my unconventional work. I am eternally grateful for the opportunities they give me to let my stories see the light of day. Thanks to Angie for her magic as the final editor to further tighten the story. She is a delight to work with. Inevitably, those pesky errors slip through, and I am thankful that Alexis Smith, the final proof editor, caught those before the book went to print. Thanks to Nancy Kaufman for the final cover. A huge thanks to all the other readers and fellow writers who have sent personal emails, written reviews, and posted nice things on Facebook (you know who you are). The Affinity authors are an incredibly supportive group and often share posts or send words of encouragement. Finally, my wife, Jody, continues her support even when it interferes with our time.

DEDICATION

To all the powerful men and women who work to keep our country from becoming a hotbed of extremist views, and may we all prevail during these scary times. And to my beautiful wife as always.

TABLE OF CONTENTS

Prologue   1
Chapter One   4
Chapter Two   19
Chapter Three   33
Chapter Four   42
Chapter Five   50
Chapter Six   64
Chapter Seven   72
Chapter Eight   80
Chapter Nine   85
Chapter Ten   104
Chapter Eleven   119
Chapter Twelve   137
Chapter Thirteen   149
Chapter Fourteen   160
Chapter Fifteen   178
Chapter Sixteen   190
Chapter Seventeen   201
Chapter Eighteen   209
Chapter Nineteen   223
Chapter Twenty   239
Chapter Twenty-one   246
Chapter Twenty-two   254
Chapter Twenty-three   266
Chapter Twenty-four   289
Chapter Twenty-five   297
Chapter Twenty-six   311
About the Author   319
Other Affinity Books   320

PROLOGUE

Twenty-Five Years Earlier

Jimena tried to keep up with Emma, but Jimena's short, stout stature was no match for Emma's long legs. Everything about her best friend was the polar opposite. Jimena sighed and watched her best friend's golden hair blow in the wind. Unlike Jimena's long, dark hair, Em always kept her hair too short for a ponytail. Pumping harder on her pedals, she narrowed the gap and skidded to a stop shortly after Em jumped from her bike and started locking it against the bike rack.

Em squinted against the sun, smiling broadly at Jimena, still huffing from the exertion. Today, Em's eyes were almost sky blue. That meant she was happy. After spending so much time with Em, Jimena could tell when she was having a good day. When they turned a stormy gray or the color of her father's gun, Jimena knew things at home had gotten out of control. She loved how Em's eyes changed color with her moods, unlike her own eyes, which were the color of poo. Em would tell Jimena to stop being a ninny because brown was the best eye color in the universe and everyone knew that. Em always told her how much she loved Jimena's eyes, and she wished she had eyes the color of milk chocolate, warm and comforting.

"Dad said you aren't supposed to ride to the beach anymore," Karl, Em's younger brother, said between breaths. He puffed even more than Jimena after coming to a stop in front of his sister.

"Shut up, you little twerp. If you tell Dad, I'm gonna pound you harder than he beats me."

"Let me play with you, and I won't tell," he offered.

Em rolled her eyes. "Fine. We're playing cops and robbers. I'll be the cop."

"I don't wanna be the robber. You always get to be the cop," he whined.

Jimena didn't want to be the robber, either. She hated being the robber. She wanted to be a cop like her papa, even though people said that Border Patrol weren't real police.

"Tough. Jimena and I are always the cops. If you wanna play, you gotta be the robber." Em folded her arms across her chest, and her eyes turned a stormy gray.

Karl placed his hands on his hips and glared at his sister. "Dad says that only dirty Mexicans are robbers, so Jimena has to be the robber."

Em pushed Karl hard, and he landed on the sidewalk. "Don't you ever say that again, or I'll make you pay."

Karl began crying and, through his tears, yelled, "I'm telling Dad."

"I'll be the robber," Jimena said, her voice barely a whisper, but apparently, Em heard her offer.

"You don't have to. Karl is just a baby. I'm not scared of him telling. I'll take my whipping. It's okay." Em shrugged like it wasn't a big deal, but Jimena had seen the marks before, and they looked awful.

"I'll tell about you playing with Jimena, too. Then you'll surely get a whipping. He told you not to play with Jimena anymore cause she's a dirty Mexican who will rob you the first chance she gets." Karl stopped crying, narrowing his eyes as he made the threat.

Em smirked. "I thought you wanted Jimena to play with us and be the robber. You'll just be telling on yourself, then." Leaning in, Em whispered in Jimena's ear, "You can pretend to be a robber, but really be like undercover or something, and then we'll make Karl be a dirty cop."

Jimena giggled. She liked when Em came up with a good plan. "If you promise not to tell, I'll be the robber."

CHAPTER ONE

Present Day

The incessant buzzing on her nightstand finally woke Emma Schmidt. She picked up the phone with the blue case, registering it was her boss since the phone with the red case remained silent. She chanced a glance at her girlfriend. Yeah, clearly pissed. Those stormy hazel eyes were a telltale sign. Grabbing her phone, she offered an apologetic shrug. The end was near. She was sure of it. Everyone claimed to understand her work meant she might have to leave for several weeks at a moment's notice. Her to-go bag was always ready in the corner of her bedroom. She still had high hopes for Gabriel. After all, they both worked for the FBI.

Gaby was in communications, but she knew everything about the missions that Em would take on because she had the highest clearance. Of course, that didn't stop Gaby's irritation every time Em volunteered for another undercover assignment. This one was particularly perilous because this group was full-on bat-shit fringe.

Gaby had lost her passion for medicine several years ago and made a surprising pivot to an entirely different career path. Em never got the complete story of why she'd left healthcare, and Em never bothered to push for details. Nevertheless, it seemed to suit both of them.

"Schmidt," she answered.

"Chatter on the web is loud. What have you learned?" Adam Carter, her boss, asked.

"Nothing yet," Em growled. "Apparently, having an in because of my asshole father doesn't replace the lack of a dick."

"So graphic." Carter sighed on the other end of the line. "Well, shit, maybe we should pack it in and try another agent."

"Just give me a little more time. I think I'm gaining their trust. I want to throw up in my mouth every time I spout all that neo-Nazi shit, but I'm managing. Thanks for the newest conspiracy crap. I believe that's been the ticket to a friendlier reaction. It's either that or they like looking at my tits."

"You need to find out their plans before they take out the governor. And I want the name of the top guy," Carter instructed.

"Understood. Give me a week."

"You may not have a week. Two days or we're sending in a special team and breaking up their little coffee klatch. I'd rather wait to get the top dog, but I'm not willing to risk the governor's life to get my man. She's tight with the president, and if they succeed, all our careers go up in a puff of smoke."

"It's a lot more than a little coffee klatch. They're armed to the teeth. They have enough firepower to take out the entire state of California."

"Don't you lecture me, Schmidt."

"Sorry, sir." Em glanced at her nightstand when the red phone rang. "Hey, gotta run. My other phone is ringing. Maybe we caught a break, and they're finally going to let me inside."

Without saying goodbye, Em pressed the end call button and picked up her other phone. She rearranged her body on the bed and tried to readjust her voice to sound like the call had just awoken her. "Hello."

"We caught one, Schmidt. Get down to the warehouse because we're giving you the honor of taking care of the dirty wetback."

Em cringed. This recent development wasn't good. No, not at all good. She knew the group was capable of a lot, including cold-blooded murder. How in the hell would she navigate the situation without breaking her cover? *Shit, fuck,* and every other swear word she could think of rolled around in her head. "I'll be there in thirty. Don't do anything. I want in on whatever you have planned."

"Your dad would be so proud. Okay, we'll hold off on the other stuff, but we might get a head start on things that wouldn't interest you. She's a pretty little thing."

Em's stomach twisted into knots as her adrenaline kicked in. She needed to get there pronto before they gang-raped the poor woman. If she blew through all the lights, she could make it in ten minutes. Em would have to take the chance because knowing what they were about to do spurred her to action.

Quickly slipping into her clothes, Em grabbed her keys and raced out the door, calling over her shoulder, "Emergency, don't wait up."

"I'm not planning to," Gaby answered with venom.

†

Em strode into the dingy warehouse, scanning the scene and quickly assessing the situation. She probably should have called for backup because she wasn't sure how to talk her way out of this one. A woman with long dark hair sat in the folding metal chair left over from whatever business had occupied the abandoned warehouse. Someone had ripped her olive-green T-shirt. Em's bet was on Petey, who held his crotch. *Good, the woman had fought back.* Darnell wiped at the blood on his nose. The red liquid streamed freely down his face and was probably due to a well-placed head butt since they had secured the woman's arms behind her back with zip ties. The dumbasses hadn't thought to bind her legs, which was probably why Petey held his nuts and grimaced in pain. That would have interfered with the *fun* they had planned for her.

Squinting her eyes at the woman, a sudden realization came to her. *Aw shit.* The woman wore a Border Patrol field uniform. Before she approached the two men and their kidnapped victim, she pulled her phone from her pocket and quickly hit the record button. If things went down the way she suspected they would, she'd need proof of the force required to subdue the situation and save the Border Patrol Field Agent.

Gathering all the bravado she could muster for this ticking time bomb, she approached. Glaring at the two men, she stated with surprising calm, "You dumb shits, that's a Border Patrol Agent you have tied to that chair."

"No, she's not," Petey declared. "The dirty Mexican probably stole it off a real agent. It doesn't even fit her right. Besides, I ain't ever seen no woman Border Patrol Agent. She's here to have babies so they can suck our system dry. We can't send back babies born in the US." Petey spat on the ground.

"Did you check her pockets for any kind of identification?" Em asked, failing to mask the iciness of her voice.

Both men hung their heads and shook, indicating they hadn't. Darnell brightened and offered, "We'll just torch the bitch like everyone else and remove any evidence. They shouldn't let Mexicans become Border Patrol Agents, especially girls. That's like having the fox watch the henhouse. You wanna light the match? I'll get the gas from my truck and be right back."

Em had suspected that Petey, Darnell, and the rest of the collection of former military vets and disgraced cops were behind the string of burned bodies, but now she had verification. Em came close to the two men and whispered, "Why don't you both go? I want to interrogate her. I think I'll have better luck getting her to talk. First, we need to make sure no one followed you or anything else that might get us caught."

"Good thinking. You sure are a chip off the old block. Smart as a whip, just like your daddy," Petey said.

After the men left, Em squatted in front of the woman, ensuring she looked her in the eye. Those eyes looked so familiar, even with the considerable swelling. The woman's eyes widened as they locked on her own gray eyes. Was that fear or recognition? But Em could not for the life of her pinpoint where she'd seen this woman. She hadn't worked with Border Patrol before, so it couldn't be from work.

"Em?" the woman whispered through her battered mouth. The full, naturally red lips were mesmerizing despite the considerable damage Petey and Darnell had already done to them. She'd taken a beating.

Em shook her head at the sudden realization. Trying to make sense of everything, she quickly pulled the data together in her head. "Jimena?"

Tears escaped from Jimena's eyes. "I don't want to die."

"Ssh. You're not going to die. Listen carefully. We don't have a lot of time. I'm undercover. Follow my lead. I'm going to cut your ties, but keep your hands behind your back until the right moment presents itself."

Jimena nodded.

†

Jimena knew that today would probably be her last day on earth. But, if she had to die, she'd do it fighting until her last breath because there was no way in hell she would let those two poor excuses for men violate her. Her mama always said patience was a virtue. Waiting until she almost gagged from the foul odor of the man with the long unkempt beard, she kicked him as hard as she could in the balls. The other man got close enough for Jimena to see his nose hair, so she head-butted him. From the blood oozing from his nose, she'd definitely scored a direct hit, enough to break his nose. What she hadn't expected was the tall woman with a commanding presence. She did not fit.

When the woman squatted in front of her, she looked into those stormy gray eyes. She knew. Perhaps Em had followed in her father's footsteps after all. That did not bode well for her, but she had to try. Maybe reach out to her and pull the last remaining humanity from the girl she knew so intimately from her past.

There was no time to find out more after Em revealed why she was really here. It wasn't to kill her. They weren't out of the woods yet, but like in their youth, Jimena trusted Em. Em had only once let her down. Granted, that was a pretty big violation, but Jimena didn't believe Em would

10

allow this situation to spiral out of control. A pang of regret sparked inside her because she knew she would cause Em to blow her cover. She must be onto something a lot bigger if Em hadn't already arrested these two. After learning of a string of homicides, Jimena had been scouring the areas where most of the desperate men and women tried to cross. Whoever was targeting the people crossing illegally, they were brutal and indiscriminate. Whole families burned alive. She'd hurled the first time she'd come across a tiny body.

The glee on the men's faces as they brought in two gas cans caused Jimena's stomach to roil. She was about to lose it if she couldn't gain control of her emotions and help Em. The men were enormous. A lot bigger than Em, despite her height. Jimena could usually hold her own, even though she was barely five foot two. However, these men were at least twice her size.

"Did you get anything out of her? Maybe she's the one who's been sniffing around, trying to collect evidence against us. Good thing we caught her, huh?" Darnell said.

Em stood and nodded. "Well, maybe, but she isn't the only one who has been gathering evidence. And you just gave me something to work with that will have you enjoying gay sex in prison for quite a long time."

Darnell's eyes grew. "You're a cop?"

Em shrugged. "Like father, like daughter. Except I took a slightly different route because I'm not a racist piece of shit like my father. May his evil ass never rest in peace."

Petey quickly tipped over his gas can and pulled a lighter from his pocket. The few seconds he took to tease the spark into action gave Em and Jimena enough time to move away from the pool of gas moving in their direction. The fire lapped up the liquid, and Jimena knew it wouldn't be long before the can exploded and ignited the other full container. Darnell had set it down before taking off in a surprisingly fast run.

Em retrieved the gun from her ankle holster and shouted, "Don't make me shoot you or chase your smelly ass. I fucking hate chasing assholes and tackling their stinky ass bodies."

Jimena hesitated for a second before running after the two men. Even with her short stature, she'd been the star of her high school track team. Neither of the men looked like they were in particularly good shape. She'd catch them, eventually. Jimena wasn't sure what she would do when she caught up to them, but she'd worry about that later.

Joining the women's rugby club paid off as Jimena lunged for the smaller of the two and tackled him to the ground. Pulling her knife from her boot, the one they'd failed to check, she shoved the edge to the man's neck and growled, "Please give me a reason to slit your throat." Then, flipping the man over, she punched him in the face. "And that's for tearing my favorite T-shirt. I used fabric softener on this, and now it's ruined."

After hearing a shot, Jimena ventured a side glance and noted how Em had brought down the other man with a well-placed shot to his right leg. She smiled at how efficient Em was in securing the man with the zip ties she must have obtained after ransacking his pockets. He groaned in agony.

"You fucking bitch. You shot me," the man whined.

"I warned you not to run. Now shut the fuck up before I give your other leg another slug." Em grinned at Jimena while leveling the gun at the man. "Hey, you need some help over there?"

"Nah. Unless you have some spare zip ties, I don't think this asshole wants me to slice his throat, so he's super cooperative for now," Jimena said.

Sitting the man up with his hands secured, Em quickly fastened his feet together and commanded, "Stay." She snickered at the man. "Good boy." Strutting over to Jimena, she handed her a fistful of ties.

"Thanks." Jimena's voice softened as she said, "It's good to see you, Em. Been a long time."

Em scratched the back of her neck. "Yeah, it has."

"You two know each other?" the man on the ground asked while Jimena efficiently secured his hands and feet.

"Did I say you could talk? You have the right to remain silent. I suggest you use that right," Jimena snarled.

"Well, fuck. That's three months of my life that I'll never get back," Em lamented as she handed the gun to Jimena. "I need to call my boss and let him know I'm blown. Can you watch these two yahoos while I make the call?"

Em moved out of hearing distance, but before she was too far away, Jimena heard her say, "Schmidt here. I have an update on the situation."

†

Backup arrived soon after Em had made her call, but she didn't look entirely pleased as they took over the scene. Jimena had only a minuscule understanding of how the FBI worked, but she assumed Em hadn't made her move to arrest the two men because the Feds were after someone much higher in the chain of command.

"You need to let a medic check you out, but I can't be here when they arrive because they're tight with the local PD. I'd blow my cover for sure if the paramedics or local police department got a whiff of this undercover operation. The medics can make sure you don't have any serious injuries. Your face looks pretty beat up." Em shifted on her feet. "Sorry I didn't get here sooner. This is one big royal fuck-fest. I probably won't have an ass left after my boss chews it to the bone."

Jimena shrugged. "I'll just grab an ice pack, and it'll be all good. I'm sure it looks much worse than it really is."

"Doubtful, but I know better than to push you to do something you don't want to do." Em shoved her hands in her pockets. "I was so damn close to breaking up this nasty hate cell," Em lamented.

"Hey, maybe you're not blown yet. How long can you hold those two? Homeland security or FBI? Can't you detain them on terrorism charges or something else while you continue to work undercover?" Jimena asked.

Em scrunched her face and answered, "FBI. How did you know?"

"I've worked with you government types before. You have a kind of air about you."

"Good air or foul air? I'd hate to be accused of passing gas or blowing hot air," Em joked.

Leave it to Em to make a joke out of this situation. Jimena shook her head but smiled at her childhood friend. "Mostly good, but sometimes you take over a case, and that pisses me off."

Em chuckled. "Well, you've certainly grown some tits since I last saw you."

"Yeah, well, that happens when a person lets fifteen years pass without a single word."

Em cringed. "Sorry. I was working through some shit. It's not like we lived down the street from one another. He moved us to fucking Idaho. Idaho! Can you imagine me in that backward corner of the world?"

Jimena shrugged. "Oh, I don't know, maybe living in the country would be better than here. Unfortunately, it's got a lot worse since we were kids. The gangs and cartels run everything. The old neighborhood isn't the same."

Shock registered on Em's face. "You still live there?"

"Someone had to take care of Mama after she got sick."

"What about your sisters and brother? You were always a tight-knit family. So I just figured they would all gather around to help."

"Well, my brother is useless with wiping asses and seeing our mother in pain. Manny also followed in Papa's footsteps and became a Border Patrol Agent. He works in a different office, but we see each other about once a month. Rosie moved to New York, and Maria uprooted her family and took them to Chicago. They have their own lives and families. I volunteered, and they happily agreed to let me take the lead. Everyone offered to pitch in for a twenty-four-hour nurse, but I didn't want Mama to feel abandoned."

That soft lilt returned, and Em asked, "How's she doing?"

"She passed six months ago," Jimena answered.

"Oh, Jimena, I'm so sorry. She was a jewel—always fed me when I would run to your house after Dad started drinking and hitting. She was like a second mom to me. More than my mother ever was, but I don't blame her anymore. Besides, what doesn't break you makes you stronger. Isn't that what they always say? And the bastard finally got what he deserved. Blown up by a bomb of his own making."

"I didn't know that, or I would have called to see how you were doing."

"Why would you call? You didn't even know where we'd moved to. It wasn't like I reached out to you."

"Why didn't you?"

"It's complicated. Maybe we can discuss it over a beer or something," Em suggested. "Right after I check in and take my ass chewing like a woman."

"I'd like that. Murphy's is still open. Maybe we can go there."

"No shit? How is that possible? Old man Murphy was like ninety years old when we were kids."

Jimena laughed. "He was not. He was like sixty-five. But he retired, and his granddaughter took over for him."

"Siobhan?" Em asked.

"Yeah."

"She still hot?" Em grinned.

"Oh, yeah, and very married to her smokin' long-term girlfriend. We hang out a lot."

Em raised her eyebrow. "Oh, so still into the ladies?"

Jimena shook her head. "You do know that straight people can have gay friends, right?"

A frown appeared on Em's face, and Jimena decided to set her straight, figuratively. "Not that it's a big deal, but yeah, I do all right with the ladies."

"So, you're, um, taken?" Em hesitantly asked.

"Now, I didn't say that. I haven't clicked with anyone since you left. That doesn't mean I'm not still hopeful, and trying a variety of flavors hasn't exactly been a hardship."

Em threw her head back and laughed with abandon. "Okay, give me a few hours, and I'll meet you at Murphy's. We can have lunch and a beer and catch up. Say one? Will that work for you?"

"Sure. I need to submit my report, too. I was picking through the evidence when those two got the jump on me. Not an impressive look for me either, but if I know my boss, Gary, he'll tell me to take the rest of the day off. Probably the only time sexism will benefit me. He gets uber protective when people beat on his female agents."

"There is more than one of you?" Em asked in surprise.

"Yup. There are a whopping two of us in our unit. I can't imagine there are that many undercover FBI agents that are women, either."

"There aren't, and I only got this assignment because of my connection to the group."

"Your connection to the group?" Her cavalier statement genuinely perplexed Jimena. The comment was almost a throwaway. How could Em have any connection to such a vile group of men?

"I'll tell you what I can over lunch," Em answered.

"Hey, maybe we can work together on this. I might have a few missing pieces to throw into the kettle."

Em shrugged. "That might be good. I'll pitch it and see where it lands."

"Me too. See you later, Em. Good luck with your meeting."

"Make sure Gary is the only one who knows about my involvement. No offense, but I don't trust the local authorities, and unfortunately, that includes Border Patrol."

CHAPTER TWO

Murphy's hadn't changed in the fifteen years she'd been away, and somehow that was comforting to Em. It was still a relatively grungy cop bar that served surprisingly decent pub fare. When her father was in a good mood, he'd take the whole family there, but his scowl marred his otherwise handsome face anytime one of the Hispanic cops entered. He especially hated the Hispanic Border Patrol Agents, thinking they were helping the Mexicans cross illegally. Often Jimena's papa was the recipient of his foul mood and comments. To his credit, Jose never gave him the satisfaction of responding. At least not until her father forbid Em from playing with Jimena and took a belt to Em when he caught them. After that, Jimena and Em were a lot more covert, and her father never knew of the times that Em would run to Jimena's home for comfort.

Em spotted Jimena in a corner booth. She still looked like she'd gone several rounds with the women's lightweight boxing champion, but the swelling seemed less than when they'd parted several hours earlier. Two frothy beers sat on the scarred wood table, and Jimena smiled brightly as Em approached.

"How did you know what beer I would order?" Em asked.

"It's the only decent one on tap, and I figured you for a woman who only drinks beer on tap versus anything in a bottle or can. Those are usually nothing more than pisswater." Jimena leaned back in the booth, never losing her grin.

"So, you think you know me so well after reconnecting and spending barely thirty minutes together?" Em cocked her head and tried for her most menacing look, but she couldn't help the slight uplift of her mouth.

"People change, but not their fundamental character. Besides, I pay attention and have a good gut sense."

Em quirked her eyebrow. "Oh really? Then maybe you can explain how those two dipshits got the jump on you?"

Jimena frowned. "High-powered assault weapon beats a handgun. Thanks for the save, by the way. I owe you. I see you came out of your meeting with your ass intact."

"How do you figure?" Em asked.

Jimena grinned. "Well, you still fill out those jeans quite nicely. Nothing missing."

Em threw her head back and laughed. "It could have been worse. He wants to see if they can hold Petey and Darnell, at least for a few days. That might give me enough time to find the head guy and break up their plans. It wasn't a huge stretch to claim those idiots were domestic terrorists. Not very smart ones, but still. The leader, who I've yet to meet, is not quite as stupid. He's eluded the authorities for years. Finally, they were desperate enough to give this undercover operation a shot."

Jimena nodded. "I managed to get ahold of my supervisor, who is quite interested in combining forces. All those burned bodies have irritated him beyond his usual curmudgeonly self."

"You're invested in this, aren't you?" Em asked.

"Yeah, I am." Jimena motioned for Em to sit.

Em scooted into the booth and lifted the beer, taking a sip. "Mm, good call on the beer. Well, that's a good thing because Gary phoned Carter while I was updating him, and he signed off on combining forces. But honestly, we need all the help and intel we can get. We know they're planning to take out the governor, and the media constantly highlighting the burned bodies is putting a lot of pressure on the FBI."

Jimena took a large sip of beer before responding, "Ah, the media. Figures. They didn't give a shit about the insignificant brown folk until the news stations caught the story."

"That isn't fair. I've been working on this case for three months. They did care. I care."

"I know you do, Em. You always have. It's just that I'm a lot more skeptical of people in government. By the way, how did you end up being an FBI agent? And how is it you're connected to this heinous group?"

"My father."

Jimena lifted her hand in the air and gestured for Em to continue. "I'm going to need a little more than that."

"Okay, do you want the short or long version?" Em asked.

"Long, always long. I have already ordered some fish and chips for us. I remember how you liked those from Murphy's. Besides, they are sinfully good here. We have all afternoon to eat, drink, and get caught up."

"Just shy of four months after we moved to Idaho, I couldn't stand it anymore. I trotted over to the nearest military recruiting office the day I turned eighteen and signed up. Unfortunately, Idaho isn't exactly welcoming to budding lesbians, even those who try their best to stay in the closet."

Jimena cringed. "Yeah, I suppose California was a lot easier on me, despite my very Catholic background. Papa had a harder time with it than Mama."

"How is your papa?"

Jimena looked away. "Dead."

Em took Jimena's hand. "Oh, Jimena, I'm so sorry. You lost both your parents, and I didn't even know about either of them passing. I'll never forget what your papa did for me. He's the only one who had enough balls to stand up to my dad."

"A couple of thugs ambushed him one night. Unfortunately, they never caught the men who killed him. I tried to look into it but didn't get very far. The local police were predictably unhelpful. After all, it wasn't one of their white officers, and in their opinion, Border Patrol isn't real police and not part of their blue lives matter mantra."

"Fuckers. Do you want me to see if I can get some of my buddies to take a second look? A few are remarkably talented at finding small clues."

Em knew Jimena was looking at her with a fair amount of awe and admiration. She'd seen that look before. Although Em allowed the flush of heat to travel her neck, she couldn't let her latent feelings for Jimena overwhelm her. Em had a girlfriend. Or at least she thought she still had one. Gaby hadn't been too pleased when she learned Em had volunteered for the undercover mission.

"You'd do that for me?" Jimena asked.

"Of course I would."

"Thanks. Okay, now back to your long tale," Jimena prompted.

"After twelve years in the Army I was a little adrift, and the FBI came recruiting. There weren't too many women who made it as Army Rangers, so I suppose I was a hot commodity. Plus, somehow, I had managed to get a bachelor's degree during my time in the Army." Em shrugged.

"Impressive. So now you're a hotshot undercover FBI agent. Married? Girlfriend?" Jimena asked.

"The latter. Although, that might be debatable. Gabriel and I aren't seeing eye-to-eye about my career trajectory. So, it would not surprise me if I came home to a few empty drawers and closets."

"Sorry?" Jimena screwed her face.

"I'm not. If I'm completely honest with myself, the relationship has been dangling on a shredded rope for at least six months now. I love Gaby, but I'm not in love with her. It's not like some epic love affair never to end and following me into my next life."

"Okay, so then why are you still with her? It isn't exactly fair to either of you."

"True. Inertia, I suppose. These last three months have taken every ounce of energy I have. It's harder than you think to pretend to be some racist neo-Nazi asshole who loves the former president and followed closely in the footsteps of her even bigger asswipe father. I didn't have enough left over to break up with her. Letting her do it is so much better for everyone involved."

"But she hasn't ended the relationship, and whether you admit it or not, that is sucking energy from you," Jimena pointed out.

"You're probably right. If Gaby's still there tonight, I'll woman up and have the convo."

"Tell me more about your current assignment and how you found an in."

"Oh yeah. So we've been following this group for a few years. Intel revealed the group was about to kidnap or kill the governor of California. I recognized a few names as former

Marine Corps buddies of my father. Then, my father got his ass blown up. The FBI connected him to this group after his failed mission. He was always so arrogant about his demolition skills. So I volunteered to pretend I was grief stricken and needed to join the group as a means of getting revenge."

"Wow! So, your father is dead?" Jimena confirmed.

"Yup. No substantial loss."

"What about your mother?"

"Oh, she's still alive. She's living in California again. Like the dutiful wife, she followed him to southern California. I have no idea what kind of work he was doing. Something shady for sure, but we haven't uncovered who funds the group. They have enormous resources. It's downright chilling how much firepower they have. Not to mention where they live. None of them is hurting for cash, that's for sure. White trash with cash."

"I never thought I would join forces with the FBI, but fighting domestic terrorists is something I can lean into. I see it as my patriotic duty. They're a bigger threat today than any foreign terrorists."

"That's what Carter keeps telling me. I need to develop a plausible story about what happened to Petey and Darnell, especially if they informed someone else in the group that they planned on calling me to take care of you. I think it was a test. Obviously, I failed, but they don't need to know that while we keep Petey and Darnell locked up. One of my colleagues is the best at getting people to cough up evidence in exchange for a lighter sentence. Let's hope they take a deal and don't blow my cover."

"Do you want to come to my place and strategize? I'll make my mother's traditional beef tongue recipe and throw in some homemade guac for good measure," Jimena offered.

"I'd love nothing better, but as you so eloquently said before, I need to deal with my relationship shit. Can I call later?" Em asked.

"Sure. I'll make it, just in case. Let me give you my digits." Jimena held out her hand.

Em grinned. "Smooth. Is this how you get all the ladies' numbers? Offer to make them incredible homemade Mexican food?"

Jimena laughed. "No, this is a work thing. Strategizing, remember? If I make a play for you, you'll know it. I don't do subtle."

Em pulled the phone from her pocket, unlocked it, and handed it to Jimena without responding. Jimena typed on the phone and then handed it back. Em pressed a button with her index finger, and Jimena's phone rang.

"Hey, hot stuff," Jimena answered. "Now I have your number, too."

"That was the point." Em lifted her beer mug. "Here's to a successful collaboration."

As their mugs clinked together and each took a sip, a waitress approached the table and set down two baskets of fish and chips. "You need anything else?"

"Ketchup," both Em and Jimena said simultaneously and then laughed.

"I think there's a rule somewhere that you can't have fries without ketchup," Em noted.

"Got it," the waitress answered. "Be right back."

Jimena glanced at Em. "Do you want another beer?"

"Nah, better not. I never have more than one drink when I'm driving."

"Good rule to have. I don't have to worry about that since I'm on foot. My place is within walking distance of Murphy's. Do you mind if I order a second beer?"

"Not at all. If I weren't driving, I'd have another."

Jimena glanced at the waitress, who nodded before walking away.

"I forgot to tell you this was a good choice." Em lifted the beer, took a swig, then cut the fish with her fork before dipping it into the tartar sauce and stuffing it into her mouth. "Hot damn. I think my tongue just slapped my brain to tell me how good this is."

Jimena guffawed loudly. "That sounds like one of those funny southern sayings."

"Maybe it is. I learned it from an Army buddy of mine. She was from the south. So, I've given my life story since we parted. Your turn."

"It isn't nearly as exciting or interesting as yours. Pretty boring, actually."

"Let me be the judge of that. Now, spill," Em ordered.

"I almost joined the military but would have chosen the Navy or Air Force. The Army seemed too, oh, I don't know, macho and not very welcoming to women. The Marine Corps seems pretty male-dominated, too."

"You aren't wrong about that. But we always made fun of the wussies in the Air Force. The physical requirements are less stringent than in the Army or Marine Corps. I can't speak to the Navy. They seem to be somewhere in the middle, but ships were never my thing."

"You always were the toughest kid on the playground. Anyway, I went to community college, then transferred to San Diego State University to finish my Bachelor's in Criminal Justice. I suppose my papa was an enormous influence in my career choice." Jimena's voice trailed off, and her eyes grew misty.

The waitress returned with Jimena's second beer, placing it on the table.

"Thanks, Darcy," Jimena said.

Em's eyebrow rose. "You know the waitress?"

"Sure. I come here all the time. Remember, I still live in the neighborhood."

Em knew it was a risk to bring up the topic, but she had a gut feeling she wanted to follow. "When did your papa pass?"

"Three years ago. Why?" Jimena asked.

"Just tugging on a string that's dangling inside my head."

"Care to share?" Jimena tilted her head.

"Not yet. I don't share theories until they're fully formed and I've gathered more evidence." Changing the subject, she redirected the conversation. "Any great loves?"

Jimena shook her head. "I had a girlfriend in college, but we parted ways when she graduated. You? Any tales of the woman who got away?"

Em chuckled and thought better of saying *outside of you, no*. Instead, she replied, "No, not really. I've moved around too much to establish anything stable."

The women continued to eat their fish and chips, and Jimena sipped on her second beer while they talked. Glancing at her smartwatch, Em exclaimed, "Wow, it's been three hours. Time flies, huh?" The cell phone tucked into Em's jacket pocket rang, and Em placed her finger to her lips before answering.

†

"What the fuck happened?" the man screamed into the phone.

"I'm not exactly sure," Em answered. "Something didn't feel right, and I never entered the warehouse. I went underground. I'm guessing you haven't heard from Petey or Darnell." Em's heart beat quickly in her chest as she concentrated on modulating her voice.

"No, I haven't, and you didn't call either." Suspicion dripped from his voice.

"Are you sure your phone is secure?" Adding to the paranoia might work as a redirection to their laser focus on Darnell and Petey. "I mean, the feds could be listening right now. I'm not getting caught because you, Petey, and Darnell are too stupid to use the right burner phones."

"I'm sure. I suppose it's possible Petey or Darnell used their personal cell phones. We need to meet and figure out what to do about this mess. We're all toast if either of them talks," he grumbled.

"I'd rather not cite a specific place or time if they're monitoring this call. Let me think." Em paused and grinned at Jimena before continuing, "Get a new phone and call me back."

"How do I know the feds haven't tapped your phone?"

"They haven't. I learned a few things from my father." Em pressed the end button.

"Wow! Someone has tits the size of Mount Everest. I guess you aren't blown yet." Jimena finished her beer. "Either they're stretching the bounds of the Quarles decision, or maybe your colleagues, and of course, I use that term lightly, are cooperating. That's great news, right?"

"Someone knows their law enforcement Supreme Court cases." Em grinned.

Jimena tapped her forehead. "Yeah, brain like a steel trap. If I remember correctly, they interrogated the guy for an hour before giving the Miranda warnings using the public safety exception."

"That's right. Since we've been following this group closely, and they're into some pretty nasty shit, I suspect they'll interrogate them for hours. The group has enough resources to pay for an attorney high-powered enough to get them released. Hard to say. I need more time to give our guys a head start at turning Darnell and Petey. I assume Darnell is still in the hospital, so that gives us more time for him to turn. Carter was supposed to call to update me, and I'm trying to believe that no news is good news."

"How about we head to my place and wait this out together?" Jimena suggested.

"You sure?"

"Yeah, of course. Oh, damn, I forgot that you have dangling relationship issues to deal with. I don't want to get in the middle of that."

Em placed her burner phone in her jacket pocket and retrieved her personal cell. "Let me call Gaby to let her know I won't be back until late tonight. Although we ate not too long ago, the offer of a home-cooked meal is far too tempting to pass up. Honestly, I don't have the energy for drama right now. I will deal with it, but later."

Jimena held up her hands. "Okay. You're a grown woman. Far be it from me to tell you what to do."

"Well, that's refreshing."

Jimena wrinkled her nose. "What's refreshing?"

"Not getting up in my face to tell me what I should and shouldn't be doing. I know that Gaby sometimes gets a little aggressive with her advice out of care and concern for my well-being, but I've been on my own for a long time, and I don't need a mother. I didn't have one growing up, so why should I start now when I'm perfectly capable of taking care of myself?" Em knew she sounded like a petulant child, but this was a sore spot for her.

Jimena placed her hand on top of Em's. "Hey, you don't need to explain anything to me. I get it. You've always been a capable person, even at sixteen."

"Thanks. I know you said that you don't live far away, but I have my car with me. Why don't I drive us both to your place?"

"Sounds like a plan."

CHAPTER THREE

Jimena ventured a side glance at Em when she instructed her to turn right onto the next street. It wasn't like Jimena felt any shame about where she lived. Instead, she wasn't sure what sort of memories it would evoke for Em to be back in the old neighborhood.

"It's the white one with the blue trim." Jimena pointed to her childhood home.

"Oh, um, you live in your parents' house?" Em stumbled over her words.

"Well, technically, it's my house now. I've made a few improvements in the last couple of years—updated the kitchen and bathrooms. Also, I'm sure you noticed I painted over that god-awful pink."

"Sorry, Jimena. I didn't mean to suggest it wasn't nice. I guess I thought you'd stayed for your sick mama. I didn't realize you'd made a home here. We always talked about moving far away from here when we graduated." Em pulled into the driveway. "It's clear that you've put a lot of care into this home. It suits you."

"No, Em, you always talked about moving away and seeing the world. That was never my dream. Look, I get it. Your family was tough. I probably would have wanted to escape if I were in your shoes. I suppose I hoped that maybe I'd be enough for you to stick around for."

Em put the car in park and turned in her seat to look at Jimena. "Oh, Jimena. I didn't have a choice. Dad moved us to Idaho. By the time I got my shit together, I figured I had pissed you off so much you wouldn't want me to get in touch with you."

Jimena opened the passenger door. "Well, you were wrong about that. Let's just forget it—old history. Come. Let me give you the grand tour. I know the neighborhood isn't quite the same as you remember, but I'm proud of what I've done to the house." Jimena looped her arm inside Em's and tugged her along the path to her front door.

Em seemed to hesitate, opening her mouth, closing it, and obviously avoiding the emotional elephant Jimena had just led into the metaphorical room. "I see your mama's purple bush grew enormous. I remember when she planted those."

"Yeah, aptly named, it's a Pride of Madeira. They're pretty common here, and Mama was very proud of how well they did." Opening her front door, Jimena waved Em inside.

"It's like I remember, but different." Em kicked off her shoes when her eyes traveled to the polished wood floor.

Jimena led Em into her cozy living room, where her large orange tabby perched himself on her plush cream sofa. "Make yourself at home. Garfield may or may not acknowledge your presence. Can I get you something to drink?"

"You have a cat," Em stated. She sounded surprised.

"I do. You don't like cats?" Jimena asked.

"Oh, no, I love them. I wish I could have one."

"Why don't you?" Jimena stood in the middle of the room, waiting for Em to answer.

Em shrugged and sat on the couch, extending her hand to pet Garfield, who miraculously stayed put. "I move around way too much to get a cat and properly care for them. Plus, I'm always gone with my undercover assignments, and Gaby was definitely not the type of person who would offer to care for my cat. Your house is very nice."

"I don't know if I'm praying for those big-city developers to come in and gentrify the neighborhood or not. A handful of people have stayed, and they can't afford the rising costs, but there's also a fair number of drug houses operating not too far from my home. They give me a wide berth. I haven't quite decided what I intend to do to get them to move to another area of the city. Part of me believes I would just be thrusting the problem onto someone else. It's all been a catch-22. I'm not willing to move, and neither are they."

"Do you want me to make some calls to a couple of DEA agents I know? They could make life miserable for your neighbors."

"I don't know. They're relatively small-time. The devil you know, I suppose. What if they move out and someone more troublesome comes along? I'll keep your offer in mind if it gets any worse. I draw the line at drive-bys. I need to get started on dinner if we want to eat at a reasonable hour. Drink?"

"Just some water. Maybe I'll have something else with your awesome dinner. I feel bad, though. I should probably wait on you and get you new ice packs. The bruising is showing more now. It might not be a bad idea to lay some frozen peas or something on your right eye." Em stopped petting Garfield and leaned forward. Garfield huffed and jumped from the couch, strutting down the hallway, likely settling on Jimena's bed. "The least I can do is help. Besides, I thought we were going to strategize. When Smitty calls back, I need to think of something to say to him. I know one thing for sure. I am not meeting them in some remote location, just in case. They still haven't trusted me with their secure base of operations. However, if he finally gave up that piece of information, I'd meet them there."

Jimena motioned for Em to follow her into her kitchen. "All right, I'll put you on onion chopping duty. I hate that task."

"Thanks a lot. You just want to see me cry."

"You always were ultra-sensitive to onions. Don't be a wimp, tough Army Ranger girl." Jimena winked before pulling out a cutting board and selecting a knife for Em.

"What about icing your battered face?"

"I'll put an ice pack on my eye after dinner. No frozen peas, but I have a lot of ice. It can wait. It's not like I'm on my deathbed." Jimena chuckled.

Em shook her head. "Still stubborn as ever," she mumbled.

†

Em leaned back in the chair on Jimena's patio, settling with a glass of wine in her hand. She'd allowed herself to have one with dinner, and now she was savoring a second glass as she let her dinner digest. So many memories flooded her brain, crashing into her like the waves on the beach. Jimena interrupted her trip down memory lane, bringing her current reality into focus.

Jimena lifted the baggie filled with ice from her right eye and turned to look at Em. "Any thoughts on what you're planning to do when Smitty calls back?" Jimena asked.

"No clue. Thoughts?"

"Do you genuinely want to pass up an opportunity to discover the location of their base of operations?" Jimena asked, wincing when she placed the homemade cold pack on her face.

Em frowned. "Not really. Going there will be a colossal risk. It's entirely possible they're playing me, but I think it's a chance I have to take."

"What if you had a different backup?" Jimena tossed the ice bag onto the small table, leaned forward, propping her head in her hand, and shot a side glance at Em.

"No way. You can't follow me into the lion's den. You're like red meat to them," Em insisted.

"I can be stealth." Jimena sat up straight and caught Em's eyes. "Come on. I know this area like the back of my hand. Every nook and cranny. Wherever they're holed up, I'll bet I've been there and can find a place to hide where they won't know I'm there, but if things go sideways, I'll be ready to storm the castle."

"This isn't like playing cops and robbers as kids. You have no idea the kind of firepower they have. Besides, how will we stay in contact with each other for you to know if I'm in trouble? Now, put that bag of ice on your face. It hasn't even been ten minutes."

Jimena grimaced and grabbed the bag, placing it on her swollen face. "Doesn't the FBI have some fancy surveillance equipment we can use?"

"We do." Em hesitated to continue. Was she truly going to agree to this half-baked plan? Even though she hadn't seen or talked to Jimena in fifteen years, she trusted her more than most of her colleagues at the bureau. "Okay, say I agree with this bat-shit idea of yours. I want you to have access to real backup if everything falls apart. And we'll need to have both our bosses sign off on this."

"Real backup," Jimena growled, temporarily removing the ice.

"I didn't mean it like that. I saw how you handled yourself with Darnell and Petey. That was impressive, but neither of us can control ten to fifteen men with assault rifles by ourselves."

Jimena nodded. "So, now we wait."

As if the universe had heard their conversation, Em's cell rang.

"I got a new fucking phone. Happy?" Smitty snarled.

"Yes, I am. So, have you learned anything more?"

"Yeah, the feds have them, and there was a fucking Mexican Border Patrol Agent involved. She needs to disappear. You up for making that happen?"

"Only if you stop treating me like an outsider. I want in on everything. I think I've earned my stripes." Knowing there was a mark on Jimena's head did not settle Em, but at least they expected her to take care of the problem, which bought her more time.

"I'll send coordinates to your phone. We'll meet tomorrow at noon."

"Why not tonight? What about Petey and Darnell spilling the beans?"

"Don't you worry your pretty little head about that. It's being taken care of." The call ended abruptly.

"Shit!" Em exclaimed. "I need to make a call." Pulling her other phone from her pocket, she punched the contact number for Carter so hard that she was afraid she might crack the screen.

"Schmidt here. They have someone on the inside. Petey and Darnell are at risk."

"Too late. I was just about to call you," Carter answered.

"What the fuck? How did you let that happen?" Em shouted.

"Don't you take that tone with me. We're looking into it. Trust me, we'll track down the leaks into the depths of hell. Watch your back, Em. Their network is far more than we imagined. Working theory is that when we finally allowed them to have their attorney help negotiate the deal, he wasn't actually an attorney. He took out Petey. Another guy posing as a nurse got to Darnell. And like two ghosts, they've disappeared without a trace. I don't know if you've blown your cover or not. I'll leave it up to you whether you wish to bail."

"I got a call. Either they're playing me, or I finally have access to real shit the assholes are planning. I have a noon meeting tomorrow, but I'll need a few things. Jimena, the Border Patrol Agent, knows this area, and she offered to be the first-level backup," Em explained.

"Did she get authorization to go all Joan Wayne?"

"Not yet, but I'll be sure she makes the call. Just be ready to move in case things don't go as planned."

"We'll be ready. I assume you need communication equipment."

"Yes, please. I'll swing by and pick it up tonight. Thanks for letting me follow through on this."

"It's your funeral, but I'd rather not attend, if you don't mind."

Em chuckled. "Your sentiments about my well-being are underwhelming."

"Yeah, yeah, just be careful. I sincerely hate having to train new recruits. Don't worry about picking up the equipment. We'll put everything you need in the safe house."

"Can you have someone bring the beater to the safe house? I'll take that to the meeting so they don't suspect anything."

"You got it."

Em ended the call without saying goodbye and turned to Jimena. "Last chance to back out. Petey and Darnell are dead. This could possibly be the biggest trap I've ever walked into. Oh, and they expect me to track you down and execute you. Either we have a few days to wrap this up, or else they already sent someone to scrub your existence. I don't think they know about the safe house we have set up. Care to join me tonight?"

"Well, since you asked so nicely, I'd love to." Jimena tossed the ice onto the table with a massive grin on her face.

Em looked around the backyard where they'd watched the meteor shower, and she'd made so many wishes. Some had come true, but the biggest one had not.

CHAPTER FOUR

Sixteen Years Ago

Pulling her jacket closed, Em shivered in the frosty night air and tapped quietly on Jimena's window, hoping she wouldn't wake the rest of the house. After a few minutes, Jimena pulled open the blinds. Rubbing her eyes, she blinked at Em, smiling outside her bedroom window.

Opening the window, she asked, "Em, what are you doing here? Did your dad hit you again?"

"No. Come out and watch the meteor shower with me. And bring some blankets. It's colder than a witch's tit out here."

"It's like one in the morning," Jimena grumbled.

"Yeah, I know. It's supposed to start soon and last for about an hour. Come on. It's our best chance to have all our wishes answered."

Jimena grabbed two blankets from her bed, quickly popped out her screen, and crawled through the window. "What are you talking about?"

"Shooting stars, Jimena. Hundreds of them. We can wish on all of them."

"I thought you said it was a meteor shower. Those aren't shooting stars, so I don't think it counts."

Em shrugged. "They're called shooting stars, but they aren't stars either. A shooting star is actually a collection of dust particles that burn up in space. Those tiny specks of dust from space are meteors."

"I did not know that," Jimena answered.

"That's why you have me as your best friend. So I can fill your head with a bunch of useless information." Em grinned as she hugged herself, protecting her body from the wind that traveled through her thin jacket.

Jimena looked down at Em's bare feet, handed her the blankets, then turned back to her window. "Give me a second," she called over her shoulder. "I need to grab something."

Crawling through the window a second time, she held out a pair of socks. "Here, Papa says you lose heat through your extremities. These socks should help."

Em laid one blanket on the ground, sat, and then patted the space beside her. Quickly putting on the socks Jimena had given her, she grinned at Jimena.

When Jimena joined her on the blanket, Em relaxed on her back, looking up at the vast sky. Jimena followed Em's lead, and their hands touched as they lay side by side on the blanket.

"It's starting." Em pointed to the sky. Her body shivered, and she wasn't sure if that was because she was still cold or because Jimena had clasped her hand and threaded their fingers together.

Jimena turned to face Em. "Are you still cold?"

"A little," Em answered.

Jimena sat up, and Em knew she was also about to let go of her hand to pull the other blanket over them. She didn't want to lose the connection and almost pulled her back but thought that would seem weird to Jimena. She reluctantly let go as Jimena grabbed the blanket and covered both of them. When Jimena retook Em's hand, Em sighed in contentment.

"Did you already make your first wish?" Jimena asked.

Em had, but she didn't want to admit to her wish. Instead, she blurted, "Are you really going to the Winter Formal with that new kid?"

Jimena's face turned to her, and Em recognized the confused expression written on her face. "He's a refugee from Iraq. Papa thinks I should do everything I can to make him feel welcome. It hasn't been easy on him. Why can't you say yes to Jimmy? Then you can meet us there. It'll be fun. I know your dad won't let us go on a double date, but we can all hang out if you go with Jimmy."

Em scoffed. "Jimmy is an asshole about stuff like that, always talking shit about all the illegal immigrants. He'd never agree to hang out with you and Akmal. I wish you and I could go together."

Jimena's eyes grew wide. "Like a couple?"

Jimena opened her mouth to say something else, but Em interrupted her before she could say the words. Em had gone too far voicing her scandalous thoughts. She had to peddle backward quickly before Jimena refused to have anything to do with her.

"No, as friends. Never mind. It was a stupid idea. Forget it."

Jimena's nose crinkled. "You know you can tell me anything, Em. I would never judge you."

"Let's just watch the meteor shower. I'll tell Jimmy I want to go with him, but only if we meet up with you and Akmal."

"Do you think Jimmy will make trouble for you by telling your dad?"

Em shrugged. "Don't care if he does. I'm not afraid of my father anymore. I'm as tall as he is now. Next time he smacks me, I'm gonna hit him right back. I might even tell his boss. I heard he could get in a lot of trouble if they knew he hits his kid. Karma, baby, karma. I'd love to see him get fired for child abuse."

"Be careful, Em. Your dad has a terrible temper. I'm afraid for you. Papa and Mama have always said that you can come live with us if it gets to be too much. We don't have a palace or anything, but you're always welcome."

"I know, Jimena, but I'm okay. I've been taking care of myself for a long time, and I'm a survivor. He'll never get the best of me. I know how much it pisses him off when I don't cry, which makes my resolve that much stronger to never let him see me break." Jimena's focus returned to the sky and the multiple shooting stars. Em vowed to never forget this night. With Jimena holding her hand, she could conquer the world.

†

Jimena narrowed her eyes when she watched Jimmy put his hand on Em's butt as they danced. Then he tried to kiss her, and Em pushed him away and stalked off the dance floor.

Akmal remained a respectable distance from Jimena as they danced and was the perfect gentleman. He was friendly and handsome, but Jimena didn't have feelings for him, not like how she felt about Em. She knew she should have confessed to Em when they watched the meteor shower. It was the perfect opportunity. At first, she thought Em was trying to tell her she felt the same way, but then Em said she only wanted to go to the dance as friends. Sometimes Em would look at her, and she thought for sure that she didn't imagine things, but Em never made a move.

"Akmal, do you mind if we stop dancing? Em seems upset. I'm going to grab her and take her outside for a bit."

"I will wait at our table. Would you like me to get you some punch?"

Jimena shook her head. "I better not. I heard the football team spiked it with moonshine or something."

Jimena stalked to the table where both Jimmy and Em were scowling at each other. She grabbed Em's hand and pulled her to her feet. Then, smiling at Jimmy, she said, "I'm taking your date. We have girly stuff to do."

"Whatever," Jimmy grumbled.

Jimena kept ahold of Em's hand as they made their way outside. "You okay?" she asked gently.

"No, I'm not. I knew this was going to happen. Now Jimmy thinks I'm his to do what he pleases. I know what the football team is saying behind my back. Jimmy bet them he was 'going to tap that before the night's end,' earning his bingo virgin card."

"What? That little fucker. Why didn't you tell me that? I would have never suggested you go with him. He was always nice to you. I thought he liked you."

"No, but that doesn't even matter because I don't like him either. It's okay, Jimena. At least you're having fun with Akmal. He seems nice. Respectful. I like that about him. You make a cute couple."

"Maybe you should have called Robbie to take you. I'd bet he would have come back from college if you asked him to."

Em sighed. "You don't get it. I don't like Robbie, either. I don't like boys at all. I like girls. There, I've said it, and I'm not taking it back. You can leave me alone now."

"But, but, it was all over the school when Shelly caught you kissing behind the bleachers in seventh grade. Then you went to Robbie's Senior Prom last year, and you were so excited when he asked you," Jimena stuttered.

"No, I wasn't. You were the one who thought it was so cool that the most popular boy in the senior class asked me to prom. The truth is that Robbie didn't like me either. We kind of both figured that out after the not-so-epic kiss. He's gay, too." Em grinned. "Yup, I caught him making out with Greg in the back of his car."

"Wow! Greg too?"

"Yeah, we're here, we're queer, and we aren't going away. We're everywhere, Jimena. Time to open your eyes and come out of your traditional Catholic bubble." Em crossed her arms over her chest and adopted a rigid stance.

"Why didn't you ever tell me before? You're my best friend." Although she tried, she failed to mask the hurt in her voice.

Em touched Jimena's arm. "Because I don't just like girls, Jimena. I like you. You know, in that way. I know you don't feel the same about me. If I confessed that to you, I was afraid I'd lose you forever."

Jimena smacked Em's arm away, and tears sprang to the corner of Em's eyes after it was clear she had misinterpreted the reason for Jimena's anger.

"You're disgusted now. I'll go." Em turned to leave.

"Wait, no. I'm not mad because you finally told me. I'm upset because you didn't confide in me sooner. Have I ever once said anything derogatory about any of those out lesbians or gay guys in our school?"

"No."

"Then what the fuck made you believe I would care one bit about you? Did you ever stop to think that maybe I've been questioning myself for years?"

"You have? Well, then, you don't have any right to be angry with me. Why didn't you tell me?"

"Cause I like you, too, but then you said we could go to the dance as friends. I thought it was just me having all those feelings."

Em pressed her forehead against Jimena's. "I really want to kiss you now."

"So do it."

Em laughed. "Okay, I will." Em caressed Jimena's jaw and directed her face, pressing their lips together in the sweetest kiss Jimena had ever experienced. Not that she had a lot of experience kissing anyone, but she would remember this night for the rest of her life.

CHAPTER FIVE

Present Day

Returning to the window inside Jimena's cozy home, Em separated the blinds a couple of inches and peered outside. Jimena approached from behind and settled so close that Em could feel her breath on the back of her neck.

"What are you doing?" Jimena asked.

"You can't be too careful. I wanted to make sure no one was lurking outside, ready to take you out."

"Good thinking. Hey, I meant to ask you about your two different cars. I've already figured out you carry two different cell phones for obvious reasons, but two cars?"

"I'd rather not take any chances. Hopefully, they know nothing about my vehicle. The other one is a loaner for my undercover work. It has a few special compartments where I store extra ammo and firepower."

"Well, aren't you the little girl scout?"

Em turned to face Jimena, and their lips were so close. All she had to do was close the distance, and those lips would be hers again, but Jimena's swollen lip appeared painful. At least the swelling around her eye looked better.

If memory served her correctly, Jimena had the softest lips she'd ever had the pleasure of kissing. She remembered their first kiss at the Winter Formal. It had been everything she'd fantasized about and more, even though it was far down on the passion scale by most people's standards.

Jimena coughed and took a step back. "So, are we clear?"

"I don't see anyone, but that doesn't mean anything. We should probably slip out the back and call an Uber."

"Or we could roll my motorcycle out the side door that opens to the backyard."

"Now I'm duly impressed. You're full of surprises tonight. Although I can't claim to feel all that good about riding bitch."

"You'll get over it." Jimena chuckled. "When we get there, you need to call your girlfriend. When I meet Gaby, I don't want her to have a negative impression of me for causing you not to come home tonight."

"Oh, yeah. I almost forgot about that dangling participle."

"You sound like an English teacher," Jimena teased.

"I've always wanted to write a book about my escapades," Em joked.

"I'd read it."

Jimena threw together a small to-go bag, grabbing it before carrying it into the living room, where Em had moved to another window to peek through those blinds. After Jimena had returned, the women quietly made their way to the garage. Em perpetually swiveled her head on high alert for anything out of the ordinary. She wasn't sure, but the hackles on the back of her neck gave Em a creepy feeling that something or someone was out there, waiting to pounce on them. Jimena unlocked the garage's side door, and Em noticed a security camera mounted in the corner. Jimena punched in her pin on the keypad by the door, grinning before removing the cover on her bike. Em recognized a gleaming Harley Softail Deluxe. She wasn't sure what year the bike was, but it was in pristine condition.

"I couldn't help but notice the security in the garage, but nothing in your house," Em noted.

"There was no way I would let anyone come near my baby. I'm planning on adding more security to the house, too, but the garage was my priority."

"She's a beaut, Jimena. Any chance I can give her a go sometime?"

"Not on your or my life. I'm the only one who will ever drive her. And be careful when you hop on the back." Jimena grabbed the second helmet, handing it to Em. "Here, put this on. It should fit your head."

"Damn, you're no fun."

After Jimena rolled the bike into the backyard, she put the kickstand down and returned to the garage. Em waited while Jimena locked up and reset the alarm. Following Jimena to the side gate, Em continued to survey her surroundings. The creepy crawling feeling never left. Through a line of trees and several large bushes, she recognized a truck she'd seen at one of the group gatherings she had infiltrated. That was not a good sign. No, not at all good. Pressing her finger to her lips, she motioned toward the vehicle. Jimena turned the bike in the opposite direction and continued to roll it down the side street until they made it to one of the major intersections.

Jimena started the engine, and the bike purred that distinctive roar of a Harley. After donning her helmet, Jimena settled into the seat and flipped the kickstand. Over her shoulder, she directed, "Hop on. Just tap my left or right side to let me know which way to turn."

Em squeezed Jimena's hips to let her know she'd heard.

†

The ride to the safe house was exhilarating, and Em wondered why she'd never bought herself a motorcycle. She'd typically move from place to place with barely the clothes on her back, preferring not to tie herself down with too many toys or belongings. The Army had taught her how to keep most of her life in one duffle. It wasn't ever too hard to find furnished apartments that suited her nomadic lifestyle.

Gaby often complained about how minimalist Em preferred to live, and it was a frequent sore spot in their relationship. It didn't help that Em never agreed to stay the night at Gaby's place, which was a great deal cozier than Em's apartment. She'd have sex there but refused to leave any belongings or inch any closer to cohabitation. Em knew this wasn't fair to Gaby, and that should have been her first clue their relationship had run its course. Gaby made all the accommodations, including being the one to spend most nights at Em's apartment.

The safe house wasn't unique—two bedrooms, two baths, a basic kitchen, and a living room. The interior had a definite eighties flair to it. It wasn't any larger than Jimena's house but definitely had more space than Em's apartment. Em knew it would be fine for a few days. Unfortunately, Em didn't have any spare clothes with her. She'd have to root around in the drawers to see if there was something left over from past inhabitants that she could toss on to sleep in. Prancing around naked in front of Jimena was out of the question.

"I'm going to see if one of the bedrooms has any extra clothes that I might fit into. I probably should have asked Hank to grab my to-go bag, but I sincerely hate anyone entering my private space," Em said.

"Sorry, I didn't have anything to snag that you would fit into with that Amazon body of yours. It looks like you got taller over the years, if that's possible. But you certainly filled out nicely."

Em decided to ignore what might have been a flirtation on Jimena's part. "Maybe you shrunk, and it just seems like it."

"Hey, I'm almost five-foot-two now. Don't make fun of my ethnic heritage. Mexicans aren't known for their height. That doesn't mean I can't hold my own in a fistfight." Jimena held up her fists, posing like a boxer.

"I would never underestimate those who come in small packages, but I am lamenting the drastic differences in our size. Not only won't I have a change of clothes, but I don't even have anything to sleep in."

Jimena shrugged. "Sleep in the nude. I do. Unless you think the sheets on the bed have creepy crawlers in them. Ew, they change the sheets in this place, don't they?"

"I think they do, but I don't know," Em admitted.

"Then they better have an extra set somewhere or a washer and dryer. I am not sleeping on dirty sheets."

Em shook her head and chuckled. "Such a princess."

After pawing through all the drawers in both bedrooms, Em found a Chargers T-shirt, gray sweatpants, a black hoodie, and a pair of running shorts. That would have to do. She never wore underwear anyway, besides the fact that it would be beyond gross to don someone else's panties or briefs. With bounty in hand, she returned to the first bedroom she'd foraged in and found Jimena pulling the sheets from the bed.

Jimena looked up from her task and said, "I'm not sure I trust the second set of sheets in the closet, so I'm opting for the washer and dryer I found. Crossing my fingers that both work." She held up her fingers in a demonstration. "Do you want me to wash the sheets in the other room for you?"

"Sure, why not?" Em answered.

"After I put the sheets in the washer, I'll make myself scarce so you can call Gaby."

"Right, yeah. I suppose I've put that off long enough. Thanks, Jimena."

†

Retreating to the other bedroom after Jimena had removed the sheets, Em pulled her phone from her pocket and dialed Gaby's cell.

"So, you haven't managed to get yourself killed yet," Gaby said as a means of answering her phone.

Em cringed. "Look, um…"

"Nope, you don't get to do this over the phone. I at least get to see your face. I'm hanging up and calling you on Facetime."

Em reluctantly hit the end button and answered the Facetime call. The first thing she noticed was Gaby lounging on her couch in her cozy home. Em wasn't sure if that was a good or bad omen. Of course, she hadn't stayed at Em's place, even though they had tentatively made plans for the weekend.

"It's good to hear you're in one piece," Gaby said.

"Uh, yeah. We're at the safe house."

"You and the Border Patrol Agent, right?"

"Yes, Jimena is her name. Funny thing, I know her. We grew up together."

Gaby raised her brow. "You know that you're probably blown, right?"

"Not necessarily, but Jimena is in serious danger. They want me to eliminate her."

"Em, you can't be that stupid. Those assholes are playing you."

"You don't know that," Em defended.

Gaby sighed. "It's not that I don't understand your desire to do your job and do it better than anyone else, but you keep signing up for the most dangerous undercover assignments, and one of these days, your luck will run out. Who do you think they called to clean up the public relations mess? I know exactly what's happened. Two dead neo-Nazis with demands from their family to know what happened does not make for a flattering story about the FBI. They've involved the right-wing press in this disaster. I can tell you the press conference wasn't a bag of giggles."

"Sorry for that, but they're rattled now, as evidenced by the elimination of Petey and Darnell. When groups are unsettled, they make mistakes. You know that. I plan to capitalize on that."

"I can't do this anymore. I've been doing all the adjusting since we first started dating. If even just once you'd met me halfway, I'd have something to work with." Gaby looked tired and defeated. She wasn't wrong.

"You're right, Gabs. You deserve someone so much better than me."

"Oh, Christ. You're actually going to bring out the 'it's not you, it's me' line. How about you own up to the fact that you aren't as invested in our relationship as I am? It's not that hard to tell the truth. I don't expect you to manufacture feelings for me. If they aren't there, they aren't there."

"Okay. It's not that I don't care about you, because I do. But you're right, I'm not in love with you, and I don't believe I'll ever get there."

Gaby sighed. "Now, was that so hard?"

"Yeah, it was because I hurt you."

"You would have hurt me far worse if we'd continued without you being honest with me. You know, I'm not placing all the blame on you. I knew. Deep down inside, I knew you were never going to love me back. I've already removed my stuff from your apartment, so you don't have to worry about an uncomfortable interaction in the future."

"Maybe we can be friends?" Em asked hopefully.

"I need a little time, okay?"

"Sure, sure."

"That doesn't mean I don't want to know that you've come out of this assignment intact. Please take care of yourself and watch your back. My gut says there is more than one mole."

"I will, and yes, I'm aware of that," Em answered.

"Don't let these fuckers win, Em."

"I won't. Bye, Gaby."

"Goodbye." Gaby clicked off, and then Em stared at the empty screen before walking into the central living area, where Jimena sat with a steaming cup of tea. The aroma of orange spice permeated the air.

Jimena lifted her tea. "Found some herbal tea. Do you want a cup?"

"That actually sounds nice. Once again, I should be the one taking care of you, and instead, here you are, making herbal tea for me. At least your eye looks a little better. You should probably ice your lip next."

Jimena's nose wrinkled, demonstrating what she thought about that idea. Em was too exhausted to push the issue.

"Sit down and relax, and I'll make you a cup. Then you can tell me how the call went. It looks like you lost your best friend," Jimena said, taking on the caretaker role once again.

"Although it needed to happen, I feel horrible. Gaby is a good person. I honestly wish I could have fallen in love with her. I think that someday we'll make it into the friend zone, but we're going to keep our distance for now. I've created a shit show for Gaby. She's responsible for communications between the press and the FBI. I don't even want to watch the press conference. Apparently, it was painful."

"Hold those thoughts." Jimena set her tea on the coffee table and walked to the kitchen.

Em wondered how terrible an idea it was to spill her guts to the one woman she'd fall hard and fast for with only an inkling of interest from her. That feeling had always been there, and now they were both grown women. This wouldn't be puppy love. No, this would be a mature love complete with the physical intimacy she longed for.

The sounds of Jimena opening the cabinet and filling the teakettle with water leaked into the living room as Em laid her head on the back of the sofa. She pinched the bridge of her nose. Suddenly, she felt drained. All she wanted to do was have a cup of tea and retreat to a bedroom. But they needed to nail down a plan. And Em felt duty-bound to tell Jimena about the truck she recognized lurking around the corner from her house. Unfortunately, it looked more and more like the meeting was a set-up. Yet, if there was a sliver of possibility, she wanted to follow through with the gathering.

Jimena returned from the kitchen with a steaming mug. "This place is well stocked. I found honey to add to the tea. You still take honey in your tea, right?"

"Yeah, splendid memory."

"Okay, what's that pinched look about? There's something you feel the need to share but don't know how I'll react." Jimena took a seat on the couch next to Em and turned to face her, capturing her eyes.

"You always could read any micro-expression on my face."

Jimena laughed. "Babe, that's not a micro-expression. The most obtuse person would pick up on the almost comical strained face you're showing the world."

For a minute, Em allowed herself to bask in the warmth of the endearing term Jimena had used. After they'd gotten together, Jimena would call her babe all the time. She liked it, even though she was a total tomboy and didn't think babe was the most enlightened term for a woman.

"I recognized a truck close to your house. I'm not sure if they were merely doing surveillance or had sent someone to carry out a contract," Em blurted.

"You're worried the meeting is a set-up, and my life is in danger," Jimena guessed. "But you aren't planning on bailing in case you haven't blown your cover because you don't value your life as much as mine." Jimena pursed her lips in a sign of frustration.

Em chuckled. "Now you're comically telegraphing your feelings."

"I think we should call the whole thing off," Jimena declared.

"No can do, but I don't think it's safe for you to go with me now. In fact, I'm going to arrange for a protective detail until we blow this entire group apart."

"Not happening. I can take care of myself. Like I said. I know this area better than any of your fellow agents. They'll pick out one of your guys quicker than a hot knife through butter."

"I don't like this," Em stated.

"Join the crowd. I want these bastards behind bars every bit as much as you—"

"I know you do," Em interrupted. "Okay, I recognize your stubborn face. Any bright ideas on how to approach the situation?"

"First, I need to know the location of the meeting. Once we learn that, I'll take my motorcycle and find a place close enough to wait things out while you meet with the group. You let me know at the first sign of trouble via your wire.

You always had that spidey sense when things were going to go sideways. That should give me plenty of time to rouse the troops. I'll need a direct line to your boss—Carter, right?"

"Yeah, his name is Adam Carter," Em answered.

"I'll get them to gather in a location far enough away to avoid detection but close enough to storm the castle." As though this was an everyday occurrence, Jimena casually brought the cup to her lips and took a sip.

Em lifted her head when she heard a vehicle pull into the driveway of the safe house. "Go into the back bedroom," she directed.

†

Jimena hesitated before capitulating to Em's order. She figured they didn't have time to argue. Besides, her gun was in her bag. By the time she'd retrieved her gun and flipped the safety, she heard laughter in the other room. Figuring it was safe, she returned to the living room to see a tall, well-muscled man talking with Em. He'd perfectly coiffed every hair on his head, and it looked as though he had ironed his jeans.

Em glanced in her direction and said, "Hey, sorry to rattle you. This is Hank. He dropped off my car for me. He's been complaining about what a pig I am." Em shrugged. "Too many empty food wrappers for his persnickety taste."

Hank lifted his hand in a small wave. "You must be the Border Patrol Agent. Impressive shiner."

Jimena nodded. "Jimena."

"I'm going to go now. Steve is waiting for me outside."
Em raised her eyebrow. "Hot date?"

"None of your damn business," he quipped.

"Have a good night, you two, and be careful, Em. I'm
starting to get used to you. Steve and I are both on standby
tomorrow. You better call in with enough time for us to save
your sorry ass if things become more of a shit show than
what Gaby had to deal with today."

"Yeah, I heard."

"Ooh, the little lady chewed your ass out, huh?"

"Something like that. Now get the fuck out of my face. I
hope not to see you tomorrow."

"Me, too, Em. Me, too."

Jimena was happy to observe that, against all odds, Em
had found people who cared about her—in the Army and
apparently now in the FBI. She'd seen firsthand how the only
people who cared about Em were Jimena and her family.
Even Em's little brother had pulled away when he got older
and didn't feel the need to follow her and Jimena around all
the time.

CHAPTER SIX

Fifteen Years Ago

Em tugged on Jimena's arm, leading her to their special place on the beach. "Come on, Jimena, we have to hurry, or we won't catch the sunrise."

"What makes today's sunrise so special?" Jimena grumbled. "I'm cold." She grabbed the collar of her jacket and pulled it up tight against her neck.

They finally reached the large piece of driftwood, and Em plopped on the sand, pulling Jimena next to her. She draped her arm around Jimena and held her close. "I'll keep you warm."

Jimena turned her face to Em. "I should be the one keeping you warm. You don't have any fat on your body like me to protect you. Aren't you freezing?"

"Nah, I'm too excited."

"For what?"

"Don't you remember? One year ago today was the first time we kissed."

Jimena blushed and smiled. "Oh yeah, and other things, too."

Em reached into her pocket and pulled out a small ring box, offering it in her palm to Jimena. "Here. It isn't as nice as the one I'm going to get you in a few years, but it'll have to do for now. I saved all year to buy it."

"Oh, Em." Jimena opened the box and found a simple gold band with a tiny diamond chip.

"It's a promise ring. One day I'm going to marry you."

"Girls can't marry other girls."

"By the time we're ready to get married, you know, after we finish college, it'll be legal. Times are changing, Em. Just three years ago, a bunch of same-sex couples married in San Francisco."

"That was only a stunt. It wasn't legal."

"Both Obama and Clinton support civil unions. I know it isn't marriage, but I'm convinced we'll get there. I'm voting for Obama. I'll be eighteen by then, and I think he will do it. Imagine, Jimena, the first black president." Em grinned. "It's a tough choice, but I like his message of hope." She thrust her fist in the air. "Yes, we can."

"I got you something, too." Jimena pulled a small box from her pocket. "It isn't a ring," she apologized.

"You didn't forget after all, did you?"

"Of course I didn't." Jimena thrust the gift forward.

Em opened the box and saw a beautiful necklace inside. "Wow. Is this a Saint Christopher medal?"

Jimena nodded. "It's been in my family for years."

Em pushed the box back at Jimena. "I can't take a family heirloom."

"I asked Papa and Mama, and they agreed that you should have it. You need it more than any of my family. You know they think of you as another daughter."

Em swiped the tear from the corner of her eye. "Okay." Undoing the delicate clasp, she put the necklace with the medal around her neck and tucked it inside her shirt. She pointed to the ring. "Are you going to put that on?"

Jimena frowned. "I haven't told my parents about us. They'll notice. What should I say about it?"

Em tapped her finger against her chin. "You can put it on a chain, and when you're ready to tell them, you can transfer the ring from the chain to your finger."

"Okay. I promise I'll tell my parents soon. It's just that they're so religious. At least Mama is. Papa seems to go along with Mama because he loves her and always wants to make her happy."

"It's okay, Jimena. I understand. You take all the time you need. I'll always be here."

"I can't wait to go to college with you. No more sneaking around. We can get a place together and be roommates. No one will suspect."

"Yeah." Em lifted her face to the sky and then noticed the sun beginning to peek. "Look, Jimena." She pointed at the horizon. "Isn't that the prettiest sunrise you've ever seen? I think God is trying to tell us He approves."

"You don't believe in God," Jimena answered.

Em shrugged. "I know, but you do."

"I love you," Jimena said. She snuggled against Em and sighed contentedly.

"I love you, too, Jimena. I always will. Forever is around the corner for us. You wait and see."

"I believe you," Jimena responded, and kissed Em on the cheek.

†

Karl Junior had followed his sister when she snuck out of the house before sunrise. He suspected she would go to Jimena's, and he was right. Karl had almost puked in the sand when he watched his sister and her clandestine lover. Then he'd crouched closer to listen in on their conversation. Something needed to be done about the two of them. If his dad had to beat the shit out of Emma, then so be it. There was no way he'd have a dyke for a sister. Running in the other direction, he made it home in no time and found his father scratching his groin as he walked into the bathroom.

His eyes tracked on Karl, and he growled, "What the fuck are you doing, boy?"

Karl answered quickly, relishing how his dad would shower praise on him for tattling. "I followed Em when she crept out this morning. I thought you'd want to know."

"What the hell is that stupid girl up to now?" Karl Senior asked.

Eager for his reaction, Karl continued, "She met up with Jimena, and they did disgusting things. They're both dykes. Em gave Jimena a promise ring," he added with revulsion.

"That's it. I don't go for that pansy-ass response of *pray the gay away*. I'm going to beat that perversion out of her. I've been on the fence for a couple of weeks now on the new job offer in Idaho, but this latest stunt by your sister just made my decision for me. Besides, my boss has been riding me lately. Excessive force, my ass," he mocked. "He will regret making my life so miserable this last year. If the gangs would only take each other out, I wouldn't have to come down so hard on them. Let's see how they manage without me. This place has gone to shit, anyway."

"Idaho," Karl Junior squeaked. "But, my friends…" This was not going the way he had hoped. All his friends were in California. He was the quarterback on the JV football team.

Karl Senior narrowed his eyes at his son. "Stop your whining. You better not turn out to be a pansy-ass, too. I'm sick and fucking tired of all the liberal, dumb-ass politicians always impeding the police who are merely doing their jobs. My buddy assures me it's nothing like that in Idaho. You can make the right kind of friends when we move. They probably have a better football team, too. One where you'll be on the varsity instead of the JV team."

Karl Junior didn't want to move to some boring-ass state like Idaho. Fuck. He knew enough not to say another word, or he'd get a beating right along with his sister. *Damn his sister for always ruining everything.*

†

Em wasn't paying attention to anything as she skipped along and made her way to her bedroom window. She'd sneak back in with no one knowing she'd even left. She did it all the time and rarely got caught. This would be the last time she would ever miss the cues of something slightly amiss. Slipping her fingers under the small crack she'd left in the glass window, she carefully pushed it up, cringing when she heard the slight squeak. As it turned out, the noise didn't matter because after she crawled through the small space, she met her father's cold, angry eyes. He was still here. She hadn't noticed that his car remained in the small garage.

"I warned you. Now I have to learn that not only did you ignore my order, but you're also a dirty little dyke. No daughter of mine is going to be *that* way." He raised his fist, and before she knew it, he'd broken her nose with a clear shot to her face. Continuing his assault, he kicked her repeatedly with his solid work shoes after she'd fallen to the ground. She'd barely had time to protect her head, which was the only thing that had kept her alive. After she had lain on the hard floor, a collection of broken bones with blood pouring from her mouth and nose, he ordered, "I'm going to work, and you're staying home from school. Karl will give the office a note saying you're out sick. You'll stay home until we move."

She knew she'd feel another blow, but she managed to get out one word through the pain. "Move?"

"We'll be in Idaho before the end of the month. I've got people watching now. If you so much as get within thirty feet of Jimena, you won't be the only one to suffer the consequences. I know exactly how to make people disappear. That is not a threat, little girl. That is a promise. Her future is in your hands."

Half an hour later, her mother offered the only kind gesture she'd ever extended to Em in her entire life when she'd silently helped her to the car and took her to the hospital. Em touched the Saint Christopher medal on her chest and thought, *big fat lot of good this did her*. But she never took off the medal. Nothing would protect Em from her father's wrath. She'd need to get away from him.

The nurse looked skeptically at her injuries, apparently not believing the story her mother had given. But when the doctor came into the room and Em recognized the man, she knew the nurse wouldn't report what she had observed to child protective services. He was one of her father's old Marine buddies.

It took Em three months to heal from all of her injuries. Fortunately for her, that was all she needed before she turned eighteen and had to pass the physical to join the Army. Em never looked back, even though she thought about Jimena every day those first three years. She'd even penned a letter explaining everything several times, only to toss it in the trash, never sending it. Her father's words stayed with her for years. Em knew he would make good on his promise. Finally, after Em had completed her first tour of duty, she convinced herself that Jimena was probably better off without her.

CHAPTER SEVEN

Present Day

The following day, Em's burner phone rang. She scrambled to answer it. "Yeah."

"Meeting's off. We can't find the bitch. She's disappeared. We'll contact you again when we learn her whereabouts."

"What about your other plans? When am I going to get briefed on them?" Em asked, trying to modulate her voice to sound nonchalant versus desperate which was what she was feeling at this exact moment.

"They're on hold until you can take care of the Border Patrol Agent."

"Why is that so important? I thought you said Petey and Darnell weren't going to be an issue. She didn't see me, so what's the big deal?"

"She's been poking her nose into stuff that isn't her concern. Boss man said she's a loose end that we need to tie up."

"I still think that isn't the smartest move—going after a Border Patrol Agent. It's almost as bad as killing a police officer. If your goal is to shine a big unwanted spotlight on us, go right ahead and knock off a Border Patrol Agent."

"You're not paid to think."

"I'm not paid at all," Em answered sardonically. "And it'll be my ass in a sling, not yours."

"No one's tying your hands. You'll do as we ask if you want in on what we're planning. I thought you were a good soldier like your father."

"Fine, whatever. Call me when you get your shit together, and you've found her." Em ended the call by stabbing the phone with such veracity that she feared she'd break the glass. She flung the phone on the bed and yelled, "Fuck!"

When Em turned around, she noticed Jimena leaning on the doorjamb with a questioning look. "Did your phone do something to piss you off?"

"Meeting's canceled." Em absently touched the medal hidden below her shirt.

"Okay. I take it that's bad news." Jimena lifted one eyebrow.

Em shrugged. "Not necessarily. At least they don't know where you are. On the other hand, I'm supposed to be the one to make sure you don't take another breath." She began pacing. "I need to think."

"Anything I can do to help?" Jimena pushed off the doorjamb and closed the distance, lightly stroking Em's arm.

Em tried hard not to let Jimena's touch affect her, but she was only human. She moved away. Catching feelings, any feelings right now, might get both of them killed. Em had to focus. "Yeah, I'd kill for a cup of coffee right now."

"Well, considering they want you to off me, I'm not sure I like you using that expression," Jimena joked, but her face screwed in confusion. Em assumed that was due to the distance she'd put between the two of them.

"Hilarious." Em knew Jimena deserved to hear the complete story, not the tiny snippets she'd shared with her about why she'd never reached out in fifteen years.

Jimena chuckled. "I think so. Relax. At least it appears as though your cover isn't blown." She made her way into the kitchen, and Em followed.

"Yeah, but in order for them to trust me, I have to execute you. Those paranoid asswipes won't let me in on their plans until I've proved myself to them. If I read between the lines correctly, that's their loyalty test." Em leaned against the counter, watching Jimena measure the ground coffee and place it in the filter.

Jimena stopped what she was doing and looked up. "What if we give them exactly what they want?"

"Are you out of your fucking mind?" Em pushed herself off the counter.

Jimena held her hand up in the universal gesture to stop. "No, just hear me out. I've learned a few things living in California, close to Hollywood. Why can't we stage my execution?"

"You mean like use blanks or something?" Em pursed her lips, deep in thought.

"Exactly!" Jimena exclaimed excitedly. "Then I can activate the squib after you pull the trigger. We can practice getting the timing right."

"I don't know whether to be shocked or impressed that you know about these things. Plus, the Jimena I used to know wasn't exactly a planner. You always flew by the seat of your pants and hoped to get where you intended to go." Em smiled at Jimena with considerable admiration for her former lover's creativity.

Jimena shrugged. "I plan sometimes, but I will admit the idea just popped into my head. I had a friend who worked in the special effects department at Paramount studios."

"A friend, huh? Female?" Em wasn't usually a jealous person, but suddenly she had an uncomfortable feeling. All those years apart, Jimena didn't exactly enter a nunnery. So, of course, she'd had lovers. Probably as many as Em.

"Okay, an ex, but we're still friends. I know she can get me a squib or several since we need to practice."

"This is crazy."

"No, I promise it'll work."

"But for this to fly, you'll need to come out of hiding and make yourself vulnerable. What if Smitty and his crew decide to send someone else to take you out?"

"They won't because they want to test you. It's a chance I'm willing to take. I'll stay inside the safe house until we stage the execution."

"I don't know if I like this plan." The foreboding feeling Em had wouldn't go away. She knew she should refuse, but a more significant part of her was excited about working with Jimena. They'd always been in sync before on so many levels. Finishing each other's sentences, anticipating what the other would do, or how they would respond, everything except not recognizing that they were in love with each other. That was certainly a blind spot that fortunately resolved itself at their Winter Formal.

"You want to catch these bastards, don't you?" Jimena turned on the stove to heat the water in the kettle.

"Yeah, but—"

"No buts, I want them behind bars as much or more than you." Em watched as Jimena ground her teeth. She catapulted back to when they were kids, and Jimena used to do that whenever she took a stance, which wasn't that often.

Em threw her hands in the air. "Fine. Let me run this by Carter. If he gives the go-ahead, you need to get approval from your supervisor, too. I'm not going to risk pissing off Border Patrol. You already dislike the FBI."

"Deal. I can kill two birds with one stone by calling my neighbor to ask her to feed Garfield while I'm gone. He's okay for a day, two tops, but he'll need fresh water and food. I can tell her I'll be back in a couple of days because I have to go out of town, but I'll return the day after tomorrow. They'll ferret this information and feed it back to you if they're smart. Then voila, we have our setup!" Jimena crossed her arms and relaxed against the counter with a massive smile.

†

"Now what?" the gruff voice on the other end answered.

Em relaxed on the couch while filling Carter in on the new plan. "We hit a tiny snag."

"How tiny?"

"The meeting is off until Smitty and gang locate Jimena so that I can prove myself and execute her."

"How in the ever-loving fuck is that a tiny snag?" Carter yelled.

Em laughed. "Ever-loving fuck. Well, that's a new one."

"Don't get smart with me, Schmidt. I suspect you have a harebrained plan you want me to approve."

"I do. I can't take all the credit for the scheme. Jimena suggested it."

"Okay, let's have it."

"See, Jimena has some contacts in the movie industry who can get us a squib and blanks for my gun."

"What the hell is a squib?" Carter asked.

"You know that special effect where blood bursts from a person's chest after being shot? That's the squib being activated. Anyway, we're going to give them a show. If I prove myself with their gruesome test, I'm in."

"I don't like it. You two are made for one another. You're both bat-shit crazy. I should have never authorized you to partner with her. They have different training, you know."

Em had tried without success to get Carter not to use the term "bat-shit crazy" but he was old school and didn't recognize how that term disparaged individuals suffering from mental illness. She liked to say "bat shit" without adding crazy to the end. However, most in the FBI weren't as sensitive. It was a losing battle.

"Your elitism is showing, Carter."

Em could almost see him shaking his head as he said, "I don't know why I put up with your insubordinate ass. You're going to do this whether I approve or not, aren't you?"

"Yeah, but it would be better if I had your support. Plus, we need someone to go to the studio to pick up the goods. Ask for Carol in the special effects department at Paramount Studios in LA. Tell her that Jimena needs"—Em glanced at Jimena, who mouthed the answer—"ten squibs and a box of blanks. We need to practice."

"I can't believe I'm taking orders from an arrogant little…" Carter grumbled as his voice trailed off.

"Now, Carter, you know I'm the best undercover agent you've got and the only chance to break up this ring of psychopaths."

"That is about the only thing we agree on," Carter grudgingly admitted.

†

With that hurdle over, Em relaxed into the couch and grinned at Jimena. "So, we have a whole day to ourselves." She waggled her eyebrows. "What kind of trouble should we get into?"

Jimena grabbed her chin. "Hmm, let me think. We're too old to play cops and robbers, and we'd need a third. By the way, have you kept in touch with your brother?"

Em could feel the frown form on her face. "Nope, he turned out to be a whiney little shit that I didn't want anything to do with. He's the one who ratted us out and caused the move. I'll never forgive him for that."

"Why do I feel you left out big chunks of the story? One day we're sharing our undying love for one another. As I recall, I got a marriage proposal, then I hear you're sick. When I tried to see you, your mother said you couldn't have any visitors because you were contagious. The next thing I knew, you and your family had moved out, and I had no idea where you were or if you even lived. I imagined you had a terminal condition or something."

"Well, at least my father didn't answer the door," Em glibly responded.

"I purposely went to your house when I knew he'd still be at work. I've never been stupid, even as a kid."

"No, you were always far too insightful for your own good," Em answered.

CHAPTER EIGHT

Fifteen Years Ago

When Em didn't show up for their fourth-period Civics class, Jimena had a bad feeling. Making a beeline for the hallway, she searched the crowded melee of high school students lumbering their way to lunch or their next class. Finally, finding the person she did and did not want to talk to, she tapped him on the shoulder and asked, "Where's Em? She wasn't in Civics class today."

"Sick," Karl Junior mumbled.

Jimena scrunched her face. Em was perfectly fine yesterday when they watched the sunrise at the beach.

Something wasn't adding up, but she knew she couldn't pursue her line of questioning any further. Karl was a chip off the old block, except he wasn't fully formed yet, and not as intimidating as Em's father. She had no doubt he would get there, though, eventually. Unfortunately, all arrows pointed in the direction of a first-class asshole. He routinely picked on any kid he thought was too effeminate or not cool enough to breathe the same air.

She knew it was stupid to show up at Em's house. But she couldn't shake the niggling feeling that something was terribly wrong. If she hurried, she'd miss Karl Senior. Em's mom wasn't as terrifying to deal with, and Karl Junior would be at basketball practice.

Bridget, Em's mom, answered the door, and when she realized who had knocked, a frown appeared on her flawless face. Flawless except for the bruise she'd nearly managed to cover with a heavy foundation. "Jimena, you shouldn't have come here," she said.

"Karl said Em was sick. So I brought her homework," she offered, desperate to see her if only for a minute.

"That's unnecessary. Karl Junior has already taken care of it. Em is contagious. We can't have her infecting acquaintances at school."

Jimena wanted to bite back that she was far from an acquaintance but knew that would only make matters worse. "Okay, um, can you at least tell her I stopped by?"

"Run along, Jimena, and don't come back."

The finality of that sentence left Jimena dejected. She would have to wait until Em returned to school or for her to sneak out and tap on her window. She waited weeks before learning the Schmidt family had moved away. Jimena was broken-hearted. Em hadn't bothered to say goodbye. She thought Em loved her as much as she loved Em, but she was wrong. She kept Em's ring around her neck, hoping that someday they would reunite and it would all be a silly misunderstanding. The Em she knew would never leave without saying goodbye. Something must have gotten in the way. She suspected that something was Karl Senior, but what could she do? She was just a stupid high school kid.

†

Em hobbled to the top of the staircase and listened while her mother told the lie Karl Senior had directed her to tell anyone who asked. Bridget had earned a beating herself when Karl learned about her brief moment of compassion. The doctor had called Karl to check on Em, asking how she was doing, and that's how he found out Bridget had taken her to the hospital. He hadn't bothered to check on her after returning home from his shift, or he would have seen the evidence himself. The cast on her arm was unmistakable.

The morning they were scheduled to leave for Idaho was hectic, with packers in and out of the house. Em decided this might be her only chance to slip out and see Jimena. She was desperate to explain everything and had convinced herself she could do it with no one finding out. After, Em would make a plan to leave the house for good. She'd already done the research, and no way was she going to join the Marines.

She knew how much Karl hated the Army, so that's the branch of service she decided she'd sign with. A way to say a big "fuck you" to her father.

Unfortunately, Karl Junior was always skulking around, and she didn't see him before it was too late.

"Where do you think you're going? Off to see your little girlfriend?" He sneered at her.

"Fuck off, Karl. I know it was you who couldn't wait to run back and tell Dad. How'd that work out for you, asswipe? Eager to move to Idaho?"

"Fuck you. If I have to give you a beating as bad as Dad, I will, but you're not sneaking out today. Just because the move has distracted everyone doesn't mean I'm not keeping my eye on you. Give it up, Big Sis. You're never going to see Jimena again." Karl moved to block her path.

"Never is a long time, Karl. Dad can't keep me on a leash forever."

Karl Senior yelled from the living room. "Em, Karl, get your lazy asses here and grab the bags for the car. We're leaving in less than half an hour. I expect both of you to be ready by then. I'm not going to tell you again."

A little over three months later, Em left the confines of her home and enlisted in the Army, never looking back. She'd convinced herself that Jimena was better off without her by that time. Jimena was headed to college, and the Army sent Em to fight in Afghanistan. She didn't know if she'd make it back in one piece, literally or figuratively. War changed people. Jimena didn't need to deal with a mere shadow of who she used to be. It was better this way.

As it turned out, she was partially correct. Physically, she had returned with all her limbs and major organs intact, but mentally she bore the scars of someone who saw the kind of carnage that would affect almost anyone with a heart. She often thought the Saint Christopher medal had protected her body, but the piece of jewelry was likely never intended to shelter her now fragile psyche. She'd always be indebted to the FBI which, after recruiting her, had recognized the signs and got her the help she needed. Years of therapy worked unless you counted her incessant need to place herself in dangerous spots. Gaby believed she should do more work with a therapist, but Em had certainly had enough head shrinkers for a lifetime. Although she had a more favorable view of them, Em wasn't budging. The argument with Gaby got old quickly and seemed to always hover above, threatening to put an even larger wedge between them.

CHAPTER NINE

Present Day

Determined to get the real story out of Em, Jimena remained on the couch and nonchalantly took another sip of her coffee before pinning Em with her most commanding stare. This had always worked for her before.

"No more subtly changing the subject. Time to spill, Em."

"We should leave old history in the dust. No good ever comes from stirring that shit up. It just makes you cough out painful memories. I've no doubt you already figured out what probably happened."

"I have my theories, but nothing specific. Why didn't you contact me in all these years? It's not like I moved, and you couldn't track me down."

Em sighed. "Is it that important for you to know?"

"Yeah, it is. I've been wondering for the past fifteen years if I imagined everything, or did we genuinely love one another? Correction. Did you honestly love me, or were we just stupid teenagers caught up in our hormones?"

"Not that you aren't creative and imaginative, but no, it wasn't a figment of your imagination, and it wasn't hormones, either. I'm sure you've already worked out that my father found out about our little rendezvous. Things got uncomfortable…"

Jimena grabbed Em's hand and stroked it. "Translation, he beat the shit out of you, and that's why he wouldn't let you go back to school. The evidence would have created issues for him."

"Bingo. You got it in one."

"That doesn't explain why you didn't try to call or anything. Unless your father beat you so bad that…" Jimena's voice trailed off as tears formed in her eyes. "Oh, Em. I wish I'd known. You know that Papa would have intervened."

Em shook her head. "No, it wasn't that bad. Although it was worse than all the other times. My mother risked his wrath and took me to the hospital, where at least they put a cast on my arm. If it weren't for her one act of kindness, I'd probably have had a lifelong injury impacting my ability to join the Army." Em lifted her arm, moving it, demonstrating that she had full motion. "I tried to sneak away on the day we left. It was my best chance at success since everyone was busy with the move and packing the truck. I wanted to say goodbye. Unfortunately, my brother caught me, and that was the end of that. But the biggest reason I didn't contact you before we left was that my dad threatened to summon hell and let it rain down on your head. You should have seen his eyes, Jimena. He wasn't fucking around. Dad would have killed you and hidden the body where no one would ever find you. I couldn't let that happen."

Jimena sucked in air and sat there, attempting to allow the words to enter her brain, maybe by osmosis. She hoped that would make them more palatable. "If your father wasn't already dead, I'd kill that son of a bitch myself with my bare hands. Did you really believe that he would try to track me down and make good on his threat after leaving if you tried to reconnect with me?"

Em shook her head. "Not exactly. By the time I enlisted, I knew they were sending me to Afghanistan, and remembering all the plans we had to attend college together, I couldn't fuck those up for you. So I thought you were better off without me. Then the war happened and, well, it changed me. It took a long time and several therapists to find the shell of the person left behind. I'm much healthier now, but I still have issues, as Gaby would tell you if she got the chance."

"You don't seem different from the person I knew way back then. Perhaps a little more badass, but that's all. All the fundamentals are still there."

Em laughed. "Well, you're a whole hell of a lot more badass than your seventeen-year-old self and beyond stunning. If I'd known you would grow up to be such a gorgeous woman, I would have come knocking years ago."

"Yup, there's that charmer I used to know. So," Jimena began slyly, "you and Gaby are really no more?"

"Yes, ma'am. I am blissfully or not so blissfully single. We were on life support for far too long. I should have pulled the plug a long time ago. I suppose I'm not as badass as you believe I am. Fortunately, Gaby had enough guts to end us."

"Good. Because I've wanted to do this ever since I saw those big beautiful silver eyes of yours." Jimena didn't wait for an answer or acknowledgment of what she was about to do. Instead, leaning in, she captured those full lips she'd dreamed about for years after Em left.

Jimena could tell that her bold action threw Em for a loop, but she felt Em lean into the kiss after the initial shock. Ignoring the sting from her injury, she allowed the kiss to grow more insistent and deepened the kiss by letting her lips suck gently on the outer edges before sliding her tongue inside to meet Em's eager mouth. It felt like their tongues were engaged in a sensual dance as they came together. Jimena had kissed many women since Em, but this felt like home. She noted that adult Em had learned a few things over the years.

As they broke apart, Jimena wouldn't precisely characterize their breathing as panting, but it was pretty damn close. "Sheesh, woman, if I'd known you learned to kiss this well, I would have jumped you the minute you ended your call with Gaby."

Em gently stroked Jimena's lip with her index finger. "I didn't hurt you, did I?"

"Oh, hell no, and even if you did, I would have to readjust my thoughts on BDSM."

Em chuckled. "Well, one thing that hasn't changed is that you're much braver than me."

"Now that's a big fat lie. You were always the one to confess first. If you hadn't told me you were a lesbian back in high school and then admitted you wanted to kiss me, I might never have had one of the best years of my life. I had fun in college, don't get me wrong, but it was never like it was with you."

"Well, for the record, I've wanted to kiss you, too since the moment I laid eyes on those sultry brown eyes of yours. I've been an idiot all these years, haven't I?"

"Yes, you have, but I forgive you." Jimena brushed her hand down the front of Em's chest, and when she felt the small round medal, she pulled it out from underneath her shirt. "You kept it?"

The caress on Jimena's cheek had never felt so intimate. "Of course I did. I credit my survival in the war to your gift. I never take it off. My dog tags sometimes kept the medal company, but I would never part with it."

Jimena reached into her shirt and pulled out the promise ring hanging from her gold chain. Holding it up for inspection, she said, "Great minds. I figured this was as good as our family's Saint Christopher medal. It's been my good luck charm, too. Although, I will admit to cursing it a few times over the years, especially in the beginning."

Em hesitated, then said, "You know this is a horrible idea—"

Jimena cut her off with another searing kiss. Not waiting for another protest, she insisted, "No, it's a magnificent idea. One I've been thinking about since last night." She grabbed Em by the hand, pulled her from the couch, and led her into the bedroom.

Although Em verbally protested, her body telegraphed a completely different message as she compliantly followed Jimena. "We both need clear heads if we're going to pull this off. It's not like we'll get a mulligan."

"Please don't tell me you're a golfer now. That would totally ruin the image I've had in my head for over fifteen years," Jimena joked.

"Be serious."

"I am being serious. I think more clearly when there isn't sexual chemistry needing to be released. I'm like one of those propane valves. If you don't release the pressure, I'll explode. You don't want that to happen, do you? Besides, after great sex, I'm like the energizer bunny. I can accomplish anything."

Em raised her eyebrow. "How do you know it will be good?"

Jimena flipped her hand in the air. "It was good when we were seventeen, and I don't know about you, but I've learned a few tricks along the way. There is something to be said about experience and more years on the planet. We were always compatible in bed, Em. Why would that change now?" Jimena concentrated on enthralling Em with her most smoldering look. It wasn't hard because she could not wait to make love with Em after all those years apart.

"Fuck it." Em pulled on Jimena's sleep shirt, and before long, Jimena found herself naked on the bed, with Em only in her baggy shorts. A tangle of arms and legs jockeyed for the best position. Jimena tugged on those shorts to remove the last piece of clothing, wanting desperately to be skin to skin with Em. The sting of her lip and other spots that were still sore from the beating faded into the background. At least she didn't have any broken bones. A few bruises would not delay her pleasure.

"Off, please," she ordered.

Em helped Jimena remove her shorts, and then Jimena climbed on top, kissing Em again like her life depended on getting this right. She wasn't sure who let out the first long, low moan, but both cries seemed to co-mingle in an almost guttural sound. There was nothing slow and sweet about their coming together. After grinding on top for a short time, Jimena worked her way down, pinching, licking, and lightly biting on Em's nipples, but Em was having none of that as she flipped Jimena over, and the two women struggled for dominance.

Jimena grinned and remarked, "I can already tell we might have a teeny tiny problem. Who gets to ravage who's body first? Since I made the first move, I say I win, and you can have your turn after I'm done with you. I promise." She flipped Em on her back.

"Fine. I never could resist those eyes of yours. Talk about the very definition of bedroom eyes."

With that settled, Jimena continued her journey until she nestled between Em's legs. She wondered for a brief moment if Em would enjoy a strap-on. Not that she'd snuck one into her bag, but the image wouldn't leave her brain. She'd initially allowed Em to top her, but being the recipient of a good fucking was a whole other breed of cat.

Using the tip of her tongue, she teased Em until she felt her hips rise to meet each flick. Then Jimena plunged her finger deep inside and got the reaction she was hoping for.

"Oh, yes. More," Em begged.

Who was Jimena to deny such a heartfelt plea? Later she could take her time, but this first release called for fast and hard. She pushed in and out with a second and third finger as Em met each thrust eagerly.

Another guttural sound emerged from Em before Jimena felt her contractions around her fingers. It had taken less than a minute. Although Jimena was disappointed that she hadn't exercised more control to keep Em on edge, she was happy to see and hear the result of finally being able to fill Em up with her love.

Em's body relaxed against the mattress as a bead of sweat remained on her forehead. Jimena slowly made her way up to Em's mouth and let her taste her own juices as they kissed more languorously than before when they'd been at the height of passion.

"Fuck, that was good. So good, Jimena. I don't usually let anyone top me. I kind of have control issues, you know."

"Sometimes, it's good to let go. I feel the same. But with someone I trust, it's a whole different experience. You know what I was thinking about a few minutes earlier?"

Em chuckled. "I'm almost afraid to ask."

"Ever had anyone use a strap-on with you?"

"Nope, but I'm very proficient with one, if you're interested."

"Oh, I'm interested, all right. But I also want to fuck you with one. Would you ever consider that?"

"I'm not saying yes or no. Let me think about it. If I'm honest, it's intriguing, but only with you. I'd never allow anyone else to do that. Now, I do believe you promised." Em flipped Jimena over and demonstrated her own sexual prowess based on what she'd learned over the years. Jimena was thankful that Em had ignored the bruising because the last thing she wanted at this moment was for Em to treat her like a delicate porcelain doll.

†

Em had lain on her back with one arm behind her head and the other wrapped around Jimena, who had made herself comfortable curled on her side with her head on Em's shoulder and one arm draped over her stomach. It was a familiar position for the two women, having settled into their favorite after-sex position the first time they'd explored one another and brought each other to orgasm. With Em being so much taller, it made sense that Jimena would snuggle against her versus the opposite.

Em's mind had been a whirlwind of both hope and trepidation. They'd reconnected like she'd always dreamed of, but Em had no clue what that meant for the future, especially now that they would enter the lion's den together. So many things could go wrong. Was this just sex for Jimena? Did coming together mean as much to Jimena as it meant to her?

"We should talk." Em broke the silence and comfort of their post-sex glow.

Jimena groaned. "All right, but I don't regret a thing. And no, my lip nor any other part of my body was too damaged to thoroughly enjoy what we just did."

Em turned her head. "Is that what you believe I'm ruminating over? Glad to hear I didn't hurt you, though. I guess I got caught up in the moment and didn't even register that you might still need to recover from what those assholes did to you. I'm not exactly feeling regret right now, but I am worried. You were always more spontaneous than me. I need a certain level of planning to feel comfortable. Even my enlistment wasn't spontaneous. It was my Plan B."

Jimena scrunched her nose as she lifted her head a little and looked at Em. "I never knew you had a Plan B."

"I didn't want you to think I would bail on you."

"But you did bail on me."

"Not by choice."

"Yes, by choice." Jimena sat up and held her hand out, indicating that Em should wait while she finished her thought. "Look, I understand your choice, but it was a choice. I've honestly forgiven you. You were still a kid and had an impossible decision to make. I might have made the same choice if I'd been in your shoes."

Em had already skootched her body against the headboard, patiently listening to Jimena. "Okay, that's fair. Now I'm an adult and feel like I'm in a similarly impossible situation. If we go through with this bat-shit plan of yours, there are so many things that could go wrong."

"Like?" Jimena prompted.

"What if Smitty or whoever shows up wants to ensure I've done the job and checks for a pulse?"

Jimena nodded. "Got it. Valid concern. What else have you got? I want you to put all your worries on the table, and then we can take them one by one."

"Smitty might decide to put his own bullet in you for good measure."

"Keep them coming," Jimena encouraged.

"They'll probably want to deal with your supposed dead body, and can you fake death for as long as it takes to hide the evidence? Which leads right into another worry that they'll want to burn your body to remove whatever evidence might exist."

"Okay, wow! You've been thinking this through, haven't you? I guess my spontaneity needs a partner who can rationally mull over the consequences. That's why we'll make a good team. We can do this."

"And how do you propose dealing with all these not-so-inconsequential issues?" Em scratched her head in frustration.

"You'll have to be the one to check my pulse and insist I'm dead. I know there isn't some fancy way to fake my death like in the spy shows where they stop a person's heart for a short time. I'm not stupid. We can buy ourselves more insurance by creating a sense of urgency to get the hell out of wherever this theater occurs."

"And how do you propose we do that?"

"We should have a backup available to hit their lights and sirens as soon as they hear the shot. I know it's a bit of a risk, but in all likelihood, they'll either choose my home or one of those seedy places they took me to before. It would not be a stretch to have patrols around my house, given that Petey met his demise at the police station."

"I think you're right about that," Em acknowledged.

"Besides, pulling me from my home, versus a quick execution once they determine there isn't a protection unit right outside, is the smartest move. Smitty seems more on the ball than Petey and Darnell. So he'll want the fastest and easiest solution."

"You're right. Smitty isn't dumb. All right, that takes care of everything besides Smitty deciding to take a shot at you." Em furrowed her brow.

"That's a calculated risk I'm willing to take. You and I will do everything in our power to convince Smitty or whomever they send that you want to prove for yourself that I'm dead. I plan for you to present the FBI Oscar to me after this is all over." Jimena grinned. "I suggest you practice your acting skills. No hesitation. The quicker you shoot, the more convincing you will be. I trust you, Em. I always have."

Em grabbed Jimena's hand. "Can we talk about something else weighing on my mind?"

"Always. You know you can talk to me about anything, right?"

"Let's say that by some miracle, we manage to come out the other side without getting our asses blown away. Have you thought about what that means for the future?"

"The future, as in our future?"

Em cleared her throat. "Um, yeah."

"Well, I admit, I've been envisioning a future. Of course, it's a little fuzzy, but I was hoping we could explore the possibilities."

"Even if I could make this my base of operations, I've always taken dangerous undercover assignments. Traveling takes me away from Southern California nearly as much as the military."

"I see. And you think that's the same as when you went to Afghanistan and believed leaving me back home wouldn't be fair to me or our relationship?" There was a hard edge to Jimena's voice.

Em cringed. "Sort of, yeah."

"Nice try, Em, but you aren't getting rid of me as effortlessly as Gaby. I'm a big girl now, and I decide what I can and cannot handle. Not you. Besides, perhaps after this is all over, the FBI will offer me a job, and we can go on assignments together."

"What about the FBI pissing you off when they take over a case? You'd be the one getting under another officer's skin." Em smirked at Jimena.

"Totally different scenario because I'd be the one in charge. You know how I like to take control."

"Yeah, that's another thing we'll need to work out. I don't let just anyone top me."

"Oh, but think of all the fun we'll have navigating that issue." Jimena waggled her eyebrows.

"So, you think we have a second chance at getting this right?" Em wasn't sure she deserved a second chance, but she'd take it if Jimena agreed.

"One hundred percent convinced we do. I've never been more sure of anything. Not that I believe in destiny or all that mystical crap because I'm far too practical for that, but I thought of you often in those fifteen years."

"Jimena, you are quite the enigma. A woman with deep faith who doesn't believe in mystical spirituality. Spontaneous and free-spirited, yet determined and laser-focused on what you want."

"Uh, hello, Pot." Jimena raised an eyebrow.

"Okay, Kettle. Point taken. Now that's settled, any thoughts on how we should spend the rest of the day besides preparing for our Oscar-winning performances?" Em asked. "Personally, I wouldn't mind spending the whole day in bed. We have fifteen years to catch up on and some serious discussions about dominance and submission." Em grinned.

"Interesting. You have evolved from that sugary-sweet seventeen-year-old." Jimena shot Em a sultry look. "I've dabbled a little but tend to stay on the more vanilla end of the spectrum. Giving or receiving pain doesn't do anything for me. You?"

"Same. Although I would not characterize edging, light biting, a little pinching, or shall we say, enthusiastic fucking, as pain. And bondage done correctly can ratchet up the sensations."

"Agreed." Jimena's stomach growled loudly. "If we're going to engage in enthusiastic fucking, I need sustenance. Plus, I really have to pee. I've been holding it in for the last fifteen minutes. I also don't want you to think that our relationship will only be about sex."

"Relationship, huh? I like the sound of that."

"Isn't that what we've been negotiating about for the last half hour? I'm not interested in another fuck buddy," Jimena declared with a measure of forcefulness Em found extremely hot.

"Another fuck buddy? I don't like the sound of that. Over the years, I might have slept with a lot of women, but only one at a time. I don't like to share. At all. That's a deal-breaker."

"Whoa. I won't be sleeping with other women, but hold that thought because I wasn't kidding about needing to pee." Jimena emerged from the bed and almost ran into the small bathroom connected to the bedroom.

†

Em strolled into the small kitchen with a big smile on her face. Opening the refrigerator, she pulled out a carton of eggs and began quietly humming "Happy" by Pharrell Williams. Then, spinning in the kitchen, she started cracking eggs into a bowl and dancing around to the tune in her head. When she heard laughing, she turned to see Jimena crossing the room. But that didn't stop her from swaying her hips and continuing to hum.

"You always were an incredible dancer. And unlike me, you could hold a tune. However, I can't quite tell what song is in your head."

"'Happy,'" Em answered. "I know we're about to run headfirst into a raging fire to save the day, but today is for us to enjoy and be happy. I'm taking a page from your spontaneity book. For once, I don't want to plan a thing. I just want to be here with you—basking in the light of your glorious glow. You know you always had this sort of, I don't know how to describe it…"

"A flame that I could never extinguish. That's how I've always thought about my feelings for you."

"God, look at us—two badass law enforcement officers getting all mushy. I'm not sure I like what basking in your light has done to me." Em stopped dancing around but continued to whisk the eggs in the bowl.

"Oh, I don't know. I like this lighter version of you. Sometimes you can get awfully serious and fail to enjoy the now. We'll have plenty of time to show off our badassery. You know you can be both. People are never one-dimensional. We are all multifaceted," Jimena explained.

"I suppose you're right. How did you get so wise?"

"Years on the planet, Em, just like you, years on the planet. Everyone has their own brand of wisdom, strengths, and weaknesses. The key is to partner with someone who can complement your strength and shore up the areas that need a little focus."

Em stopped preparing the eggs and grabbed Jimena's face to kiss her. "God, I love you."

The minute the words slipped from her mouth, she knew it was a premature declaration, but she couldn't exactly say she didn't mean them. Jimena stared at her, open-mouthed.

"Was, uh, was that a spontaneous assertion because you're in a good mood, or did you mean that?" Jimena stuttered.

"Shit, sorry. It just slipped out."

"So you don't still love me?" Jimena's eyes dimmed a little.

"No, no, fuck, I suck at this. Yes, of course I still love you. I never stopped. I only thought it might be a little soon to make sweeping pronouncements of love."

Jimena's mouth formed a lopsided grin. "Ooh, look at you, failing to plan a romantic moment. Just for the record, I never stopped caring for you, either. Only this time around, my feelings are a little more mature."

"Really?" Em asked.

"Yeah, really. I think we could have something amazing. I'm not asking you to marry me or anything. That would be ridiculously impetuous, but why is it so out of the realm of possibility that I would still care deeply for you? You were my first love. Isn't it common knowledge that a person never forgets their first? By the way, what the hell are you making?"

Em laughed. "Got a little too intense for you, huh? I'm making the best omelet you've ever tasted. Although, it is missing a few key ingredients that would make it more spectacular."

"You realize it's way past breakfast time? We pretty much spent all morning…reconnecting." Jimena winked.

"Brunch? I say omelets and pancakes are universal foods that we can eat any time of the day. Besides, they're the only choices if you want something remotely edible. I never quite learned how to cook. But I can call for takeout like the best of them if you'd prefer to eat something else."

"No, no, please show me your culinary skills with an omelet and pancakes. I'm too hungry to wait for takeout."

"More coffee?" Em asked.

"Sure, why not? But I can make it."

"No, let me do this. Sit down and relax, and I'll bring the coffee and food to you. Maybe you should check in with Gary, considering we altered our plans. You didn't exactly have time to do that. And don't you also need to get hold of your neighbor to get the ball rolling?"

"I do. Okay, I'll let you pamper me. It's been a long time since anyone did that for me. You always were the more attentive one. Dare I say the consummate romantic between the two of us? I loved that about you."

"I sure hope that use of loved isn't past tense."

"It's not." Jimena grabbed a kitchen towel and playfully smacked Em on her ass. "Now get back to cooking for me, wench."

Jimena hadn't come out and declared her undying love, saying things like caring for Em deeply, but Em sensed Jimena felt the same. She was simply being overcautious. Em couldn't blame her. She was the one who'd left all those years ago. Now that she'd decided to do whatever it took to gain Jimena's trust and make a go of it, she wasn't letting go anytime soon.

CHAPTER TEN

Why hadn't she just come out and told Em she loved her, too? Maybe a part of Jimena was still pissed that Em had left without an explanation all those years ago. Logically, she understood, but seventeen-year-old Jimena, who had cried for weeks, still held some real estate in her heart. On the other hand, it was Em, the only woman she would ever love so wholly. This was her issue to resolve on her own, and by God, she would.

Jimena practiced her deep breathing before gathering the energy to call Gary. She knew it would be a hard sell because he hadn't exactly jumped on the previous bandwagon. Had it not been for Jimena pointing out how much good press might come out of successful collaboration, he might not have gone for it. She would have loved to be a fly on the wall during the conversation between Gary and Carter. Gary was like a politician, always looking for the best angle in any situation.

"Evans," Gary answered briskly.

"Hi Gary, it's Jimena. We've run into a slight complication. The meeting is off between the agent and the domestic terrorist group. They want her to execute me before letting her further into their inner circle."

"What?" Gary screamed. "Then we're out. Let the FBI clean up their own mess."

"Before you say that, can you just listen for a minute? We have a plan."

"I'm not going to like this, am I?"

"You will when we catch these bastards and Border Patrol shares in the accolades. I promise this will reflect very well on your leadership."

"You ass kisser, but go on, I'm listening."

"If Hollywood can make it look like someone has been shot and killed, I know we can duplicate my fake death. I have a friend that will get us blanks and a squib. It'll look as real as on TV or in the movies. We've also talked about every contingency for something going awry. The less you know, the better. I know you have to keep those above you informed, but can you please not share anything about this new plan? There are leaks not only in local PD, but the FBI also suspects Border Patrol may have a few rogue agents. For everything to work, we need to keep this under wraps for now."

"Are you telling me how to do my job?"

"No, sir. Please, Gary, this may be our only chance to catch them red-handed."

"What about your brother? You know what a hothead he is. He'll come barreling into my office, ready to take off a few of my favorite body parts. Are you sure you want to do this? They aren't putting on pressure, are they?"

"No, sir. It was actually my idea. Manny is off on his annual deep-sea fishing trip. By the time he gets back, I'm convinced we'll have resolved all of this. Of course, my brother will chew my ass for getting involved, but at least he won't believe I'm dead because he won't know."

"All right. You have my permission, and I won't say a word until I hear again from you. When is this big event supposed to play out?"

"In a couple of days. I'm calling my neighbor to care for my cat for a few days since I will be out of town. If they're as smart or connected as we think they are, they'll find out and make their move in two days when I return to my house. You can help by letting that information slip. Then, hopefully, whomever they have on the inside will pick up that intel and run with it."

"I don't like believing that someone in our agency is working with these scumbags. I might have to do my own reconnaissance to figure that out. God help that person when I catch him."

"Or her. Don't be sexist," Jimena teased.

"Fine, but the odds are it's a him. You be careful, Jimena. I'd rather not train a new agent."

"Yes, sir. I'll call you in a few days with a report. We're close, Gary. I can almost taste it."

"Let's hope that it won't be your blood you're tasting in a few days."

"Bye, Gary." Jimena sighed and punched in the number for her neighbor, Mrs. Rodriguez. "One down, one to go."

"Hello," the wavery voice answered.

"Hi, Mrs. Rodriguez. I was wondering if I could impose on you for a favor? I had to go out of town unexpectantly, and I left Garfield alone in the house. He's pretty self-sufficient, but could you check on him and fill his food bowl? Also, maybe give him fresh water. He's a picky little bugger and likes cold bottled water. There's plenty in my refrigerator. For some reason, that fountain I bought isn't good enough for him." Jimena chuckled. "I know he's spoiled, but he's a good boy most of the time."

"Of course, dear. Is everything okay? Nothing's happened to any of your sisters or brother, has it?"

"Oh, no, not at all. Just some things I need to take care of."

"New girlfriend?" Mrs. Rodriguez teased. "I won't tell anyone."

Jimena had to slap her hand over her mouth to keep from laughing aloud. Mrs. Rodriguez was the biggest gossip in the neighborhood, and that's why she was asking her to take care of Garfield. She'd let anyone around know when Jimena would return.

Ignoring the question, Jimena barreled on. "I'll be back the day after tomorrow, probably around noon. Okay?"

"Yes, dear. I love Garfield. It will give me a chance to pet his handsome head."

"Don't give him too many treats. Garfield is already as big as his namesake, and the vet said I should put him on a diet. But that seems kind of cruel since he loves his food. And my food," Jimena added while chuckling.

"Bring that new girlfriend around for me to meet. You know I'm one of the hip ones. I've never cared who you dated. Back in the day, I had my own walk on the wild side—"

"Listen, Mrs. Rodriguez, I've got to go, but we'll have tea when I get back, and then I want to hear all about it." If Jimena let her continue, Mrs. Rodriguez would tell her the story of when she'd kissed a girl at her Catholic school. Jimena had heard the tale so many times she could recite it word for word, like an old beloved movie she watched every year.

"Okay, dear. Have fun."

"Bye, Mrs. Rodriguez, and thanks for doing this for me."

Just as Jimena laid the phone on the coffee table, Em placed a steaming plate of pancakes topped with a massive square of melting butter and the fluffiest omelet Jimena had ever seen, directly in front of Em. The scent of garlic and something else she couldn't quite detect wafted from the plate. Next to the breakfast foods, she placed a cup of coffee with steam still rising from the top.

"I hope you like it." Em turned and began walking to the kitchen, only to return with her own plate and cup of coffee seconds later.

"It smells almost too decadent to eat. What's in it?"

"Well, I had to improvise and work with what I had. There were some roasted red peppers in the refrigerator, garlic, and a little bit of spinach. I would have preferred goat cheese, but I made do with Swiss gruyere. Sorry, no blueberries for the pancakes, but there was vanilla and syrup in the cupboard. You'll have to be satisfied with plain pancakes."

"I plan on eating this whole plate. I'm ravished."

"Well, then dig in. I couldn't help but overhear. Was that Mrs. Rodriguez you were talking to?"

"Yeah, I left things kind of vague. She's a nosy one," Jimena answered. "My snooping neighbor wanted to know if something was wrong with my sisters or brother."

"Shit, I didn't think about that. They'll think you're dead. I can't have that guilt on my head, too. Fuck. We have to call it off."

"No way. You might not have considered that, but Gary did. It just so happens that Manny is fishing right now and won't return for another week and a half. By then, hopefully, this will all be a distant memory. And I already told you both Rosie and Maria live far away. Surely this will not make the national news." Jimena grabbed Em's hand to squeeze it and reassure her. "Besides, I barely got off the phone with Mrs. Rodriguez. So if I call back now, I might as well kiss my afternoon goodbye," Jimena explained.

Em chuckled. "I didn't know she was still around. Remember when she used to look at us and then wink like we shared some big secret with her?"

109

Jimena laughed. "Yeah. Do you want to know what the big secret was?"

"God, yes. I don't believe I will survive another day without learning that little mystery," Em joked.

"Apparently, she feels a kindred spirit to us dykes. I heard her scandalous story about kissing a girl at her Catholic high school—practically every year since I came home from college one year with my girlfriend. She told me the story and said nothing was wrong with a little woman-loving-woman action. The best kiss she ever had was from that girl. Or so she insists."

"No way."

"Yup. She's the biggest gossip in the neighborhood. So, I was outed before I knew it. Actually, she did a big favor for me. If it wasn't for Mrs. Rodriguez, I don't think my parents would have come around to having a lesbian for a daughter as quickly as they did."

"So you didn't come out to your parents?"

"I believed that was what I was doing when I proudly introduced my girlfriend to my parents, but they said they had already suspected. It was such a letdown. Literally, no one in the neighborhood was surprised."

"I'd love to chat with her again. She was kind of fun, as I recall. A little quirky."

"Don't worry. I promised to have tea with Mrs. Rodriguez when I return, and I'm sure she'll nearly trip over herself to share the story with you."

Em pointed at the plate in front of Jimena. "Eat before it gets cold."

Jimena used her fork to slice off a piece of omelet and placed it on her tongue. Chewing slowly, she remarked, "Oh my God. So good. Like orgasmic good. I'm never making omelets again." Jimena waved her hand up and down and said, "I dub you Queen Omelet Maker."

Em bowed. "Accepted. I usually save making a big breakfast for lazy Sundays when I am not on an assignment, but today seemed like a good day to break out my skills. I was hoping we could relax and watch movies all day, or perhaps some other things." She waggled her eyebrows.

"I vote for a little of both. Not that I don't have the stamina for more bedroom sexthenics, but snuggling with you, and a good movie, sounds heavenly. Remember when we used to do that?"

"Yeah." Em sighed with pleasure. "Those were some of my more relaxing and comforting times. Unfortunately, I haven't had much of that lately."

"Who stocks the safe houses?" Jimena asked.

"You know, I don't actually know. Choice of movies could be limited. Cheap bastards don't even spring for premium channels. I'm afraid it's old-school DVDs for us. Let's see what they've got." Em walked to the cabinet the TV sat on and opened the doors below. "Horror, thriller, comedy. Looks like a little of everything except lesbian romance," she teased.

"Thriller?" Jimena suggested.

"My life is a thriller. How about a nice relaxing comedy?"

"What? You don't enjoy seeing blood and guts? No horror, either?"

"Yeah, I forgot how you loved horror or action flicks." Em chuckled. "I only tolerated them for you."

"What?" Jimena put her hand over her mouth in mock surprise. "You mean all those times I dragged you to another *Halloween* the ninety-ninth, or whatever version came out, you hated it?" Jimena belly laughed. "I knew, but I didn't want to burst that badass bubble you wanted me to believe about you. I always understood that a bigger part of you was this big romantic softie."

"Ha ha, hilarious. Never repeat that, or I'll have to cut out your tongue. I have a reputation to maintain."

"Go ahead and pick a romantic comedy. I'm sure I'll survive," Jimena said.

"How about *When Harry Met Sally*? It's a classic. Maybe someday they'll make a lesbian version, like *When Hilda Met Sally*?"

"Hilda? Really? Why not Harriet? Hilda sounds more like a horror movie with badass witches. Now that would be something I'd watch for sure."

Em shrugged. "I'll simply use my imagination trick and picture myself in the lead role instead of Billy Crystal."

"Why am I the Sally character? You should be Sally because you're blond, and I should be Hilda because I have dark hair and am clearly the bigger womanizer."

"Sally is too fem for me to pull that off," Em insisted.

"Oh my God. Listen to us. If this is not the most ridiculous conversation. Just put the movie in, and I'll endure. We can keep rewinding the scene in the restaurant. Now that was classic." Jimena grinned.

"Perfect. We can put *Saw* in next. That should satisfy your gruesome taste in movies." Em slid the DVD into the player and stood. "Hey, you too full for popcorn? I think I saw some microwave packets in the cupboards."

"I always have room for popcorn, but I wouldn't want you to miss a minute of your sappy romance. I'll make the popcorn." Jimena jumped from the couch, grabbing the empty plates.

†

Halfway into the movie, Em's burner phone rang, and she gestured for Jimena to turn down the TV and remain quiet. Jimena nodded her understanding and grabbed the remote to mute the television.

Em pushed the button to answer the call. "Yeah. You got information for me?"

"We've tried to find out where she is, but nobody knows. What we know is that she'll be returning to her house the day after tomorrow, around noon. I'll call you when I have her subdued. Be ready to meet me there," Smitty said. "Where are you right now?"

"None of your fucking business. I have a life, you know."

"The bitch lives in your old neighborhood. How about that? Just wanted to make sure you aren't far away when I call. You need to come prepared to take her out. Quietly. We don't need any nosy neighbors calling it in before we have a chance to make sure everything is clean. The old woman next door seems to know everything that happens in the neighborhood. Maybe I should have you take care of her first."

"I'm not offing some old woman because you're a paranoid asshole. The less attention we create, the better. More bodies mean more evidence to clean up. So don't be stupid."

"She's Mexican, too. Probably another illegal," Smitty said, as if that made his idea to kill her an obvious solution.

"Fucking think with your head, man. If she's old, she'll die soon enough, anyway. It's not like she can breed new little Mexicans." Em cringed when she said that, chancing a quick glance at Jimena. "I'm not buying us more trouble. You want to off her? Be my guest." Em held her breath, hoping he wouldn't take her suggestion to heart. She didn't want another innocent woman's death on her conscience. If Smitty pushed the issue, she would have to find a way to get Mrs. Rodriguez a protective detail without her knowing they were there.

"Fine. We'll let the old bag live. She did provide the information we needed. I guess that earns her a few more days on the planet. Although two shootings in the same neighborhood where druggies are just down the road would have been a perfect way to blame the deaths on the gangs. But you're right. Too much time and effort to set up both scenes. I managed to secure drugs and paraphernalia to make it look like a drug deal gone bad."

"Good thinking." Em let out the breath she had kept inside. Jimena squeezed her hand, and Em felt the support she was being given. "What's the address? I might want to take a look before she returns. It's always good to be extra prepared if we need an escape route."

"Why the fuck would we need an escape route?"

"If there is a lot of drug activity in the area, police patrols are more frequent. Hopefully, they're stuffing their faces at that time since it will be around noon."

"Maybe we should grab her and take her somewhere more secluded," Smitty suggested.

"And take the chance of getting caught kidnapping her? I don't think so. I'd rather stick with your plan of setting up the scene as a drug deal gone bad. Forget calling me. I'll meet you there around noon. The address please," Em prompted.

"455 Second Avenue West. See you at noon. Look for my truck a couple blocks from the house, and don't park next to me. Find another place at least two blocks away."

"Don't talk to me like I'm one of your stupid bimbos. I know how to make myself invisible. You just worry about yourself." Em ended the call, not wanting to have a lengthy conversation with Smitty.

†

Jimena could see the discomfort written all over Em's face. She'd heard enough of the conversation to know that playing this role was hard for Em. The things she had to say and the derisive tone she'd used to maintain her cover had to wear on her, especially since she'd just fucked one of those Mexicans she was supposed to despise.

Em tossed the phone on the coffee table like a hot potato she needed to rid herself of. Disgust was written all over her face, but was it loathing over what she'd said or aversion to the whole ugly situation? "I'm sorry," she said.

"For what?"

"For you having to hear that. You know I'm only playing a part. I don't believe any of those things I said."

"Oh, Em. I know that. You don't have to explain."

"I feel like I need to scrub myself with pure lye every time I communicate with them."

"Babe, you need to watch those micro-expressions of yours. You telegraph revulsion. I know I am particularly adept at picking up how you genuinely feel, but you will blow your cover if you don't neutralize your face." Jimena grabbed both of Em's hands and captured her attention.

"I am much better at it when I'm face-to-face with them. I can throw up a shield or adopt an impassive expression. With you, it's different. You've always been able to cut through my defenses and see everything clearly."

"Okay," Jimena said hesitantly. "Will you be able to show that impassiveness when I'm in the same room as you? There can't be a second of hesitation when you pull the trigger. You know that, right?"

"Yup, that's why we're going to practice this so much that my muscle memory will take over, including my carefully constructed resting-bitch face."

"Resting-bitch face, huh? Now, this I have to see."

Em lost all humor and glared at Jimena. Not a hint of a smile touched her lips, and those silver eyes turned gunmetal gray. The look sent shivers down Jimena's spine, and she wondered if the Army had fundamentally changed the sweet young woman she used to know.

"Please tell me that is your resting-bitch face, and you aren't genuinely angry with me."

One corner of Em's lips turned up, and her eyes melted back into their light silvery gray—the color that had always caused Jimena to swoon. "Well? What do you think? Do you still believe I can't pull this off?"

"Nope. Not a slice of doubt in my mind. Holy shit! That look is downright petrifying. Where did you learn that?"

"The Army taught me a lot of things. One of those was how to react if captured. I figured adopting an expression of a coiled snake ready to strike was better than a blank expression. Psychological warfare is a powerful tool when used properly." Em shrugged. "It also worked quite well when one of the men or women in my unit was fucking around at the wrong time. I never had to say a word."

"You failed to mention your rank in the Army. It must have been up there for you to be responsible for a whole unit."

"It isn't that hard to reach Captain. Do your time and keep your nose clean is all it takes." Em shrugged. "I'd had enough, though, and even with them dangling Major in front of me, it wasn't sufficiently enticing to re-enlist. I wanted something different after seeing so much senseless destruction. It was time to pursue another career. Undercover work for the FBI suits me."

"I can see that. I know Border Patrol has a long way to go regarding hiring women, but half of Border Patrol is Hispanic. Even if I had joined the military, the FBI would never have come knocking on my door. You people are whiter than *Casper the Friendly Ghost*. I suppose Border Patrol suits me, too. Although there is something romantic about being an FBI agent. Hollywood certainly loves to make you the heroes and heroines. I don't think I've ever seen a series about a badass Border Patrol Agent saving the day."

"I've no doubt the FBI will stand and take notice after we've locked this up and destroyed this little hate cell. One down and likely a hundred left to deal with in various stages of threat. If you wanted to join the FBI, I'll bet they'd love to have you."

"We can cross that bridge if it ever comes to pass. I'd only be interested if I got the chance to work with you again. Otherwise, I think I'll stay put right where I'm at," Jimena said. "Time to finish getting your sappy romance fix." Jimena playfully bumped Em as she promptly relaxed into the couch and draped her arm over Jimena's shoulder. Jimena pressed the unmute button, and they snuggled together on the couch while they watched the rest of the movie.

CHAPTER ELEVEN

Over the next day and a half, Jimena and Em settled into an almost normal domestic routine, cooking and cleaning together between marathon sessions of making love. Em hadn't been this relaxed or slept as soundly in years. However, when the morning rolled around on the day they had arranged for Jimena to return to her home, Em's anxiety rose. Could they do this? The FBI had looped in two local police officers in addition to agents Em trusted with her life. They would swoop in, clear the scene, and provide details to the local news outlets. Em hoped it would make the evening news, setting her up to gain final exposure to the group's imminent plans.

Even with a solid strategy, she almost phoned Carter to call the whole thing off. Em trusted her gut, and it told her there were too many variables beyond their control. What if the local police they'd chosen were connected to the group, or somehow the informer in Border Patrol caught wind of the plan? Too many people were in the know for her comfort.

Jimena was uncharacteristically quiet as she taped one squib over her heart and two more in her abdomen and below her sternum. They'd decided to activate all three, making it look like there was no way Jimena would survive three shots. Em would initiate three quick shots in a row, making it difficult to ascertain which bullet hit first since it was likely all three squibs would activate simultaneously.

"It's not too late to call this off, you know?" Em smoothed down a piece of the tape against Jimena's heart.

"And ruin my chance of getting into the FBI and satisfying one of their diversity quotas?" Jimena teased.

"I have a funny feeling about this."

"That's indigestion from the spicy food I cooked last night. I forgot what a spice wimp you are. I remember telling Mama she needed to tone things down for you." Jimena turned to face Em and brushed her hand over Em's jawline. "Babe, we've talked about this. If needed, I can always improvise. And so can you. Do you have another weapon you can use if things fall apart?"

Em nodded.

"Good, just make sure you don't mix the two of them up? Oh, and I've heard you need to be far away, or that blank will hurt like a mother," Jimena said.

"I might have the two officers hit their lights and siren before the shooting starts. I want to guarantee the urgency of leaving before Smitty gets any bright ideas to check your pulse."

"Okay. How will the officers know when to do that?"

Em grinned. "The FBI has an array of gadgets at our disposal. A little button on the bottom of the gun, once activated, will tell them I'm ready."

"See, you've totally got this. And so do I. I'll fight him just enough to make it seem real, but not enough to prematurely activate any of the squibs." Jimena pulled the T-shirt over her head and winked at Em. "Let's do this, partner."

Em touched her lips to Jimena's in a soft kiss of reassurance. "I'll see you soon. They're going to bring you back here after staging the whole body bag in the ambulance. You'll need to remain here until we resolve everything."

"Shit. I almost forgot about Garfield."

"We'll figure that out later. I promise," Em said.

†

Jimena was tempted to take the long way on her Harley to clear her head of any doubt they would pull this off, but she wanted it to all be over, so she didn't. Unfortunately, the short ride was not nearly enough time to calm her increasing anxiety. Em had given her the perfect opening to back out, but she couldn't do it. The tiny body she'd found in the desert had been burned beyond recognition except for the clear evidence that it was a child. A small child, probably no older than five. She'd nearly lost her lunch that day and hadn't been able to scrub that picture from her mind ever since. When she thought about that innocent child, her resolve crystalized to do whatever necessary to take down the monsters responsible for the atrocities she'd seen rise sharply over the last six months.

Activating the garage door opener clipped to her bike, she understood perfectly that she would telegraph her arrival. She was ready to put on a show. Carefully easing into the garage, she put the kickstand on and removed her helmet. The blow to the back of the head wasn't entirely unexpected, but she needed to remain conscious, or she'd set Em up for a harder sell. Maybe Em would adjust and aim perfectly for each squib, causing the blanks to activate the fake blood. She shook her head to keep awake. But that wasn't the only thing that could go wrong now that he'd chosen to attack her in her secure garage.

Em was always on time, and she hoped she wouldn't disappoint today because, since she was not able to reset her alarm, the real police would arrive in short order. Her alarm system was on a timer. Whenever she activated the garage door, she had three minutes to reset the alarm before it would alert the security company, who would promptly phone the police if Jimena didn't answer her phone.

The man who grabbed her from behind was huge, and Jimena didn't have enough strength to put up much of a battle, but she got in one good elbow to his gut and stomped hard on his toes with her heavy boots. Neither made much difference when he tossed her on the ground as if she were a pesky mosquito.

Jimena had enough awareness to register that the gigantic man was zip-tying her hands behind her back. *Fuck, I hope Em is good at improvising.* Jimena still had faith that Em would know she couldn't activate the three squibs with her hands out of commission.

The man kicked her in the ribs, missing the squib attached to her stomach by mere inches, and yelled, "Get up, bitch. Time to meet your maker."

For a flicker of time, Jimena thought this might be it. The man didn't sound like he was going to wait for Em. Instead, he roughly pulled her to a standing position and pushed her forward. Jimena stumbled but regained her footing quickly as he led her into her home. The man shoved her onto one of the kitchen chairs, then pulled another one out and smirked at her. He had a gun pointed at her head.

Jimena prayed the police would not run their sirens before Em was ready. Certainly, the FBI would monitor the police scanner or have a direct line to the officers they'd chosen to convince everyone that Jimena had died. If another set of officers answered the call first, that could be a disaster for all involved.

"Now we wait."

"Fuck you," Jimena spit out. She looked around her kitchen and saw a bag of cocaine sliced open with powder spilling over onto the table. Smitty had apparently also scattered several bags of what looked like prescription narcotics across the table. There was a trail of powder leading out of the kitchen to her back door. Although a cursory glance would initially lead an investigator to believe a drug deal gone bad, she didn't think anyone worth their salt would buy that story if they only dug deeper. But Jimena had to trust that it would not come to that. *Why couldn't this asshole wait until I entered the house and had reset the alarm?*

"What did you say to me?" He stood menacingly over her. "I should pop you right now and be done with it."

Whoops. Come on, Em, where the hell are you?

Just as Jimena thought she'd overplayed her resistance and was about to learn what death was all about, she heard Em's steady voice.

Em had managed to enter the house without making a sound. Not only had she startled Jimena, but Smitty had also jumped.

"Hello, Smitty," Em said. "I see you've set the scene. Now, why don't you tell me what the authorities will think about the restraints?" Her voice was laced with ice.

"Um, I don't know. Probably that the gang bangers got a jump on her," Smitty said.

"Really?" Em raised an eyebrow. "And left all these drugs just lying around for the police to find. Did you even use gloves?"

"No need." Smitty grinned. "My prints are not in the system like yours."

"Get those zip ties off her. What the hell is she going to do with two guns pointed at her head? I believe that gives us a distinct advantage. The story will sell a lot better without her tied up."

"Whatever, but then you need to pop her, and we can get the hell out of here." Smitty made his way to Jimena, pulling out a switchblade and not so carefully cutting the zip ties. Jimena could feel the trickle of blood seep down her hand from the cut Smitty had made while releasing her hands.

"You'll get no argument from me. Now stand back. I wouldn't want you to catch a stray—"

Jimena heard sirens from inside the kitchen, causing Smitty to jump. "What the fuck, cops?"

Em raised her gun and aimed with an imperceptible nod directed at Jimena. Reacting quickly, Jimena had barely enough time to activate the squibs simultaneously with Em's three successive shots. Jimena slumped in her chair. She heard the second set of sirens and tried not to react.

"Time to go, Smitty. There's a back door leading out of the garage," Em barked.

Smitty glanced at Jimena's body.

"What the fuck are you waiting for? An invitation from the president? Go, go," Em shouted.

There was a moment's indecision before Smitty ran to the back door with Em close on his heels. Jimena waited for the two police officers to find her in the kitchen before barely lifting her head. They were good, playing to an invisible audience in case Smitty and Em remained close enough to hear or see. But then she realized why they were acting this way when two more officers entered the house, guns drawn. She resumed her slumped position.

"We need a bus at 455 Second Avenue West," the female officer spoke into her shoulder mic.

The other officer put his fingers on Jimena's neck and said, "No pulse. No rush on the bus. She's dead." He pointed to the other officers who'd just arrived. "Check the back. They can't have gone far."

Jimena hoped they weren't fast enough to catch Smitty or Em because that wouldn't help the carefully laid deception. But at least it left her alone with the man and woman in on the ruse.

The man touched her arm and said, "All clear."

Jimena nodded her thanks to the two officers. The woman winked at her and nodded in acknowledgment. The worst part of the whole deception was when they zipped her into the black bag before shoving her into the back of the ambulance. The minute she heard the doors slam, she clawed at the zipper. Jimena thought she knew what being buried alive might feel like. She felt a firm hand stop her frantic efforts to untangle herself from this premature coffin before the person on the other end unzipped the bag. Jimena breathed in the stale air in the back of the ambulance. That air had never felt so good. At this moment, it was better than the one trip she'd made to Northern California, where she had been surrounded by greenery and fresh mountain air.

Jimena couldn't gulp enough oxygen before she finally croaked, "Thank you." She recognized the man dressed as a medic. Em trusted Hank, so Jimena did as well.

"Sorry, we had to make it look real. I know it doesn't feel like it, but good fortune is on our side. Brilliant luck

126

with the garage alarm. Em can use that to explain why the police arrived so quickly. You must have a guardian angel. So far, this is working out well."

"I worried that the alarm would cause issues," Jimena mumbled and felt a sharp pain in her ribs when she tried to take a deep breath.

"Nope, our officers intercepted the call and took it before anyone else responded. Since they were already close, it made perfect sense to the dispatcher, but to make it look real, they had to announce, 'shots fired,' which brought the second unit."

"Yeah, I heard."

"Fortunately for us, some eager journalist must have listened to the police scanner. There was a news crew right there recording everything. But, just in case we still have eyeballs on this, we have to take you to the hospital for them to certify you are dead. A vehicle will wait at the loading dock to whisk you to the safe house," Hank explained.

"Any news from Em yet? I know it's still early, but I hoped she would call in when she was safe."

Hank shook his head. "Not yet, but don't worry. It appears as though everything went according to plan. It's been a slow week in the news. I wouldn't be surprised if they led with this story."

†

Smitty wasn't as stealthy as Em, and she cursed him as he lumbered along. At first, she thought the silent alarm

Jimena had attached to her garage was a lucky break for them. It would explain why the police arrived on the scene so quickly. When she'd approached the house, she had peeked into the garage first and noticed the lights blinking. She'd had the brilliant idea of setting off the alarm before she arrived as one more reason the cops would show lickety-split. Then the FBI could carefully leak that detail, or Em could make sure Smitty knew. Fortunately or unfortunately, that had already occurred. Smitty must have grabbed Jimena in her garage and didn't notice the silent alarm.

Em quickly popped a com into her ear and alerted Hank, directing him to make sure their chosen officers were first on the scene.

"We're on it, already. This isn't my first rodeo, you know," he grumbled.

However, two additional police officers had responded and were now making their way closer to Smitty and Em. Thinking on her feet, Em grabbed Smitty by the arm, "Stop running," she hissed. Then she roughly pulled him next to his beater truck and kissed him.

At first, the kiss had shocked him, but then his slobbery mouth was all over hers, roughly kissing her back. She nearly gagged but kept up the display until she heard one of the officers speak.

"Hey, did you hear gunshots earlier?"

Em shrugged. "Yeah, so? It's not that unusual in this neighborhood."

"See anyone running this way?"

"Even if we did, what's in it for us if we tell you? We're not getting involved in some gang-banger war." Smitty sneered.

The larger officer took a menacing step in Smitty's direction. "Maybe you'll be more cooperative when we haul you down to the station for questioning."

Smitty started to reach for his gun, and Em subtly stopped him. The last thing she needed was a trigger-happy Smitty shooting two police officers.

Em pointed to the adjacent side street. "Two dudes. Went that way. One was wearing a black hoodie and the other a baseball cap. They were both Hispanic. I couldn't read the writing on the cap, but if you hurry, you might actually catch them this time," Em stated with a touch of attitude.

The officer who had threatened Smitty hesitated, then turned to his partner. "Come on, we're not letting those little punks get away." They both took off with remarkable speed.

"Where did you grab the Border Patrol Agent?" Em hissed. She wasn't taking any chances, even though she'd bet all she owned that the FBI would leak that piece of information to the press.

"In her garage. Why? What the fuck does that matter?" Smitty grumbled.

"It matters, you fuckwad, because she has an alarm system there, and I'll bet you didn't have her disarm it. When I cased the place earlier, I traced the wires and figured that out. Then I checked her house for alarms, which I guess she hadn't gotten around to installing yet. Why the hell do you think the police arrived so soon? I didn't even have a chance to put on my silencer. We're lucky I had enough wits about me to send those cops in another direction. What the hell were you thinking, reaching for your gun? We don't need that kind of heat on us."

Smitty smirked. "Is that why you kissed me? I got some heat for you, baby." He grabbed his crotch. "You know I got more to offer you. You aren't too bad on the eyes. I could fuck you."

"In your fucking dreams. I suggest you pull your head out of your ass and get the hell out of here. I plan to do the same and lie low for a few days. Call me when we're ready to move forward with something more meaningful than eliminating some insignificant Border Patrol Agent, or chancing bringing the whole damn police force on our heads for shooting one of their own." Em pivoted sharply, taking off at a brisk pace in the opposite direction of the cops. She sighed in relief when she reached her car. Once on the road, she put the ear mic in and contacted Hank. *Guess today was not a good day to die.*

"If Smitty is one of the best they've got, we should have no problem taking this domestic terror cell down. His stupidity might have worked to our advantage. Although, I didn't like that two police officers saw my face and Smitty's. Smitty almost drew his gun and shot them. These paranoid assholes are likely to find out who they are and execute the poor bastards. Can you make sure that doesn't happen? I don't want their deaths on my head."

"All good on this end. We even got the media recording everything. We'll make sure they know about the silent alarm in the garage, too," Hank answered.

"Yeah, thanks. I thought about tripping it myself. I'm sorry I didn't let you know about that sooner. It just came to me on my way over."

"No worries. Everything worked out fine, thanks to my quick response. Although Jimena wasn't too happy when they zipped up the body bag. She's a bit claustrophobic."

"Don't be an ass, Hank. You would be, too, if they stuffed you in a bag, reducing your oxygen to a bare minimum."

"Okay, okay, sorry. We're on our way to the hospital now. Want to talk to her?"

"Yes. Put her on," Em directed.

"Hey," Jimena greeted.

"Hey, yourself. You doing okay?" Em softened her tone, the recent adrenaline rush calming now that she heard Jimena's voice.

"Yeah. How about you?"

"Peachy. Listen, you did an outstanding job in there," Em said.

"Me? I'm not the one who had to think on her feet. Thanks for getting me out of those zip ties. I didn't even consider that he might restrain me or that he'd grab me before I entered the house."

"It's okay. It's what I'm trained to do. Undercover work is a series of pivots. Thinking on one's feet is crucial to the success of an assignment. I might not be as spontaneous as you, but I am trained to change tack in a split second when required. You didn't get hurt, did you? Blanks can still cause discomfort if they hit the right spots without a barrier to protect you."

"Nah, I'm good. A few ice bags and some rest and relaxation is all I need."

"Hank let you know that he'll take you back to the safe house, right?"

"Yeah, he did. Will you be joining me?"

"Yup, I'll be there later today or tonight." Em glanced in her rearview mirror. "I should make sure Smitty isn't following or anyone else. Plus, I need to swing by my place and grab my to-go bag. I'm unsure how long it's necessary to stay at the safe house. After that, I may detour to a less populated area to ensure I'm not tailed, then maybe stop for a bite to eat. You'll probably reach the house before me." She'd wanted to say, "I love you," but didn't want Hank getting all up in their business if Jimena said it back. Em ended the call and breathed a sigh of relief. Jimena was alive. Everything seemed to go well. Not exactly according to plan, but close enough for Em. Maybe planning everything to a T was not the be-all-end-all. Sometimes, a person just needed to go with the flow, Em cogitated. Jimena was good at that, and now, so was Em.

†

"You ready?" Hank asked.

"Yeah, sure, zip up the plastic coffin. I'll practice my meditation. But you might want to hurry because I don't think dead bodies hyperventilate."

"I promise. We'll be fast. Someone is on the inside to make this happen quickly. We'll get you to the back loading dock, pronto."

Jimena took a deep breath before Hank closed the bag, wincing when it caused pain. It took all her effort to slow the pounding of her heart as she swore she could hear every tiny click of the zipper. After Hank closed her off from the antiseptic air in the back of the ambulance, Jimena decided she would never ever complain again about the smells in a hospital.

The bump of the gurney sent a sharp pain into her right side, and she could barely silence the groan. Moving along the bumpy surface of what she suspected was right outside the hospital entrance didn't help the pain in her ribs. Yup, definitely broken or fractured. She'd have to tell Em not to make her laugh. At least not for a few days while she recovered. Not much a person could do for broken ribs besides let them mend on their own. Six weeks, give or take a week, and she'd be ready to spar again. Finally, they must have reached the inside of the hospital as the gurney rolled more smoothly along the surface of whatever flooring the hospital had chosen. She was grateful for that but coming close to the point where her panic would return. Not that she could take a deep breath without pain, but she longed for that antiseptic smell inside the hospital. She'd gulp for air the moment Hank unzipped the bag. Fuck the pain that would cause to her right side.

She almost kissed Hank's smiling face when he opened the plastic coffin. Instead, she winced as she crawled from inside the small enclosure, and he led her to a waiting car.

"Are you hurt?" he asked with concern in his eyes.

Jimena shrugged as she gingerly climbed into the passenger seat. "A kick to the ribs. Probably fractured, but not much to do about that anyway, so, no, I don't need medical attention." She touched the sore spot at the back of her head, and it felt a little sticky. *Crap, I'll just have Em take a look when she arrives. No sense in telling Hank about that injury.*

Hank jogged around to the driver's side and quickly slid in. "Uh huh, and what about your head? Yeah, I noticed the fresh blood on your hand after touching your head, even though you tried to hide it. And there's dried blood on your other hand. Going for a matching pair, are you?" Hank shook his head. "You're as stubborn as Em. You two really do belong together."

Jimena whipped her head around to face Hank. Bad idea, when the pounding inched forward in the race between which injury would cause the most pain. "What?"

"Jeez, Jimena, give me some credit. Even if my observational skills weren't finely tuned, the two of you ooze love from your pores." He held up his hands. "Gaby and I are close. She told me about their break-up, and I figured you were probably a factor. Em hasn't said anything, but I could tell. I've worked with her for a few years, and the woman rarely smiles. Damn, I think the first time I saw her smile was when she looked at you. I didn't have to spend a lot of time with you guys to notice that. One brief trip to the safe house was all it took. The love vibe is definitely there." Hank buckled up and eased out of the loading dock.

Jimena sighed as she belted herself into the car. "Is that a problem?"

"For who? Me or the FBI?"

"Either, both, I guess. I didn't want to be the cause of Gaby and Em splitting up," Jimena answered.

Hank lifted his shoulder and grinned. "I didn't think you were. Gaby knows that, even if she doesn't know about the two of you. They weren't meant to be anything but good friends. It's pretty much what they've been for almost six months now. No sex usually means the demise of a relationship. So it's not a problem for me. I'm glad Em is finally getting some. Gaby will find her person."

Jimena playfully punched Hank's shoulder. "Better not let Em hear you say that." Jimena chuckled. "And the FBI?"

"Don't worry, I'm not planning to let them in on the secret. It's none of the agency's damn business, but I suspect they might have concerns. They don't let couples work together for good reason. Not that I always agree with that. You both did well today. I believe you can handle it. That's all that matters to me. Besides, I would be a massive hypocrite to have an issue with you two since Steve and I ignore that unwritten rule. And it should be all the FBI cares about, too. When everything is said and done, the only thing of any import is that we catch these bat-shit sons-a-bitches."

"You'll get no argument from me about that," Jimena agreed.

Hank chuckled. "Wow! You are good. Got us talking about something other than your injuries. I know some basic first aid. Let me look at your head when we get to the house. Okay?"

Jimena shook her head. "I didn't lose consciousness, so I'm not too worried. A few Steri-Strips, ibuprofen, or aspirin, and I should be good to go."

"Probably, but you better let Em know the extent of your injuries, just in case. Head injuries are nothing to fuck with. Em should be on the lookout for a concussion that turns into something life-threatening."

Jimena appraised Hank. "Do you have kids, Hank?"

"Not yet. Why?"

"Because you'd make a great father."

"Someday, maybe. It's harder for two dads to create a family. Getting harder every day with the current political climate. I don't mean to lecture you about this stuff, cause you know…"

"I do. Don't give up on the dream, Hank. Kids need loving parents regardless of the family makeup."

Hank nodded and smiled. The rest of the journey to the safe house was relatively quiet, as both people were lost in their own private thoughts.

CHAPTER TWELVE

Jimena must have looked like an old lady walking into the safe house. Although she would never admit this to Hank, she was grateful for the steadying hand he lent her. Immediately after emerging from the car, she felt an alarming amount of dizziness. She might have passed out or stumbled to the ground if he hadn't been there. Not a good look if she wanted to convince him to leave after dropping her off. It wasn't that she didn't enjoy Hank's company, but she wanted to be alone to decompress a little before Em arrived. It was Jimena's way to regain her bearings and be completely present with Em.

Hank seemed to sense her desire to be alone but left her with a parting comment. "Don't hide your pain from Em. Let her check you out. It isn't good to start off whatever it is you two are doing with secrets."

Jimena scoffed. "Downplaying one's injuries is not exactly a relationship-killing secret."

"Slippery slope, my friend. First, you leave out the unimportant details, and then before you know it, you avoid talking about the big stuff." He winked and then left.

An argument was now ensuing between her head and her ribs. Each one demanded attention, but since she couldn't see her head, she rooted into the freezer, looking for a frozen bag of anything to place on her ribs. She'd never be caught dead with frozen vegetables in her home, but she suspected the safe house wouldn't be as particular about the types of foods they stocked.

"Aha, this will do nicely." Jimena pulled out a bag of frozen corn, made her way to the couch, lifted her shirt, and placed the corn on the angry-looking bruise. She shivered when the cold seemed to burrow into her skin. Flipping her wrist to check the time, she vowed to remove the uncomfortable frozen vegetable ice pack from her ribs the second her twenty minutes were up. The afghan they'd used the day they had cuddled on the couch to watch a movie was neatly folded across the back of the sofa. She pulled it on top of her body, hoping to stop the chill.

Jimena almost readjusted her body to lie on the couch when she remembered the back of her head was sticky with blood. "Fuck," she grumbled, then ambled to the kitchen to grab a towel. Hopefully, the bleeding had stopped, and the towel would keep the blood from getting on the sofa. She touched the back of her head before grabbing the towel. Yup, it was still sticky but didn't appear to be hemorrhaging. Surely, she would have felt that.

I'll just take a quick nap. Returning to the couch, Jimena placed the towel behind her head, then sprawled her short body across the sofa. Once she'd settled the afghan on top, she added the bag of corn and promptly fell asleep.

†

Em smiled when she saw Jimena curled on the couch, sleeping peacefully. Light snoring sounds reached her ears, which made her smile wider. Jimena was absolutely adorable with the afghan clutched around her body. Then Em noticed the tea towel and frowned. After setting her to-go bag on the floor, she swore under her breath, "Shit."

Either Jimena had heard her, or maybe she sensed someone else was in the room. Her eyes flung open, and she popped up, wincing. A bag of corn fell to the ground.

Em crossed the room and sat next to Jimena. "Is there something you failed to tell me when we talked earlier?" She pointed to the blood-stained towel.

Jimena lifted her shoulders in dismissal. "A welcome home gift from your colleague, Smitty. It isn't that bad. Just a little headache, and you know how head wounds bleed a lot."

Em pointed to the bag of corn on the floor. "And what is that for? I know you must have more than a minor bruise if you grabbed an ice pack. I'm going to strangle Hank. Did he at least have someone check you out?"

"And how were we going to do that? I'm dead, remember? Maybe a few broken ribs, which there isn't much to do besides ice them."

"We have people who could have examined you. Sometimes broken ribs cause punctured lungs, and that's serious, Jimena." Em blew a puff of air in exasperation and yanked her personal phone from her pocket. Then, punching the number, she said, "Hey, I know I'm the last person who should ask you for a favor, but…"

"What do you need?" Gaby asked.

"Um, well, the Border Patrol Agent I've been working with, who is supposed to be dead, has a few injuries that I was hoping you could check out. We're at the safe house on Twenty-second Avenue. Suspected broken ribs and a head injury."

"Yeah, I saw on the news that she died. Set-up, I presume? I'm surprised they haven't called me yet to speak to the press. Never mind, I'll wait for the call, and they can give me the details. It won't be long before the press connects the dots to your Border Patrol Agent. I'll be there in fifteen."

"Thanks, Gaby. I owe you."

"Yeah, you do. I'm just happy it isn't you I'm patching up." Gaby ended the call, and Em breathed a sigh of relief before returning her focus to Jimena.

"Gaby?" Jimena scrunched her nose in confusion.

"Yeah, she's a doctor, or she was a doctor," Em answered.

"I thought she was the FBI's communication liaison."

"She is. I guess healthcare has as much of a disillusioning effect as joining the Army. So Gaby left it to pursue other opportunities and made her way to the FBI. She's a few years older than me."

"Okay. Um, does Gaby know about us? Our history?" Jimena asked.

"Yes and no. She knows that you're a childhood friend. I told her that when we, uh…"

"Ended the relationship," Jimena finished.

"Yes. Gaby doesn't know we were a thing."

Jimena lifted her eyebrow. "Were?"

"Are," Em corrected. "When I talked to her, we weren't, you know, so it would have been a 'were' when we broke up."

"So, how would you like to play this? Am I an old friend now?"

"No, no, of course not. I would never want you to lie or deceive anyone. Correction, deceive anyone that is not in a domestic terror cell." Em smiled. "It's just that I don't think it would be nice to rub salt in Gaby's wounds. We only broke up a few days ago, and now she's coming over because I asked her for a favor."

"I get it. I'll be careful. Just so you know, Hank already picked up on"—Jimena gestured between the two of them—"you and I."

"He's an intuitive bastard. Figured he would. Which is why I am pissed at him. He should have told me you were hurt."

"Don't blame him. I promised him I would tell you about my injuries and let you check them out. Also, Gaby told him about your break-up."

"Yeah, they're close. I'm glad Hank can be there for Gaby. Turn around." Em twirled her finger. "Let me look at your head." She palpated the back of her head. "You've got a good-sized knot, but the bleeding has stopped. I can't tell if you need stitches. Gaby will know."

"I feel like a home-wrecker." Jimena held her hand up. "Hank already tried to tell me I'm not, but it will be hard to look your ex-lover in the eye and not feel like the worst human being on the planet."

Em stroked Jimena's cheek. "You're not. You just risked your life to salvage my undercover operation. Plus, I know you, and you are far from the worst. In fact, I'd put you in the top ten percent of humanity."

Jimena arched her eyebrow. "Top ten percent, huh? Not the top one?" she joked.

"I thought you Catholics saved that accolade for saints, popes, and other religious leaders. Did you become a saint in the fifteen years we've been apart? I can believe it. Saint Jimena, the patron saint of hot lesbians."

The tentative knock on the door interrupted their banter. Em placed her hand on Jimena's knee. "Hang on. It's probably Gaby, but I want to make sure."

Em quickly made her way to the front door and looked through the peephole, opening the door to Gaby, who looked utterly put together, as usual. Not a single hair was out of place. Em wondered what Jimena would think of Gaby, who was almost her exact opposite in physical appearance—tall, blonde, and willowy. Today her eyes almost appeared blue to match her silk blouse. She carried an enormous first aid bag that Em presumed had more supplies than would typically appear in the most extensive kit on the market.

"Thanks, Gaby," Em greeted. When she turned around, she noticed Jimena sizing up Gaby with a tiny frown on her face. The grimace quickly turned into a forced smile as Gaby made her way across the room to sit beside Jimena.

"Hello, you must be Jimena. It's nice to meet you. Em told me you were old school friends. She doesn't talk much about her time in California before moving back." Gaby pulled a penlight from the bag and a pair of gloves. Quickly donning the gloves, she said, "Let's check your pupils first. I want to make sure they're dilating properly."

"Um, yeah, we grew up together. Both of us were little terrors. Thank you for coming by. I told Em I was fine, but she's always been a bit overprotective."

Gaby arched her eyebrow and glanced over her shoulder at Em before shining the light in Jimena's eyes. "Looks good. Any blurry vision?"

Jimena shook her head and winced. "No, just a pounding headache."

"Did you lose consciousness?" Gaby asked.

"No, although sometimes I feel a little dizzy, especially when standing up."

"It looks like you have several injuries a few days old, but they appear to be healing nicely," Gaby noted.

"Yeah, compliments of the two suspects that unfortunately expired before you could obtain any useful information from them," Jimena stated.

Gaby quirked her eyebrow but continued her examination. "Okay, can you turn your body and let me look at the back of your head?"

Jimena twisted her body as Gaby continued her rudimentary examination. She efficiently cleansed the wound, shaved the area, then washed it again.

Em noticed Jimena gritting her teeth, but it looked like Gaby might be able to place a few Steri-Strips on the cut beneath the large swollen knot.

"Doing okay?" Gaby asked.

Jimena nodded. "Yeah, I'm good."

"It doesn't look like I'll need to stitch you up, but you should have Em watch the area for infection. I could probably get you some pain medication, but I'd recommend ibuprofen or Tylenol for the discomfort. Would you mind lifting your shirt so I can look at your ribs? An X-ray would be nice, but hopefully, we can get away with a few questions and my years of experience with thrill-seeking surfers."

Em appreciated Gaby's attempt to lighten the mood. However, tension radiated from Jimena, and Gaby was intuitive enough to recognize the signs, maybe even guess about their connection to each other.

"I'm sorry that Em dragged you all the way out here for basically nothing." Jimena lifted her shirt.

"I know it hurts to breathe or laugh, but I need you to take a deep breath and tell me if you feel a sharp pain in your chest or pain radiating to your shoulder or back. Looks like someone kicked you with a boot."

Jimena nodded, and Em watched her clench her jaw as she sucked in air. "Um, it's uncomfortable, but mostly where he kicked me."

"Good, good. All right. Your injuries won't be a barrel of monkeys, but I'm not seeing anything life-threatening. If you start to have blurry vision, confusion, or the pain I described earlier after taking a deep breath, you'll need to figure out a way to have the hospital treat a dead person." She turned to Em. "I don't suppose it would be worth it to you to break your cover if Jimena loses her life in the process."

"Of course not," Em barked before immediately regretting it.

Apparently, Em wasn't the only one to feel remorse, as Gaby quickly said, "I'm sorry, that was totally uncalled for."

"It's okay, Gaby. I probably deserved that jab," Em quickly responded.

"No, you didn't. I'm still working through…" Gaby's voice trailed off.

"I'm so sorry," Jimena interjected, looking miserable as she said the words.

Gaby stood, removing her gloves and then tossing them into the bag along with her penlight. She started to clean up the mess with the alcohol swabs and other discarded cleansing supplies.

Em quickly approached and gathered the pile of tossed-away items. "I got this." She gathered Gaby in an awkward hug. "Thank you."

Gaby stepped away and said, "Take care of each other. I'll call when I'm ready. It's okay, Em, we're okay, really. Or we will be." She touched her arm, glanced at Jimena, and then left without another word.

"I'm worse than the dogshit you scrape from the bottom of your shoe after stepping into it. Because we both stomped all over that pile of shit today."

Em ran her hand through her hair. "Yeah, I know. I'll make it up to her somehow."

"How, Em? How will you do that? The woman is clearly still in love with you."

"I don't know. Find Gaby someone she deserves."

"I don't think you need to be her wing person. She looks like she'd have women falling at her feet. Why didn't you tell me how attractive she was? I just met someone who could own the runway as a model. Who, coincidentally, could not be more opposite in looks from me." Jimena's eyes gave away her emotion.

"Yes, Gaby is beautiful. I won't deny that. She's also kind and a good person." Em sat next to Jimena and grabbed both of her hands. "But, Jimena, she's not you, and that was the problem. If I'm perfectly honest, that was the problem with every relationship I tried over the years. None of them were you. You might be the opposite in looks, but you're

146

every bit as beautiful. More even. For years, I went for women who looked very much like you. That never worked. So, I thought I'd try a different tack with Gaby. That didn't work either. Because only one woman has ever truly captured my heart. And that's you, Jimena."

A ghost of a smile appeared on Jimena's face. "Good answer. But, damn, did she have to be so gorgeous?"

Em laughed. "I know, right? Why in the world would she pick me?"

Jimena brought her forehead against Em's. "Because you're kind, funny, generous, loving, and runway model material yourself, in that sexy, androgynous way that all lesbians go for. Even the butches can't resist someone who looks like you."

Em placed a gentle kiss on her forehead. "Flatterer. Time to ice your ribs. Have you taken any Tylenol yet?"

"Not yet."

Em jumped from the couch and made her way to the bathroom. She rooted around in the cabinet until she found what she was looking for. After returning with the Tylenol bottle in her hand, she shook out two capsules and handed them to Jimena. "I'll get some water for you. And then, how about a movie as I wait to hear from Smitty?"

"Sounds perfect. Pick something I won't mind falling asleep to."

"You got it."

It didn't take long for Em to relax to the faint snoring sounds as Jimena cuddled against her while they watched a movie that neither was invested in. Before Em knew it, she'd followed Jimena into dreamland. When she woke, the room was dark, so she turned off the DVD and helped Jimena into the bedroom, guided her into bed, and pulled her close, wrapping her arms around her stomach, careful to avoid her ribs.

CHAPTER THIRTEEN

Jimena opened her eyes when a ringing cell phone roused her from sleep. She realized two things. She had slobbered over Em while sleeping, and Em's arm had wrapped protectively around her back shoulder.

"Yeah," Em croaked after disengaging from Jimena to retrieve her phone. "Why all the cloak and dagger?"

Sitting, Jimena strained to hear what was said on the other end but couldn't decipher everything. Em must have figured out that Jimena was trying to listen as she repeated what the person on the other end was saying.

"Okay, okay, tomorrow at two o'clock. I'll drive to La Jolla and wait for your call." Em paused, listening to the man on the other end. "No, I don't have any more information than you. Why would I know about the FBI's reasons for

149

taking over the investigation? Don't they get involved in drug trafficking on a larger scale? Maybe the Border Patrol Agent actually was involved in big-time drug trafficking."

Em sighed loudly into the phone. "How the fuck would I know? Could be you started a shit storm by knocking off Petey and Darnell and then making me prove myself by killing that woman. I know how to disappear. Do you? But before I do that, I'd like to know my efforts meant something, and that I was part of a larger plan. Dad died for the cause because he was working on a broader scheme than knocking off some insignificant Border Patrol Agent. This meeting better be worth my while, or I'm out. Fine, two o'clock." Em ended the call and returned the phone to the table.

Jimena shook her head. "I don't like the sound of that. La Jolla is a sizeable area. One I'm not very familiar with. How will you have backup if you don't know where the meeting will be held?"

"They can track my phone."

"La Jolla is full of gated communities. A person can't simply roll into one of those without the gate code, which your backup will not have."

Em frowned. "I'll admit, it's a little riskier."

"You're going to at least have a comlink to let them know the gate code and address, right?"

"Yeah, of course. But then, I'll have to remove the link, and I can't wear a wire because they'll pat me down."

"So, you're not going to take a gun with you?"

"No, I don't think so because I'm sure they'll take it. Maybe I can get away with a backup in an ankle holster."

"Let me go with. I can hide in the back seat and jump out along the way before you reach the final destination."

Em started shaking her head before Jimena finished. "Nope. You're still recovering from what Smitty did to you. Anytime you're around these assholes, you get hurt. I can't allow that to happen a third time. I can take care of myself. Once we learn their plans, my backup will swarm the place. Even if they have to bust down the gate."

"How will you do that if you aren't wearing a wire or your comlink? I thought you were the one who always plans for every contingency. Unfortunately, there are holes in this scheme that you can drive a semi through."

"I'll call Hank and get him over here to strategize. I know the FBI has a lot of gadgets at their disposal, including one to alert backup with a hidden device." Em pulled her Saint Christopher medal from her shirt. "We can attach it to this, and one smack to my chest will activate the alert and bring in the Cavalry. We'll get maps of every gated community in La Jolla. Maybe that will give us some clue why the meeting is over there. It doesn't seem like the kind of place these dicknobs hang out. They're more the survivalist types."

"Everything smells all wrong about this," Jimena insisted.

"Maybe, but you have to cut off the head to kill the snake. And considering we don't know who that head is, this is our best chance of finding out."

"At what cost, Em? Your life? I would never tell you what to do. That isn't my place, but I'd like to think that since we started this together…well, almost. I suppose I jumped in mid-assignment." Jimena captured Em's eyes. "The point is that I need to see this through with you. Neither of us gets to dictate what the other is or is not willing to do. Partnerships don't work that way—even under the guise of love and protection."

"Okay, but we're both going to make sure backup is there for us if this goes sideways. I trust Hank and his team to do their job. There are still going to be a lot of on-the-fly decisions. Like the best time for you to exit the vehicle."

Jimena grinned. "Spontaneity is my middle name."

†

Em was a controlled ball of energy, as she kept finding reasons to get up off the sofa, allowing her to pace the room. The first knock had her scrambling to the door to peek through the peephole. She assumed it was Hank or the pizza delivery person. Em opened the door to a smiling Hank, who held up a twelve-pack of beer.

"Got the beer. Where's the pizza? I'm starved."

Jimena tilted her head and scrunched her nose. "I sure hope you two aren't planning to drink the entire half case of beer. I don't think heading into the meeting tomorrow with a raging hangover is the best plan."

Em laughed. "No, silly, you'll have a couple, right?"

Jimena shook her head. "Nope. I'm already trying to keep my massive headache at bay. The last thing I need is alcohol. That will only temporarily mask the pain."

"It's tradition," Hank said. "Whenever Em and I work on an assignment and have to get our ducks in a row, we have pizza and beer. Don't let the fact that Em is a woman fool you. She can drink me under the table, and I've got at least fifty pounds on her. She must have developed that skill in the Army."

Em grinned. "True dat. If I wanted to gain any acceptance from the boys' club, showing my beer-drinking prowess was essential. It took a lot of practice." Em winked. "But if it makes you feel better, I will stop at three."

"Me, too," Hank added.

"Do the two of you actually come up with clear-headed plans while you satisfy this inane tradition?"

Both Em and Hank nodded and grinned. "Although we'd prefer to smoke some weed for the ultimate inspiration, but the FBI does random tests, and the fact that it's legal in California does not make a bit of difference to them. The tests are rare because, recently, they've seemed to relax their stance on marijuana use." Em shrugged. "But neither of us wanted to take the chance."

A knock on the door interrupted the discussion, and Em went through her usual practice of checking before answering. The delivery woman retrieved two large pizzas from the warmer, and handed them to Em, who pulled a fifty from her pocket and gave it to the woman.

"Keep the change," Em said before closing the door and crossing the room to set the boxes on the coffee table.

"One of those better be Hawaiian," Hank remarked.

"Of course, dude. The other is meat lovers' special. No vegetarians in the bunch. Thank goodness," Em answered.

Jimena flipped open the box on top. "True. Even though I can practically feel my arteries harden with a mere glance at all the meat on that pizza."

Em walked into the kitchen. "I'm pretty sure I saw paper plates and napkins in the pantry. Does anyone need a fork?" she asked.

"Nope. I classify pizza as finger or hand food. The Queen declined our invitation, so no need to get fancy," Hank joked.

"I don't need a fork either," Jimena added.

"Alrighty then." Along with the paper plates and napkins she found, Em grabbed a bottle of water from the refrigerator and handed it to Jimena, who had already declined the beer. Hank was in the process of taking a large bite of the pizza he had pulled from the box below the meat lovers' special. Crumbs fell on his lap.

"Heathen," Em ribbed.

"You were way too slow," Hank mumbled around his bite, then reached for a plate and napkin.

After Jimena and Em had loaded their plates with two pieces each, Em started the discussion. "So, you know I got the call earlier to drive to La Jolla. Did the geeks find out anything unusual about that location? Have you picked up any chatter that would give us a clue about where the meeting might be?"

Hank set his pizza on the plate, swallowing his second bite quickly. "Yeah, and it isn't great news. The governor's mother lives in La Jolla."

"Coincidence? I think not," Em answered. "What else you got?"

"Other than your death, Jimena, and how it made national news, not much. The reporter who caught the scoop was trying to make a name for themselves, so Gaby had to do a press briefing. Somehow, the reporter learned you were the Border Patrol Agent connected to the Darnell and Petey situation. She's like a dog with a bone."

"Shit," Jimena muttered.

"What?" Em asked.

"Um, my sisters."

"Uh, yeah, from what I heard, shit is right. Your brother lost his shit with your boss. Rosie called him while he was out at sea. Your bro rushed back and made a beeline to Gary's office. Gary had to yank him inside and tell him you were fine. Your sisters know, too. Manny called them right after he left the office. It's not ideal, but, hopefully, they all understand the gravity around keeping this under wraps," Hank explained.

"Have we warned the governor about a possible plot that might include an attack on her mother?"

Hank sighed. "We have, but she isn't taking it seriously. Her mom lives in one of those gated communities known for their high level of security. We insisted on adding another person to Governor Murphy's security team. That's the best we could achieve. And get this, living in La Jolla isn't the only coincidence. Apparently, the governor was invited to a late lunch tomorrow at her mother's house. Her mother is a powerhouse in politics and the major reason for Governor Murphy's success. An invitation is more like a command."

"Okay, wow!" Em exclaimed before taking a large gulp of beer. "That's two coincidences that are hard to ignore. Can we get details on the community? Jimena was going to hide in the back seat and can be another link to you and your team since I won't be able to maintain communication once I enter the meeting. But maybe we can send in additional agents under the guise of fixing cable, water lines, whatever story you come up with. I'll still attach something to my Saint Christopher medal, and if activated, you need to come in hot because that means I'm in trouble. Although, handling this quietly is preferable. The FBI gets enough bad press, and if we go in blazing to an upscale neighborhood, that is bound to cause us issues. I'll do the best I can to give you intel before entering the lion's den."

"We'll be there. Don't worry. I always wanted to crash through one of those hoity-toity gates." Hank lifted his beer and guzzled half the can. "I prefer our agents handling this and leaving Jimena out of everything."

Em glanced at Jimena, who shook her head.

"I just thought of a better idea," Jimena said.

"Good, because, no offense, you hiding under a blanket and then sneaking around a gated community is pure amateur land," Hank gently chastised. "Like they're not going to notice a little Hispanic woman roaming around in their bushes."

"Fine. I agree it might not have been one of my better ideas, but give me some credit. The blanks and squibs worked. Didn't they?" Jimena defended.

"So, what's your idea?" Em asked.

"Well, you've already said it's probably not a coincidence that the governor's mother lives in La Jolla. What if we play into their biases? A Mexican woman showing up to clean someone's home wouldn't raise any suspicion."

Hank leaned back in his chair. "Now that idea is something we can work with. I feel more comfortable having additional resources around Governor Murphy. We'll arrange that with the governor's mother because her community has a security checkpoint instead of merely a gate with a code. However, if we're wrong and the meeting is not in the same place as where the governor's mother lives, you won't be any help at all. We'll have put all our eggs into the La Jolla community, which will leave Em on her own."

"My gut says it's too much of a coincidence. Whatever they have planned is likely going down tomorrow," Em insisted.

"I agree. I just thought I should put it out there if we're all wrong about this." Hank grabbed another piece of pizza and put nearly half of the slice in his mouth.

✝

After Hank left, Jimena blurted, "Why didn't you tell me how lame my idea was to hide in the back seat?"

Em smiled. "I knew Hank would blow holes in it, and then I wouldn't have to be the unsupportive girlfriend. Besides, you came up with something much better. So, it all worked out."

"I watch too many action flicks," Jimena grumbled. "That would be something that would definitely work in the movies, but this isn't Hollywood, is it?"

"No, hon. But you're awfully cute." Em sipped her beer and smiled. "We did make one of your hair-brained Hollywood ideas work. Frankly, I'm surprised they went for it because that would not be typical FBI protocol. That tells me how desperate they are to catch these guys."

"I guess since Governor Murphy is the hands-down favorite for the Democratic nominee for president, protecting her is crucial. Everyone believes it's finally time for the first woman to take office. Rumor has it that indictments are coming down any day now, and the net is rather large for the Republicans. That ought to decimate MAGA world and make it highly volatile for anyone remotely involved in their demise," Jimena added.

"Yes, but when cornered, like a wild animal, that's when these guys are the most dangerous. He'll play the victim again and whip them up. Every terror cell we break up is one less threat to deal with." Em frowned. "Based on past interactions with this group, they were already plenty fired up."

"Desperation breeds mistakes," Jimena said.

"I certainly hope so."

CHAPTER FOURTEEN

Em woke early the next day and went for a run to burn off the excess energy. Needing her wits about her for today, she had to calm her nerves. Unfortunately, adrenaline wasn't always helpful because then the amygdala took over. Rational thought flew out the window when that happened, and pure rage prevailed. Em could not let that happen. The stakes were too high, including the possibility of death or severe injury to the woman she loved.

After a six-mile run, Em returned to the safe house, wiping her sweaty face as she walked through the back door that led to the kitchen. The fry pan clattered to the floor after she closed the door.

Jimena bent to clean the mess. "Shit, you scared me. I was making pancakes." She pointed to the coffeepot sitting on the bamboo hot pad. "I just transferred it over, so it should still be hot. I assumed you'd be back any second because you've been gone nearly an hour. Run?"

Em nodded.

"Yeah, I figured. Some things never change. You always did go for runs when you needed to calm down."

"Better than meditation. It helps center me."

"I wish I could enjoy long runs, but I don't. Not even a little bit. My body type was always more suited to sprints." Jimena chuckled. "And that's why you look like you do, and I look like, well"—Jimena ran her hand down her body—"this."

Em crossed the room and kissed Jimena's shoulder, running her hands over Jimena's body. "Is this okay? I'm a little ripe right now. I hope you know how much I adore your curves. I'm not attracted to emaciated-looking women who spend all day at the gym."

"Um, Gaby certainly looked like she visits the inside of a gym quite often," Jimena noted.

"Why, Jimena, I didn't know you had such a jealous side to you. I thought this was settled law. You're it for me. The whole enchilada and more. Like a super supreme enchilada." Em playfully nipped Jimena's neck. "Delicious."

"Charmer." Jimena gently pushed Em away. "Go take a shower because you are stinky. Pancakes will be ready by the time you get out."

"After breakfast, we can look over Hank's aerial maps. We should pay special attention to the area surrounding the governor's mother's home. By the way, Hank and Steve dropped off a beater car for you to use. It's out front. The keys are on the dinette."

"Sounds good. I still wish I could go with you. I don't like being separated and don't trust this isn't some kind of setup."

"I know." Em pecked Jimena on the lips. "I'll be quick."

†

Driving to La Jolla seemed surreal to Jimena. She used her cell phone because the beater car did not have a functioning GPS system. Since the FBI had kindly provided the vehicle that would match her cover as a housecleaner, beggars couldn't be choosy. As Jimena approached the gate, she sucked in a mouthful of air and slowly let it out. She repeated her go-to technique several times before rolling down her window to speak to the man at the gate. Em had her running, and Jimena centered herself with deep breathing exercises.

"Magiclean Maid for Mrs. Murphy," Jimena mumbled, adding a heavy Mexican accent. She tried hard not to look the man in the eyes, but she noted how his eyes had narrowed.

"You're not her regular house cleaner."

"I don't know, sir. They call me today to come clean."

The man glanced at the papers on the desk and said, "Yeah, she phoned this morning to let me know. It's just odd that you aren't even from the same agency and her regular person was here only two days ago."

Jimena lifted her shoulders but didn't respond. Finally, the gate lifted, and Jimena rolled through, pushing out the air she'd held inside while the man opened the gate for her.

The minute she moved far enough away for him not to see, she placed the comlink in her ears and informed the team she was through the gate.

"I'm in, but he was skeptical. I didn't like how he grilled me. I think I spot the rest of the team. There's a van a block down the road from the house with a Viasat logo on the side."

"Copy that. Yup, that's us," Hank answered.

"It's not too late to turn around and back out of this," Em's voice came through the link.

"I think that would look odd. We better stick to the plan," Jimena answered.

"Okay. I'm approaching the gate now. Don't worry if there is radio silence for a few minutes while I get through," Em explained.

Jimena drove to the address shown on her phone and put the car in park. She grabbed her cleaning supplies and went to the front door. She waited a minute after ringing the bell. Finally, a stocky man answered and waved her inside. "Jimena?"

Jimena nodded and looked around the large entry. After he led her to a sizeable living area with overstuffed couches, she noticed the two women sitting quietly with a teapot in front of them.

Governor Murphy looked in her direction and arched an eyebrow. "So, you're the woman causing quite a media stir."

Jimena smiled. "Yeah, the reports of my death were grossly overblown, Governor. May I ask your mother a few questions, please?"

Governor Murphy barely nodded.

"Mrs. Murphy, if you don't mind me asking, have you noticed any individuals who seem out of place in your neighborhood?"

"No." A line appeared in the center of her forehead.

From the comlink, Em interrupted her interrogation by stating, "I'm inside the community now. Bad news. The guy at the gate is someone I recognize from other gatherings. I'll keep my eyes peeled for any landscapers trolling around this neighborhood. Can someone quietly take out this security guard before this shindig starts? One less person to deal with will make me feel better."

"Copy that," Steve answered. "We'll remove him from the gate and detain him for now."

Jimena held up her finger while she listened in, then turned to Mrs. Murphy and asked, "Is anyone else invited for tea or this late lunch today?"

"Why, yes. I invited my next-door neighbor. She mentioned her daughter was coming over today, and well, I thought it would be nice for Sandra to meet her."

Governor Murphy pursed her lips. "Mother is trying to control my personal life. Apparently, this woman would make the perfect companion. She's some kind of war hero. Unfortunately, I've indulged in my mother's schemes far too often. She recently sprang this little meeting on me today."

It didn't take much to put two and two together. There was no doubt in Jimena's mind that Em was the woman Mrs. Murphy hoped to introduce to her daughter. They were expecting Em to be a part of whatever they had planned for Governor Murphy.

"Well, what do you know? I see Jimena's car. The address given to me is right next door. "I'm taking my coms out now," Em said.

"Wait," Jimena interjected. "I just learned you and your mother, whoever that is, were invited for tea."

"I don't think she's on anymore," Hank noted.

Jimena sighed. "Okay, I guess we'll have to wait this out."

"Copy that. We're ready. Don't worry."

†

Em tried not to let the niggling sensation of impending doom get to her as she emerged from her car. She'd already stuffed the comlink into her glove compartment. Locking the door, she looked around and noticed the glint in an upstairs bedroom on the east side of the house. There weren't any men milling about, but that didn't mean they weren't loaded up and ready to go. She suspected whoever was on the second floor wouldn't hesitate to shoot first and ask questions later.

Em rang the bell, and Smitty answered the door, letting it swing open as she entered. He smirked at her as if he was dying to spill a big secret and couldn't wait for her reaction. That didn't help her queasy feeling.

"Well, I'm here. You finally going to let me in on why you felt the need to create all the smoke and mirrors?"

Smitty sneered. "Time to meet the boss. You've certainly attracted his attention. He has special plans for you today."

Em wondered who owned this house. It was undoubtedly more opulent than any home she'd ever owned or visited. *So, this is how the other half lives, or more accurately, the one-percenters.* Em could have fit her entire place in the foyer.

To say it shocked her to see the man casually lounging in a chair would have been a massive understatement. She hadn't seen him in nearly fifteen years, but he hadn't changed much. That obnoxious sneer and the barely contained rage that hovered beneath the surface remained present. However, his face had narrowed, and the scruff of a carefully manicured five o'clock shadow was evidence of the years that had gone by. He was no longer a boy. The resemblance to their father was startling, but she would be damned if she'd let him see that.

Working hard to keep her face a mask of indifference, Em greeted, "Hello, Karl. Long time."

"Hi, Sis. Pat her down. I want to make sure she isn't packing." The sneer on his handsome face deepened. "Carrying a gun," he clarified. "Although, I wouldn't be surprised if my perverted sister wasn't stuffing her panties with a dildo. Isn't that what your kind does? Secretly wished you'd been born with a dick? Check for any wires, but don't get too handsy inside her bra. After all, I am her brother. And a brother doesn't want to watch that kind of shit." Karl shook his head. "I had hoped this would be a family affair, but alas, you've disappointed us all. Again."

A large man that she didn't recognize stepped forward and patted her sides, removing both cell phones from her pockets. "No guns, only phones. Two," he said, holding both cell phones in the air. He reached inside, and Em seethed at his enormous calloused hand groping under her shirt and inside her sports bra. "No wires."

Karl waved his finger. "Two phones, huh?" Taking both phones, he placed them on the floor and brought his heavy boot down on them, smashing both to tiny bits. "Just in case there's a tracking device on either one. We can't have that, can we? Although, I'll bet the gated community cut into your careful plans for backup, huh? There are so many prominent citizens who live here, including the governor's mother." His maniacal laugh sent shivers up Em's spine. "Barreling through the gates and storming the homes won't play well on live TV. Did you honestly think I wouldn't follow my big sister's illustrious career? I couldn't believe my luck when I learned who the Border Patrol Agent was. I wondered how far you might go to keep your cover."

"Fuck you, Karl."

"I've heard about people so deep undercover, they begin to believe their own cover story. It stops being an act as they get in deeper. Addiction to drugs, violence, you name it. They don't even recognize the agent when they pull the poor schmucks out. I didn't believe that was possible for you, being a hero and all. But then, you surprised me. I thought you'd actually done it. I'll admit that one had me scratching my head until I figured it out." He shrugged. "No matter, she's a loose end that'll take care of itself in short order. We have patriots everywhere willing to do their duty."

"Now what?" Em asked with a fair amount of ice in her voice. She still didn't know his end game. Suspecting it had something to do with the governor, she wanted him to lay out his plans before she smacked her chest and alerted Hank and his team. Screw the possible lousy press. Hank wouldn't give two shits about alerting the media if an agent was in trouble.

"Now we strap explosives on your chest, and you're going to accompany Mom over to her best friend's house for afternoon tea. She's been bragging about her daughter, and the governor's mom is eager to meet you. Did I happen to mention that the governor is visiting today? How convenient for us. Isn't it nice that the moms wanted their two dyke daughters to meet? An out and proud lesbian wasn't enough to tank the governor's career, but mommy dearest worried a single lesbian wasn't as appealing as someone in a committed relationship. You are apparently the perfect companion. Attractive. Accomplished. A war hero. Mom wanted a non-violent solution. She thought you could influence the governor. But I've decided to go in a different direction."

Em had a sick feeling. *Could my mother be a part of all of this, or is she another victim of Karl's sick view of the world? Is he actually going to blow up his own mother?* There was no way she would allow this to play out. They hadn't strapped on the suicide bomb, and she wasn't about to let them go further with this insane plan. Em lifted her arm to smack her chest and alert backup, but Karl was too fast as he roughly yanked the chain from her neck, and the Saint Christopher medal fell to the floor with barely a ping.

Karl sneered. "Your little medal isn't going to protect you now. Do you know you are so predictable? Always grabbing for that little trinket whenever you're stressed. I'll bet you're thinking about warning everyone and getting them out before I have a chance to activate your vest. Then you can be the hero again. I'm not a total monster. Remember when we were kids and played cops and robbers? Let's play another game. It's called beat the clock. I'll give you five minutes to deactivate the bomb attached to your chest as long as no one leaves the house. Well, except Mom. You can let Mom go. I'll allow that. We have shooters ready to take out any rats attempting to escape their sinking ship, so don't test me, Big Sis."

Em kept her calm. She had five minutes. Karl had factored in time for her mom to escape in his plan, giving Hank's team time. He wouldn't activate the bomb the minute she entered the house. Jimena would size up the situation and call for backup. Her team was trained. They would know how to take out Karl and his minions before he got the chance to activate the bomb. She had to trust in her backups.

Em tried to keep her face neutral because she had the better hand in this scenario. Karl hadn't wholly done his homework, or he would have known that Em was part of an elite bomb squad. She ate, drank, and breathed demolition. Deactivating a bomb was completely doable and a skill-set she'd never lose. That wasn't the only ace Em had up her sleeve.

Hopefully, Karl didn't realize that Jimena and her fellow agents had already breached the community. The security guard checking each guest in was a person Em recognized. She prayed he hadn't pegged Jimena as the dead Border Patrol Agent. Em knew her shit, and one thing she was incredibly proficient at was noting every little thing in her immediate surroundings. The shooters that Karl referred to were on the second floor. As soon as she entered the house, she would grab one of Jimena's comms and let her team know to take them out first. Maybe she wouldn't need to disable the bomb after all.

Karl clapped his hands. "Let the games begin. Smitty, bring the car around. We don't want to be close when the bomb goes off."

Smitty nodded and exited the room. Karl pointed at the other man she'd seen before at one of the earlier gatherings. "Time to strap on the vest and tell Mom that her precious daughter is here. Be careful with the vest. We wouldn't want it to blow prematurely. Grab that ugly flannel shirt to go over the vest. Isn't that what you dykes wear these days?" Karl lifted the gun he almost carelessly had in his lap and pointed it at Em. "Honestly, I have no problem shooting you between the eyes and going to Plan B, so I suggest you not make any grand gestures. By the way, Plan B is attaching the vest to Mom and sending her over without you. I'd miss her, but there is always collateral damage in a righteous war."

The large man nodded and picked up the vest and shirt from the chair in the corner of the room. Em allowed the henchman to slip the vest on and click it into place. He handed her the shirt, and Karl motioned for her to put it over the explosives.

Karl laughed. "Perfect. Looking good. Although I believe Mrs. Murphy was looking for someone not so obvious, perhaps a little more sophisticated. By the way, I've heard you know your way around explosives. That's why there are two detonation wires. Redundancy is key, Big Sis. Remember that. I couldn't very well make it that easy on you. Unsnap the vest, and one of them goes boom. So, I wouldn't recommend that."

†

Although Em's mother had aged and looked more fragile than Em remembered, she was still a beautiful woman. Em gawked at the expensive designer outfit she wore.

"I'm happy you decided to help us, Emma. While I still don't condone your lifestyle, in this case, if you're able to have an influence over the governor and her immigration policies, I can look the other way. We'll have to find something else for you to wear, though," Bridget said with a frown on her face.

"I'm sorry, Mother, but we've decided to go in another direction. Unfortunately, we don't have time for a makcover." Karl turned his angry eyes on Em. "You'll need to send Mom out the side door on the east side of the house. That's where the car will wait for her. I suggest you not dally, or you'll be responsible for Mom's untimely demise."

Bridget's eyes widened. "Karl. What are you talking about?"

"Don't worry, Mother. Em's a war hero. Just listen to her, and you'll be fine. Explosives are her thing. Now run along to your tea, and I'll see you in a couple of minutes. The clock starts ticking the minute they let you inside."

On the way over to the target house, Em thought she saw a glint of metal in the greenery surrounding the back of the property. That was two exits covered, but hopefully, Karl's men would not see Hank's team if they approached the west side of what Em presumed was Karl's house. There wasn't a need to have shooters on the west side. There wouldn't be much time for Hank's team to take out the shooters in the upstairs rooms and at the back of the target house, but that was all she had to hang her hat on.

Em continued to look around, trying to pick out additional threats, when her mother interrupted her intense focus on her surroundings. "I didn't know," her mother insisted.

"Not the time for teary reunions or confessions. I assume you know which door you're supposed to exit once we get inside the house. Don't hesitate to make a beeline to safety.

You've always been a survivor, Mom. Why change that self-preservation gene that you have an abundance of?"

"That isn't fair. I had no choice. Your father would have killed me if I'd stepped in."

"I don't want to get into this right now." Em shook her head sadly. "You've always seen only two choices. That has been your fatal error. Now, it's literally about to be my fatal error. Unfortunately for you, Karl is now a marked man, regardless of the outcome. If they don't catch him today, he'll be on the run for the rest of his life until they do. You've attached yourself to that life now. Good luck with that."

Em lifted her hand to press the bell and breathed deeply to calm herself like she'd seen Jimena do so many times. It always worked for Jimena, and since she couldn't very well take another long run, this trick would have to do. Before the man opened the door, Em had set the stopwatch on her wrist for five minutes.

†

Jimena kept watching for Em. She saw Em walk over with an older woman who looked exactly like Em's mother, at least what Jimena remembered about the woman. They were in a terse conversation from what Jimena could observe. Something was off about the way she made her way up the path. Em moved slowly and had an ugly flannel shirt over her clothes—one she hadn't been wearing when she left the safe house earlier.

Later, when Jimena tried to recreate what happened in sequential order for the FBI, she couldn't quite make all the pieces fit. Nothing seemed to occur linearly. Instead, it was a jumble of barked demands and impossible mayhem simultaneously evolving.

Em didn't stride into the room with confidence as Jimena expected. Instead, her entrance was slow, almost methodical. She pointed to Jimena and began to control the situation.

"No time to explain. Jimena, I need one of your comms." She held out her hand, and Jimena removed her right earbud. Em's steely gray eyes landed on the woman Jimena was now sure was Mrs. Schmidt. "Go," Em ordered as she placed the earbud in her right ear.

Em's mother's eyes landed on Jimena and widened for a second before she headed for the sliding glass door on the east side of the house. "I'm so sorry," she said as she left.

"What the hell is going on?" Governor Murphy asked.

"I'm wearing a suicide vest. None of you can leave because Karl has shooters ready to pick you off if you try to exit. Wire cutters?" Em asked.

"I bought Mom a toolkit. I think there are wire cutters in the kitchen—bottom drawer."

"Does this house have a basement? Any place you can go if I can't disarm this in time or my team can't take out the shooters?" Em fired the questions at the governor since everyone else seemed frozen in place, including the extra security person the FBI had sent.

"There's a panic room," Governor Murphy answered.

174

"Good, go, go." Em turned over her wrist and glanced at her watch. "You have four minutes."

Jimena hesitated. She wanted to help Em but didn't know how. Em cut her off before she said anything. "Please, Jimena, take care of everyone. That's what I need from you right now."

As Jimena followed the governor, her mother, and the large man who hadn't done much in his protective detail role, she heard Em bark, "Hank, hopefully, you're hearing all this. Go slowly to the west side of the meeting house. At least one shooter is upstairs on the east side and another at the back of the target property. Karl Schmidt Junior is the leader. His car will exit from the east side of the target house…"

†

"Alpha team has the shooter at the back of the house. Clear."

"Good job," Em responded as she pulled open a bottom drawer in the kitchen. Not finding what she needed, she pulled a second drawer open and screamed, "Fuck, what else can test me today?" Finally, the last drawer she opened contained a small toolkit. She flipped it open, and sure enough, there was a small wire cutter pressed into the molded plastic.

Carefully unbuttoning her shirt, her eyes focused on the bundle of wires attached to the clasp in the vest. It was a clever setup. Sizing the situation, she noted she would need to cut two wires instead of one to open the clasp and remove the vest. Most people would not have noticed this, but Karl had already tipped his hand with the redundancy quip. *Redundancy is key, Big Sis.*

"Shit," Em said. The cogs had now slipped into place. "Hank, even if I disable the vest, I'm sure he wired this whole place to blow." She flipped her wrist and noted the time. "Two minutes, Hank. I need those shooters incapacitated if I have any chance of making it out alive, or I'll have to take my chances by dodging their fire."

"We're working on it. Forget the car. Bravo team, move, move, to the west side of the house," Hank yelled.

Em winced when the order came through loud enough for the entire block to hear. There was a crackle in Em's earbud, and she thought it was going to stop working, but then she heard Jimena say, "I'm coming out."

Finding the first wire, she snipped it, and almost clipped the wrong wire next to it when Jimena divided her attention by declaring she was coming out. "No, Jimena. Please stay in the panic room."

Returning her concentration to the second wire that she needed to cut to unclasp the vest, she found the tiny wire and efficiently snipped it, then quickly unclasped the vest. It didn't matter anymore if she disabled the bomb in the vest. There was no point, since Em knew there were more bombs that she couldn't possibly get to in time. Redundancy.

†

Jimena ran into the kitchen, and when she saw the vest lying on the counter, she leaped into Em's arms. But Em pushed her away and flipped her wrist over.

"Damn you, Jimena."

The rebuke stung, but Jimena didn't have time to react because Em shouted, "Hank, we need the area clear. Sixty seconds." Em grabbed Jimena by the arm and led her to the front entrance. "We don't have more time, Hank. We're coming out."

"Clear, clear, east side shooters disabled," Hank yelled.

"Thank fuck," Em responded. She bent to retrieve her gun from the ankle holster.

Jimena had also grabbed a gun from inside the panic room. It was always good to be prepared if Hank's team had not eliminated all the shooters. They might still need to shoot their way out, regardless of whether Karl's men had the better angle. Apparently, Em had the same idea. Although Jimena still hoped there weren't additional shooters ready to take them out when Hank said clear.

The minute they burst through the door, Jimena heard the shot. She glanced to her right and saw Em grab her leg, spin, and aim at someone in the bush. She fell to the ground, and although Jimena wasn't the biggest person in the world, adrenaline must have kicked in because she immediately slung one of Em's arms around her shoulders and lifted her. Dragging her away from the front door, they made it far enough to avoid most of the threat from the explosion, but pieces of the demolished house rained down all around them, and one large object hit her head. The world went black.

CHAPTER FIFTEEN

Right after they'd attended to her leg, Em had insisted on rolling herself into Jimena's hospital room. It was considerably more difficult with the IV pole she had to drag along. She'd only agreed to stay in the hospital because she wanted to be with Jimena. Gaby had thrown up her hands in exasperation. Hank apologized for missing the final shooter and for letting Karl escape. She told him of course she forgave him, but only if he could get her another cell phone since Karl had demolished hers. Now she'd have to load all her contacts and apps on the new one which increased her irritation.

The panic room had done its job far more effectively than the agent sent for additional protection. Em was in a bad mood. She knew she should give the guy a break. What was he supposed to do? Throw himself over her to protect the governor?

Em had much bigger fish to fry besides being there for Jimena when she woke up. Karl had known about Jimena being alive, and he was still out there, prepared to wreak havoc. Again. That reinforced the theory about a leak in her office, the police, or Border Patrol. Since this operation involved the most trusted agents and officers, finding out how Karl had learned Jimena was alive moved to the top of the FBI's list of secrets to unravel. Maybe there was someone in all three agencies. Em never had the patience for interrogations. She'd leave that to someone more skilled than herself.

With her leg propped up in the wheelchair, Em navigated to the side of the bed. The doctors were concerned about the swelling in Jimena's brain. A second hit to the back of her head so soon after Smitty had clocked her had caused the concerning condition. They'd performed surgery to reduce the swelling, and now it was wait-and-see time. Em grabbed Jimena's hand, holding it as she murmured her apologies.

"I'm so sorry, Jimena. You did not deserve to get caught up in this Shakespearian tragedy. Unfortunately, my family always has taken things to the extreme, and they placed you directly in the crossfire. I'm hunting my brother down as soon as I'm released for duty."

Not that Em expected Jimena to wake, but seeing her so pale and vulnerable left Em worried. Were all the doctors'

179

assurances that Jimena was likely to make a full recovery accurate or just pretty words to get her to calm down? No matter, Em would wait all night if she had to.

A harried nurse bustled into the room, and her screwed-up face told the story of her displeasure at seeing Em almost glued to Jimena's bed. She wagged her finger at Em.

"Aren't you supposed to be in the next room recovering?" the nurse asked.

"What's the difference between lying in bed and sitting in a chair?" Em pointed to her leg. "Look, it's all propped up with a pillow, just like in that uncomfortable bed."

"You plan on staying here all night?" she challenged and then made her way to the IV pole, checking the bag. The nurse's eyes roamed over the monitors she had hooked to Jimena after returning from surgery.

"If I have to, yes. I want my eyes to be the first thing Jimena sees when she wakes."

"Can I at least have maintenance bring in a more comfortable recliner?" she asked.

"Well, I wouldn't turn down something more comfortable than this wheelchair." Em grinned.

"Cop, right?"

"FBI agent," Em answered.

"Figures. You guys make the worst patients. What about her?" The nurse pointed to Jimena.

"Border Patrol."

"Great, I can look forward to taking care of both of you." The nurse rolled her eyes.

Em chuckled. "Minimal fuss with me, and we'll get along just fine. You can put all your nursey energy into Jimena. At least for right now you won't get any pushback."

"I'll have maintenance bring the recliner."

†

At first, Em thought the light knock on the door was maintenance with the recliner, but then a short, stocky man with a tuft of nearly jet-black hair poked his head into the room. He looked vaguely familiar. A spark of recognition reached his eyes, and a slow grin appeared on his face.

"Well, look what the cat dragged in," he whispered. "Where the hell have you been?" The smile melted from his face. "Nice of you to show up now. Where were you when Jimena cried in her room for two months straight?"

"Hey, Manny. It's good to see you, too. I know." Em held her hand up and continued in a low voice, "I have a lot of explaining to do. Jimena and I reconnected several days ago. She's been helping us out. We honestly thought we would have wrapped this up by now, and you, Rosie, and Maria would not be the wiser. But, unfortunately, things got out of hand. I'll take all the blame."

"While I appreciate you taking accountability for this fucked up situation, I know my sister, and I've no doubt whatever she got involved in was half her doing. Doc said her prognosis is good. But, I had to see for myself. She hasn't woken yet, has she?"

"Not yet, but I'll be here when she does," Em answered.

181

"They aren't naming names yet, but both of you are being heralded as heroes. Heroines," Manny corrected. "Sorry, my sisters are always getting on me for being a sexist man-child."

Em chuckled. "If it helps for you to forgive me, I'm not leaving your sister's side. I'm sticking to her like superglue. Not that it's any of your business, but we've worked through my fifteen-year disappearance. Jimena is probably more forgiving than you, not that I blame you. At least Jimena won the brother lottery. I always envied the relationship you two had."

"It's not your fault your brother is a psycho. We all knew you were nothing like your father or brother. So, rumor has it you're FBI, huh? Guess that fits. I want in on whatever manhunt you have planned to capture your douchebag brother. I'd love a few minutes alone in a room with Karl Junior before you take him in."

"You and me both, but I would much rather make sure our case is rock solid, and we send him away for life. Death would be too easy for him," Em insisted.

"One hour, that's all I need," Manny said with a big grin. "Listen, Rosie and Maria made arrangements to fly into San Diego and arrive tomorrow. While I've always had a soft spot for you because I knew how much you cared about Jimena, they might not be as forgiving. I'm not sure it would be that wise for you to stick to Jimena's side while they're here."

"Sorry. No can do. Um, when I said we reconnected—"

Manny waved his hand in the air. "Nope, don't need or want the details. Got it. But I'm warning you, Em, if you disappear again, I will track your ass down and beat the shit out of you. See, I've evolved. I'm willing to pound on a woman now. Equality and all."

Em chuckled. "I swear I'm not going anywhere. I love Jimena. Always have, always will. Once Karl is behind bars, we'll be able to start our life together as a normal lesbian couple. Besides, I wouldn't want to insult your manhood. I learned a few things in the Army. I'm surprisingly good in a bar brawl."

Manny pointed to Em's leg. "Not as good in a firefight."

Em shrugged. "Flesh wound. I'll be good as new in a few weeks. Pretty sure I won that fight, too. It's almost too bad. I would have liked to ask the guy several questions."

Manny crossed the room and placed a kiss on Jimena's temple. "Just take care of her. Not only her body but her heart. I'll be back tomorrow with Rosie and Maria. Call me if anything changes with her condition."

"Will do. Leave your number."

Manny pulled a card from his pocket and set it on the side table.

After maintenance brought in the recliner, Em settled in and let her eyes close while she held Jimena's hand.

†

Jimena felt like she was clawing her way through the mud. A sticky, claustrophobic feeling threatened to overwhelm her, and she thrashed about until she felt a sharp pain at the back of her head.

"Whoa, whoa, you need to stay on your side," the soft voice said.

The woman's voice was vaguely familiar. She concentrated hard on that voice. When she opened her mouth to speak. No words came out. It was as if she was fighting hard to wake from a nightmare.

Feeling the brush of fingertips on her forehead, Jimena focused on the calming touch and managed to open her eyes.

"Hey, you. Welcome back," Em said.

Jimena blinked once. "Em? Shot?" She tried to recall the correct words to string together that would allow her to form complete sentences, but her brain was still foggy. She remembered seeing Em get shot, then attempting to drag her farther away from the house. Bits and pieces started coming back slowly. Yeah, the place that was about to blow to smithereens.

"I'm fine. On the other hand, you took the brunt of the raining debris. Or, more precisely, your poor head. They had to do a quick surgery to reduce the swelling. Something called a ventriculostomy. There's a small incision with a tube coming out of your brain to drain the fluid. Or something like that. It was much less invasive than the other surgery they considered. Manny made the call," Em explained.

It took a lot of effort, but Jimena brought her right hand to the back of her head and felt the large bandage. "Am I bald now?"

Em laughed. "Is that what you're concerned about?"

Jimena managed a ghost of a smile. "Karl? Your mother?"

"Got away. Gaby has been busy. The FBI already leaked Karl's picture to the media. Hank and Steve are following up on calls coming in through the tip-line. They're also trying to find out who leaked your fake death."

"It's a small group to investigate. I'm sure we can eliminate you and me," Jimena joked. The fog was finally lifting, and Jimena felt more clear-headed. "Do you think it's possible the security guard recognized me and alerted Karl?"

"Yeah, that's possible. The local police have Jack, that's his name. He's in custody right now. The full authority of the FBI is going to make sure they don't repeat what happened to Petey and Darnell. Hank can be a pretty scary dude. If there is anything to find out from Jack, I will place my bets on Hank. Since we suspect a leak in the local police, Steve is watching the comings and goings. He is particularly skilled at noticing odd behavior. I've said he should try to get into the Behavioral Analysis Unit, but he'd rather work alongside Hank."

"So, I guess nothing to do but wait and heal. I'm assuming the governor and her mom got out okay."

"Yup, not a single scratch on either of them. The governor is a lot savvier about security than I thought. She had the panic room built after her mother bought the house. And she went through a private contractor, without registering permits or anything else that would tip off anyone about its existence." Em shifted in her chair and grimaced.

"They didn't admit you, too?"

Em bit her bottom lip. "Um, they did, but I only have to stay for another day, maybe two. My room is next door."

"Why aren't you in your room?"

"Duh, I was waiting for you to wake up, and then I could bring you up to speed on everything."

"Done. Now get your ass back in your room," Jimena ordered.

"I'd rather crawl into bed with you, but I don't think Nurse Ratched will allow that."

The door opened, and a new nurse said, "No, Nurse Brandi will not." She pointed to the whiteboard. "That's my name. You were both asleep when I started my shift at seven. Carla already gave me the scoop about you two at the evening report."

"Whoops, busted," Jimena giggled.

"Glad to see you're awake. Mind if I ask you a few questions?" The nurse moved to the side of the bed and pressed a button, readjusting Jimena to an almost sitting position. This allowed Jimena to roll carefully onto her back without putting additional pressure on her head.

Once settled, Jimena answered, "Sure, the fog has lifted slightly."

"Do you know what year it is?" Brandi asked.

"Twenty twenty-two."

"Good. And the president."

"Biden."

"Excellent. These days, sometimes I have to accept Trump depending on the person's political leanings," she joked.

"Ugh," both Em and Jimena groaned.

"Can you wiggle your toes for me?" Brandi directed as she moved to the end of the bed and flipped the covers off her feet.

Jimena wiggled her toes, and the nurse nodded. A smile formed on her face. Anticipating the next test, Jimena wiggled her fingers while lifting her arms.

"Everything looks great, Jimena. I'm happy to see movement in your extremities. Can you move your legs now?"

The small effort it took to move everything was tiring Jimena, but she followed Brandi's directive and moved her legs.

"Perfect." Brandi turned her attention to Em. "How about if I make a deal with you?" Brandi offered.

"A deal? I like making deals," Em answered.

"You get one more hour to visit with one another, then I roll you back into your own room. I need to check your bandages, too."

"Two hours," Em countered.

"It's already eight-thirty."

"Yeah, so. It's not like we both haven't been snoozing most of the time we've been in this torture chamber." Em grinned to take the sting out of her description of the hospital.

"Careful, or I'll tell the doc to order a rectal exam," Brandi countered. "If she starts to tire, don't keep her awake."

Em made the sign of the cross. "I promise, I won't."

After the nurse left, Jimena giggled. "Adopting my Catholic faith, are you?"

"It seems to give more weight to promises. Besides, I believe that your Saint Christopher medal kept me safe all these years, so there are parts of your religion I don't dismiss as fairytales." Em frowned and touched her chest.

"What's wrong?"

"Shit. I forgot. Karl ripped the medal from my neck. That's why I couldn't call the team, which actually worked out well. The shooters might have picked them off like ducks on a conveyor belt if they'd come in hot. I need to call Hank. Hopefully, his team found my necklace."

Jimena couldn't resist teasing Em. "That's why they had to dig a slug out of your leg, huh? You didn't have my Saint Christopher medal to protect you."

Em's face lost its humor as her lips formed a thin line. "I think I should give it back to you. I'm not the one who keeps getting beat up."

Jimena touched her throat. "Where's my necklace?"

"I don't know. Maybe the nurse had to remove it during surgery. I'll ask her when she comes back in."

"That's okay. I'll ask. I think you got on the wrong foot by calling her Nurse Ratched. Perhaps we should have a priest bless it or something. You know, a priest can bless any piece of jewelry."

"Seriously? You honestly believe all that mumbo jumbo?" Em asked.

"I do, yes. A blessing will simply give the ring more meaning, reminding me of God's love. I honestly believe the necklace with your promise ring has saved me on multiple occasions. I'm still alive, aren't I? That must have been due to your love. You have a similar power to a priest's blessing, but what the hell? It can't hurt to have that extra boost from a man of the cloth."

"Whatever you want. I'll take you there personally if you believe it will keep you safe. The power of positive thinking. Stranger things have happened. Belief is a powerful thing, and that is something I can get behind. Organized religion, not so much."

"I know, babe. I know. I'll carry the faith for both of us." Jimena grinned.

CHAPTER SIXTEEN

Jimena had finally convinced Em to go to her room and get some rest. The pointed look from Nurse Brandi did not make a difference to Em, but the truth was that Jimena was exhausted. It took all her effort to stay focused while talking with Em.

Finally, Jimena said, "Em, I love that you're here by my side, but I'm completely knackered, and it's tough to stay in the conversation. I want us refreshed tomorrow so we can put our brilliant minds together and figure out where the leaks might come from. Don't forget a tornado is coming tomorrow as well."

"Tornado?" Em wrinkled her nose adorably.

"My sisters. You remember Rosie and Maria, right?"

Em cringed. "Yes, and they are far scarier than Manny, who asked for one hour alone in a room with Karl. He also threatened to kick my ass if I ever ghosted you again."

"Manny wasn't kidding, was he? Never mind. I don't want to know the details. Plausible deniability. Will you please go back to your room? I think I'm going to need my strength and wits for when my entire family descends on this room."

"You could close your eyes. I'll hold your hand while you sleep."

"No, that's just it. I can't sleep knowing you're in that uncomfortable recliner. Please?" Jimena turned her pleading eyes to Em.

"Okay, but I'll be back tomorrow morning. I told Manny this was all on me. I'll make sure Rosie and Maria know that as well."

"But that isn't the truth," Jimena insisted.

"That's what Manny said. He places the blame on Karl. I knew I liked your brother." Em smiled. "He actually let me off quite easily."

"Well. I'm not letting you put this all on your shoulders. I was there with you every step of the way. It was my idea to fake my death. You all simply went along with it." Jimena yawned.

Em leaned in to kiss Jimena lightly on her lips. "I'm going to let you sleep now. I love you and will be back before you wake."

†

Em lay awake in the hospital bed, listening to the murmurs at the nurse's station. They were laughing about a blind date one of them had gone on. She didn't know how anyone could sleep in the hospital. Jimena had looked like it was hard for her to keep her eyes open, so Em hoped she was having better luck. She almost tossed aside the covers and finagled her way into the wheelchair to double-check. But Brandi came in and wagged her finger just as Em reached for the chair.

"Don't you dare make your way into Jimena's room," the nurse ordered. "She's sleeping peacefully, and that's what she needs right now."

"Fine," Em grumbled. "Although I can't imagine how anyone can sleep in a hospital. You people keep coming into the room and bugging us. Plus, I have to listen to your bad blind date stories."

Brandi had the good sense to flush with embarrassment. "Sorry. Would you like me to give you something for the pain and to help you sleep?"

"Now, that's the best suggestion I've had all night. What the hell. Sure, load up the IV. Just don't give me one of those highly addictive opioids that'll turn me into a raging maniac."

Brandi chuckled. "Nope, we save those meds for us, having to deal with pain-in-the-ass cops like you," she joked.

"Jimena is going to fully recover, right? No residual effects from the surgery or anything?"

"There are always risks post-surgery, but we'll keep an eye out for infection or any other complications that would affect her recovery. Don't worry. Jimena had one of the best surgeons in the state perform her surgery. She's lucky."

"Not really. Lucky would be not getting beat on twice within a week. And not having a large piece of wood or whatever it was fall on your head."

"You have a point, but worrying after the fact only serves to keep you awake, which then makes my job harder," Brandi teased.

"Fine, fine. Give me the magic sleeping potion, and then leave me be. How about if I make you a deal?" Em inquired.

"This should be interesting." The nurse placed her hands on her hips.

"Get the doc to discharge me tomorrow morning, and I'll do my best not to be a pain in your ass when hanging out in Jimena's room. You won't have to worry about me busting stitches or whatever if I'm discharged because I'll no longer be your concern."

"We'll see." Brandi left the room, returning a few minutes later with a vial that she efficiently plunged into the IV line.

"Sweet dreams, PIMA." Brandi grinned.

PIMA? What the hell is that? I mean, I wouldn't mind being called a puma, a sleek, powerful predator. Cats always have an air of mystery about them, too. Jimena has a cat. She'd like it if I was a puma.

Em's rambling thoughts bounced around in her head until PIMA clicked in place for her. *Pain in my ass, PIMA.* A ghost of a smile formed on Em's lips. She'd definitely met her match in Nurse Brandi. Maybe she'd introduce her to Gaby. Em liked Brandi's spunk. That was the last thought she had before falling into a deep sleep.

†

The rickety cart in the hallway squeaked loud enough to rouse Em awake. Em blinked twice before glancing at her watch. "Shit," she muttered. It was half-past eight. Jimena was probably awake already. Almost forgetting about her leg, she roughly pushed the covers away and swung her legs over the side of the bed. She felt a twinge, but because it wasn't a stabbing pain, she continued on her mission to roll into Jimena's room and check on her.

A commotion right outside her door had Em on high alert. Em's heart raced as she thought she heard Jimena call for help after what sounded like an entire wall of cups were tossed on the floor. Then she heard Manny's voice loud and clear.

"Call security," Manny yelled.

Em hopped on one leg and made her way into the wheelchair, not bothering to settle her leg properly onto the elevated side. Now she felt that sharp pain. She'd deal with that later. Her gut told her something was terribly wrong. Reaching for the door, she pulled it open and rolled her way to the middle of the mayhem. Manny had a man pinned to the ground and was punching him repeatedly.

"If anything happens to my sister, I'm going to tear you apart. You fucking piece of shit!" Manny screamed at the man.

Em wished she had her gun, but they wouldn't let her bring it into the hospital. She recognized the man as one of the "patriots" that worked with Smitty. Quickly piecing together what had probably happened, Em felt sick about leaving Jimena alone. She'd have a word with the hospital staff, and when she was done with them, none would dare make a peep about her assigning herself as Jimena's personal security. And that meant she'd call Hank to bring her a gun. Any gun. At this point, she'd take whatever he grabbed.

An overweight security guard came huffing to the scene, and Manny skeptically glanced at the man. Then, with one meaty hand still on the attacker's throat, Manny put out his other hand and ordered, "Give me your cuffs."

Wide-eyed, the guard handed over his handcuffs from his belt. Manny roughly turned the man onto his stomach and efficiently cuffed him.

Em rolled quickly over to where Manny had secured the intruder and asked, "Jimena?" She could feel the desperation in her voice.

"The nurses are checking her out right now. I think I caught him before he put whatever he had in his syringe into the IV. Where the hell were you?" Manny's eyes reflected his intense anger.

"You can yell at me later. I know I deserve it. But right now, I need to see Jimena, then I have to make a call to my colleague in the FBI. For the remainder of her stay in the hospital, she will have round-the-clock security. I will personally guarantee her safety."

"You fucking better," Manny retorted. Although his voice seemed to moderate a smidgeon from its previous fury.

Em didn't know how Manny had thwarted Karl's attempt or why the intruder hadn't gone for Em first, but she thanked the universe that he was there. Rolling quickly to Jimena's room, she sighed in relief when she saw Jimena raise her hand in a small wave.

†

Jimena had woken early, recognizing the morning noise that accompanied shift change. She'd spent enough time in hospitals with her mother when the end drew near. Her new nurse was more timid than Brandi, and she chuckled at the thought of Em running roughshod over the poor young woman. Yet that didn't stop her from pleading with the woman to see if the doctor would release her today. She didn't want to spend another night in the hospital. She also wanted her necklace. After never taking it off in the fifteen years since Em had given her the ring, she felt incomplete without it.

"How are you feeling today?" the new nurse asked.

Jimena glanced at the whiteboard to address the nurse by name and answered, "I'm doing really well, Denise. A slight headache, that's all. Maybe the doctor will discharge me today?" she asked hopefully. "Could you check on that and find my necklace if it's not too much trouble? It has special meaning to me."

Denise rummaged in the side table drawer and pulled out a plastic bag. Jimena saw her name on the label and breathed a sigh of relief when Denise handed it to her.

"Could you maybe help me put this on? By the way, are there priests who make rounds?" Jimena asked. *No time like the present to get this blessed.*

Denise scrunched her face in confusion. "Um, yeah, but you're not terminal or anything." Denise pushed the button to bring Jimena to a sitting position and then removed the necklace from the plastic bag. She carefully opened the clasp and placed it around Jimena's neck, reattaching the chain. "There you go."

Jimena chuckled. "Yeah, I know I'm not terminal. But I wanted a priest to bless this necklace. A little extra insurance to make sure I stay alive. Not that I don't trust the care you all have given me," Jimena added.

"Oh, okay, sure. Father Kelly checked in a few minutes ago. I'll see if he's available to see you."

"Thank you, Denise. Oh, and don't wake the sleeping bear next door. You might as well get a few hours of peace before she wears on every last nerve of yours," Jimena joked.

"The sleeping bear?" Denise asked.

"Your colleague Brandi didn't bring you up to speed?"

Recognition dawned on Denise's face. "Oh, you mean Ms. Schmidt." Denise chuckled. "Don't worry. Brandi gave her something to sleep last night. I've already checked on her this morning. She's snoring away."

"Good. Em needed the rest."

"Breakfast should be here soon. How bad is your headache on a scale of one to ten?"

"Maybe a seven," Jimena answered.

"Okay, I'll get you something that should take care of that. Any nausea?"

"A little."

"We'll take care of that, too." The nurse bustled out of the room, and several minutes later, the priest arrived.

Father Kelly was surprisingly young. He had kind eyes and a roguish smile.

"Good morning, Ms. Aguilar." His deep baritone did not match his youthful good looks. Father Kelly looked more like a surfer dude than a priest.

"Jimena, please call me Jimena. You don't look like a priest, except for the collar. I suppose that's a dead giveaway.

Father Kelly chuckled. "Yes, I get that a lot. I'd rather do my ministering without wearing this collar. It's worse than a necktie." He tugged at the white collar to emphasize his point. "But if I don't wear it, the older men and women don't believe me. So what can I do for you today?"

"I'd like you to please bless this necklace," Jimena answered.

"A true believer. I haven't had that request in ages."

"Can't be that long. What are you, eighteen? Did you just take your vows?" Jimena asked.

Another rumble of laughter erupted from the priest. "Twenty-seven. I think I can handle your request. Then perhaps we can pray together."

"I'd like that."

After Father Kelly left, breakfast arrived, and Jimena sent Denise away, telling her she could feed herself. Within five minutes, Jimena heard the door open and wondered if Em had finally woken. They must have given her a powerful sleep aid if she slept through the morning activities. Hospitals were definitely not places to get rest. But it wasn't Em who entered her room.

Although the man wore scrubs and could have been a hospital employee, bells and whistles blared that something was off about him. He didn't acknowledge Jimena and went straight for the IV line, pulling a syringe from his pocket.

"Hey, who the hell are you?"

The man turned around and sneered, "Your day nurse."

Jimena did the only thing she thought might draw attention to her room because she knew she was in trouble. Flipping her breakfast tray, the tray and contents slammed to the floor, making a loud noise. At the same time, Jimena yelled, "Help!" Then she pressed her call button.

She expected the nurse to answer the call and was surprised but pleased when Manny barreled into the room, quickly evaluating the situation and slapping the syringe from the man's hands.

The two men traded punches until Manny landed a devastating blow. He dragged the man out of the room, and Jimena heard him call for security. Jimena panicked. What if the man who tried to harm her had already been in Em's room? *Oh God, Em.* Just as Jimena was about to rip out her IV line and every other wire attached to her body, the door to her room swung open, and Em rushed in.

CHAPTER SEVENTEEN

A rush of relief filled Em as she rolled to the bed and awkwardly embraced Jimena. Karl wasn't going to stop his assault on them. He would never give up. Would the FBI ever catch him, or would he be allowed to operate with impunity? This had to stop.

It was a long shot, but after they took away the would-be assassin, Em wanted to talk with Manny. She needed to know if he had unwillingly leaked the information about his sister. After the house had blown, Em had asked the ambulance crew to take them to a different hospital than Scripps or UC San Diego Health in La Jolla. She had feared something like this would happen, that Karl would try to get to one or both of them.

Even though UC San Diego Health was a top-notch surgical center, Em wasn't above asking the governor's help in getting the renowned surgeon to treat Jimena at the lesser-known hospital. However, until they unraveled all the leaks and caught Karl, Em and Jimena would need to return to the safe house. So far, the only people who knew the safe house location were Hank, Steve, Gaby, and Carter. Gary didn't even know where Jimena had stayed before everything went to shit again.

Em released Jimena from the tight hold she had on her. "If they don't discharge me today, I'll check myself out against medical advice. Besides having another agent that I will personally hand pick, I'm not leaving your side until you get released."

Jimena smiled. "Okay. I won't even try to talk you out of it. I was so worried that the man had already gotten to you. At least if you're with me, I know you're okay."

The flustered nurse entered the room, followed by Manny, who pushed his hand through his hair in a nervous gesture. Em noticed his anger had abated, and his eyes only showed concern for his sister.

"I'm going to check the IV lines and hang a fresh bag. Just in case. Okay?" Denise said. "I am so sorry…"

Jimena held up her hand. "Whatever you need to do, but what he was trying to inject into the IV, Manny smacked it out of his hand before he could put anything into the line." She pointed to the corner of the room where the syringe lay innocently on the floor.

"Hey, Little Sis. Are you sure you feel okay? No funny sensations or anything?" Manny's eyes grew misty.

Jimena absently touched her necklace with the promise ring. "I feel great. I don't even have a pounding headache anymore." She cringed. "But I kind of made a mess of my breakfast tray. Sorry. I'd kill for a burrito filled with eggs, cheese, and sausage. You know, like Mama used to make."

"You didn't hear me say this, but there's a little Mexican stand about two blocks away. They might have what you're craving," Denise answered.

"I'm on it." Manny pointed his thick index finger at Em. "Don't leave her side while I'm gone."

"I don't plan to. Plus, I'm calling Hank to pull Steve. I trust Steve to keep us both safe. When you get back, I want to talk to you. Don't make any calls on your phone, okay? Especially not calls that update your sisters on what happened today. Critical information is finding its way to Karl, and I want to know how that's happening."

Manny nodded once and left the room.

†

Jimena opened her mouth wide and chomped down on the steaming burrito. "Mmm, so good. Thanks, Manny."

Her brother grinned at her as he pulled one of the heavy vinyl chairs closer to where Em had positioned her wheelchair. Em had made the call to Hank who said that Steve would be there within the hour, and then they would figure everything out together.

203

Em cleared her throat. "I don't want to piss you off any more than I already have, but I need to recreate as much as possible. I'll try not to act like I'm interrogating you. Can we go back to the day you heard about Jimena's fake death? Walk me through every conversation you had and with whom. No detail is too small."

"Okay." Manny looked to the ceiling as if someone had miraculously written the answers there, neatly, in perfect script. "I've been thinking a lot about this. I was distressed when I went into the office, so I wasn't paying much attention to my surroundings, just made a beeline for Gary's office."

"Can we try an exercise that I sometimes use to help me remember things? Our brains usually pick up more than we think. So, did you take your own car, an Uber, bus? How did you get to the office?"

"I drove my car." Manny paused. "It took me a few loops around the block before finding a parking space. That stressed me even further."

"Okay, you were upset when you exited the car, right?"

"Yes, I couldn't get to Gary's office quick enough."

"Do you remember any smells or sounds that stood out? How about anyone hanging around either before or after entering the office? Anyone that seemed out of place?"

Manny gritted his teeth. "No, only a few Border Patrol Agents, but there's always a few in the office at any given time."

"Who? Did you know these agents?"

"Not really. Jimena and I work in different areas. She hangs in the desert, and I'm on marine patrol."

"Describe everyone that was there in the office. Everything you can remember before you stalked into Gary's office."

Em waited patiently as Manny sat quietly before starting a monologue describing what he was recreating in his head. "There was a tall blond man to the right. When he looked up, I remember thinking his expression was hostile, but then I imagine I had a kind of intensity when I barreled into the office. I'm pretty sure I've seen him at Murphy's when I would occasionally meet Jimena for a drink."

"Do you know his name?"

Manny shook his head.

"It's probably Keith. He and I are never paired together because he makes it well known what he thinks about women field agents. So, for the most part, I've ignored him," Jimena added.

"Okay, who else was there?" Em prompted.

"Jesus was there!" Manny exclaimed as he obviously remembered something. "He tried to talk to me, tell me he was sorry to hear about Jimena, but I wanted to learn what happened directly from Gary. I was pissed and blamed him for your death. He's always looking for some angle to get more funds for Border Patrol, and I knew he was ass deep in whatever got you killed. The veiled suggestion that Jimena was part of some drug ring had me seeing red. So I brushed him aside and flung open Gary's door."

Annette Mori

"Do you remember if Gary closed the door or left it open?"

"He closed it right away and told me to sit my ass down while he explained everything." Manny paused as Em watched him trying to recall the details of that traumatic day.

"Okay, then, after he told you, what happened?"

Manny shrugged. "I left. I was eager to get out and make a phone call to Rosie and Maria. They needed to know that Jimena wasn't dead."

Em leaned forward. "Manny, this is important. When exactly did you make the call? Try to remember everything you can. Was there anyone around? Was it noisy? Again, what did you see? Hear? Smell?"

Manny was silent for a moment, and then as if a clear picture had formed in his head, he began reciting, "The traffic noises were loud enough that I looked around for an area away from the street because I didn't want to wait until I reached my car to call. I felt an urgency to let them know what was happening. So I searched for somewhere quiet. There was an alley next to the office building. I noticed that guy, Keith, coming from the Border Patrol office. He seemed nervous as he pulled cigarettes from his shirt pocket. I wasn't focused on him, though. I ducked into the relative quiet of the alley and phoned Rosie first."

"Were you speaking loudly?"

"I didn't think so at the time, but I guess I could still hear the traffic noise in the alley. Although it was quieter than the sidewalk. I was quick with my call, just giving the basics. I told Rosie that Jimena was fine, and that it was all a ruse, and she was working with the FBI. I didn't know any more than that, so I couldn't answer any of Rosie's questions. She said she would call Maria and that I should keep in touch if I learned something more. I said I would, and that was it."

"Did you see Keith after you exited the alley?"

Manny frowned. "Yeah, I did, and I remember smelling smoke from a cigarette while I talked with Rosie. Keith had moved closer to the alley, and right when I exited, he turned away from me and stubbed out his cigarette on the pavement. The asshole left his butt there and scurried back into the building. I remember because I picked the damn thing up and deposited it into the trash."

Jimena and Em shared a look, then Jimena voiced what Em was already thinking. "I think we should check Keith out. Is there any way they can tap Keith's phone? He might have overheard you, Manny, and then fed that information to Karl."

"Agreed," Em said. "I'll call Carter and get the wheels in motion for the phone tap. I still believe there are others. Catching him will not address all our issues. Karl is extremely well-funded. I want our techs to start following the money trail. Maybe we'll learn of other assets and get lucky."

"Shit, I'm sorry, Jimena. It's my fault you're hurt." He hung his head.

"No, it is not. You didn't plant those bombs, and you didn't decide to involve yourself in FBI business. I went to that house of my own volition because I wanted to help. That is not on you or Em," Jimena argued.

"We're going to find Karl, and when we do, he won't get away a second time." Em gritted her teeth. This was a promise she knew she shouldn't make, but it was the only thing she had to offer. Em was under no illusion that either Manny or Jimena would hold her to her promise. She'd broken too many of them to be taken seriously anymore. Maybe this one would stick, and Em could start again with a new slate. If only she could erase the last fifteen years and her most recent broken promise of sticking to Jimena like glue.

CHAPTER EIGHTEEN

Not knowing who the other leaks might be, Hank and Steve had both shown up at the hospital to personally handle Jimena and Em's transport to a new safe house. No one wanted to take the chance that Karl had discovered the previous location through his vast network of spies and misdirected "patriots." Steve was still beating himself up for missing the second shooter in the back bushes. Jimena thought too many people were taking the blame for what Karl had put them through. The only person Jimena believed should face up to his actions was Karl, and maybe several of his associates.

Jimena looked around at the new safe house. It was more contemporary but smaller. None of the four seemed bothered by the fact that there were only two bedrooms. Hank and Steve would share one and Jimena and Em the other.

Em hobbled into the main living area on her crutches while Steve fussed around in the kitchen, making tea and coffee for everyone. Hank fidgeted in his seat. Jimena had told Manny to go home to his wife with the promise that she would let him know the minute they'd captured Karl, so he could rest easily. He'd also agreed to take Garfield to his house until she could return home. That had been an enormous relief to Jimena. She felt terrible about continuing to deceive Mrs. Rodriguez, but she would worry about that later.

Rosie and Maria weren't as easy to convince to return home, but Jimena had finally managed to send her sisters back to their families. After she explained her need to go into hiding, both had reluctantly agreed as long as Jimena promised to call when the danger subsided. They hadn't been too warm around Em, clearly placing the blame squarely on her shoulders, but Jimena would deal with that later. One problem at a time.

With her leg propped on the coffee table, Em started the conversation. "All right, Hank, give us an update. There's something you learned when you took that call earlier."

Hank sighed. "I followed up on a hunch. Since the group of people in the know is tiny, and every member is someone I'd trust with my life, I kept wracking my brain over who might screw us. Then it dawned on me that we depend on tech support to gather information."

Em frowned. "Teddy? That little pipsqueak? Is he the FBI leak?"

"Maybe. I called a friend of mine. When Teddy left for the day, I had her hack into the system, looking for anything that might give a clue."

"Her? I thought I was your only female friend," Em joked.

Steve brought steaming cups of tea and coffee, set them on the table, took a chair, and quietly listened to the conversation. Steve was a true introvert, only talking when asked a question or when he had something important to add.

"I met her during a sting operation I was a part of. Total geek. She was a friend of Sophie's, the lead agent. Unfortunately, we lost a young agent that day, and the snitch she was working with got hurt pretty bad." Hank lifted the cup to his lips and blew on it before taking a small sip.

"Was this when you were in DC?" Em asked.

"Yeah. So, the story gets kind of interesting. This medical team that was not ours showed up, but we were too focused on saving the young girls who were part of the human traffic shipment. Unbeknownst to us, one target was part of an underground group that was rumored to be responsible for taking down several human trafficking rings. After that shit show, Sophie left the FBI, and I didn't see her or Toni for many years. I always wondered if Sophie and Toni joined this shadowy organization. There were a lot of rumors about them, but the FBI did not seem interested in tracking them down."

"I heard those rumors. But they were more like fairytales by the time they made their way to California." Em relaxed on the sofa with her hands wrapped around the tea.

"Anyway, Toni and I bonded in the van together. When Steve and I went back to DC last year to visit friends, we ran into Sophie and Toni at this café. Toni gave me a card with a number I could call to reach her. She told me to call her if I ever needed anything." Hank shrugged. "For some reason, I kept her card. We've sort of kept in touch. I called, and she came, blessing us with her genius."

Jimena sighed. "Do all gay men take forever to provide important updates? Can we skip to the crucial part now?"

Hank laughed. "Impatient much? All right, so here is the critical information. All calls that come into the hotline are supposed to be forwarded to either Steve or me. We've asked that none are deleted, no matter how insane or improbable they might sound. Toni found that a call had come through, and Teddy had apparently tried to erase it. He didn't know that I'd put a backup system into place or that we'd have an expert hacker in to check his computer. I suppose, deep down, I never trusted the guy."

"Did you learn something important from the call?"

"Not really. It was an older woman, and the call was garbled toward the end. We're not sure if Teddy did something to the call and then decided to simply erase it. They're still working on it. Toni put in a shadow program that tracks every single keystroke on Teddy's computer. We've also gotten authorization to tap his cell phone. So, if Teddy is involved, we'll know eventually."

"Hopefully, there is only one person in the FBI feeding Karl information. Hey, I just thought of something. Can this Toni person get me a roster of all the police officers in the local precinct? If the FBI asks for that list, it will cause suspicion. I'd rather we not alert any of them to our distrust of the local PD. I know we handpicked the officers to respond, but I might recognize the names of those who worked with my father back in the day. They would most likely be individuals to check on. How long will the phone taps on Keith and Teddy's phones take?"

Hank frowned. "At least two to three days."

"He could be on his way to Germany or Moscow by now."

"Moscow? Come on, Em, don't tell me you've bought into those conspiracy theories about Putin funding militia groups in the US." Hank shook his head.

"It's a known fact that Russia interfered in our election. Karl is well funded if the house he and Mom were living in is any indication. I would not toss any theory, no matter how outrageous it might seem on its face."

"Wow! Okay, then I guess we might have to draw outside the lines," Hank conceded. "Toni hinted at some new tech that we could use to monitor Keith and Teddy."

Em leaned forward and excitedly declared, "Let's do it. I'll take the blame if Carter finds out. But, for now, I want to keep our circle as tight as possible. You trust Toni, right?"

"As much as I trust you, yes," Hank answered.

"Jimena? What do you think?" Em asked.

"I think we ought to meet this tech genius and see what else she recommends. Does she have any way to track where that odd phone call came from? It might be your mom trying to do the right thing. And, if she's with Karl, tracing where the call came from may help."

"If my mother made that call, it was likely only for self-preservation. She must be getting a clue that Karl is not firing on all cylinders. But, yeah, I thought of that."

Hank grinned. "So, do you want to meet Toni?"

"Hell yeah. We could use a genius person on our side. Maybe she'll tell us about this secret organization," Em teased. "I can't believe you call me out on my theories about Russia, but you buy into this shadow organization fairytale."

Hank crossed his arms over his chest. "You weren't there for the sting operation. After we took the girls to safety, we returned to the meeting location, and it was like nothing had happened. There wasn't a trace of what went down. Not even a spec of blood to analyze. That kind of effort takes a great deal of organization. Just saying." Hank reached into his pocket and held Em's Saint Christopher medal in his hand. "Hey, I almost forgot, here's your necklace. I had Steve grab it before the forensics team came in. You know they would have taken it into evidence. It's not like we need to dust it for fingerprints. I imagine Karl's prints are all over that house."

Em snatched the necklace from Hank's hand. "Thanks, Hank. You're a prince. This means a great deal to me. Did you happen to get Carter to issue me another phone?"

"Oh yeah, it's in my bag." Hank stood and walked over to a leather shoulder bag and retrieved a small box.

Em leaned back and started laughing hysterically. "Hank! You bought a man purse."

Hank pulled the box and held it to his chest. "It is not a man purse. It's a utility bag. I've got shit I need to carry. Just for that mean comment, I'm keeping this phone."

"What the hell do you need to carry that can't be in a pocket or strapped to your chest? Shit, bro, I don't even carry a bag."

"That's because you're a lesbian. Everyone knows lesbians stuff all their shit in their many pocketed pants."

"I'm a lesbian, and I carry a bag. Horrible stereotype, Hank," Jimena interjected. "It's a nice bag, Hank. Where did you get it?"

Em rolled her eyes. "Oh, brother, can we talk about the shopping network another time?" Em rubbed her hands together. "Now, give me my new phone. I'm stoked the cheap bastard flipped for the latest smartphone. How come?"

"Guilt requisition. Carter knew you wouldn't be pleased sitting on the sidelines," Hank admitted.

"Not for long. Since the bullet did not hit any major nerves, arteries, or bones, I anticipate a full recovery. I'll be back on the trail soon enough."

Hank quickly changed the subject, and it surprised Jimena that Em allowed this. If Jimena had to guess, she presumed Carter had given Hank strict instructions to steer Em clear of further work on her brother's domestic terror cell.

†

Jimena did not expect the tall, dark-haired woman to be so attractive. She needed to check her stereotypes. When she thought of computer or technical experts, the last thing she imagined was a woman who looked like a model. Toni had a playful, roguish smile as she greeted Hank with a hug.

"So, you're dipping your toes into the rebel pool, huh?" Toni asked.

"Come in. I want you to meet Jimena, Steve, and Em. This is our small team. For now, we want to keep information very close to the vest. So many leaks, we're not exactly sure where the poison is coming from."

Toni entered the room and glanced at Jimena and Em before answering Hank. "Understood. Betrayal can be a bitch. I remember when that bastard Ted betrayed Soph. She got him, though," Toni said.

"Fuck me. So that's what happened to Ted. I only heard snippets because I was already in the process of a transfer to California, and my focus was on that. I never liked the guy. Total prick," Hank answered.

"Yeah, may he not rest in peace," Toni quipped.

Jimena stood and offered her hand. "Hi, I'm Jimena. It's a pleasure to meet you."

Toni shook her hand and said, "Same."

Steve stood and offered his hand. "Steve."

"Good to finally meet you, Steve." Toni shook his hand.

Em gathered her crutches to stand, but Toni gestured for her to remain sitting and strolled over to greet her.

"Thanks for helping us out," Em said.

"I'm happy to. It aligns well with some work I've been doing lately. We've been following the events closely and might know a little more than the FBI. So I was happy when Hank called. We entertained the idea of sticking our nose into FBI business again. Sometimes they don't exactly like our methods." Toni chuckled as she took a seat in the swivel chair perpendicular to the couch.

Em tilted her head and looked closely at Toni. "Who is this we?"

"I could tell you all about it, but then I'd have to kill you. Or someone else I work with might have to do it, not my thing," Toni teased.

"So, there really is this shadow organization. I knew it. You and Soph are part of it now, right?" Hank exclaimed.

Toni smiled. "Not confirming or denying it, but I have been authorized to help. You guys ever heard of nanobot tech?"

"Aren't nanobots used in medicine?" Jimena asked.

"They are, but there are many more uses, like monitoring and tracking," Toni answered.

"So, you mean like surveillance? How does that work?" Em asked.

"I've developed a special tracking nanobot. Once injected or put into the system, the bot will travel to an opening in the body, seeking light. Then we can see or hear whatever is happening from the host's eyes," Toni explained.

"Holy shit. Like being wired only so much better. How do we get these bots into Keith or Teddy?" Em asked.

"That's the tricky part. I'm just the tech guru. You guys need to find a way to inject or get the target to ingest the bots. I'll give you a vial with more than one. It's better to have multiple bots in the unlikely occurrence they all don't make it to the optimal spots for tracking and listening."

"Leave that to Steve and me," Hank offered.

"I feel like I just traveled to 2092. This is like futuristic stuff," Jimena enthused.

"Not even close to the gadgets we now have at our disposal. No offense, but the FBI are toddlers in the tech game."

"Well, it's what we've had to work with. I'm glad you're here to help, but where were you three days ago? We could have used some assistance," Em grumbled.

"Sorry about that. We were working a different angle," Toni admitted.

"And what angle was that?"

"Trying to cut off their money supply." Toni shrugged.

"Please confirm it's the Russians," Em pleaded. "Hank thinks I'm a conspiracy theorist."

Toni smiled. "Hank, you should listen to your colleague. Not a conspiracy theory at all. You can leave the Russians to us, and we'll lend a tech hand to help you capture Karl Schmidt." Toni turned to Em. "He's your brother, right?"

"Unfortunately, yes." Em stuck her tongue out at Hank. "See, I told you the Russians had their fingerprints all over this. Hey, Toni, instead of us asking for Teddy to run down the money and figure out who owns that house Karl was living in, could you hack some systems to get that information?"

Toni grinned. "Already started. Unfortunately, the Russians may be many things, but there is no shortage of cunning in their toolbox. There are multiple layers of shell companies. The good news is that we've been able to link several properties to some of those companies. For example, there is another house in that same neighborhood owned by Thomas Smith, the CEO of one of those companies. But, the man is a ghost, or at least he was until five years ago. The house next to the governor's mother's house is owned by Gabriel Jones, the VP of that same company. And guess who he has a surprising resemblance to?"

"My brother," Em answered.

Toni tapped the tip of her nose. "Ding, ding, ding, give the woman a lollipop. She got it in one."

Em pursed her lips and glanced at Hank, who appeared deep in thought. "Hank, are you thinking what I'm thinking?"

"Maybe," he hedged.

"Is it possible that in the confusion and mess on the day of the bombing, Karl and Mom simply traveled to the other house in that community?" Em asked.

Hank nodded. "It is possible. I told my team to focus on the shooters and not the car."

"How in the world did the FBI miss finding all this out? Shit, a detective worth half their salt would have connected those dots," Em grumbled.

"Oh, they didn't miss it at all. Your buddy, Teddy, tried to scrub it from the system. It almost worked, too. He replaced the documents with different ones, sending everyone, including us, on a wild goose chase. You see, it was for selfish reasons I was so eager to help. Once I was able to dig into his computer, I found a plethora of helpful information. I made a copy of his hard drive. There was far too much to analyze in the short time at his desk. I plan on taking the drive to my lab, and I'll do some more digging."

Em smacked her hands on her thighs. "Okay, I say we don't go off half-cocked to this other house. We have the advantage of surprise now. They have no idea we are homing in on their accomplices in the FBI, police, and Border Patrol. Let's see what additional gems we can find in the next couple of days after tagging those fuckers. Plus, it'll give my leg time to heal before we go in guns a-blazing."

Jimena narrowed her eyes. "You can't be serious. I would think the FBI has you on light duty, and I'm pretty sure that does not mean you get to join the SWAT team."

Hank laughed. "She's right about that. Carter gave me explicit orders to keep you out of this now. I wasn't even supposed to bring you up to date on any further intel. He thinks you're compromised by a direct tie to the suspects. That might not play well to a jury. Of course, I ignored him. But are you sure you want to take the chance to piss him off enough to fire your ass?"

"I'm not leaving his arrest up to anyone else. I want to look into Karl's cold gray eyes while I read him his rights and cuff the bastard a little too tightly for comfort."

"Okay." Hank nodded. "I just thought I should give you all the facts, including the ones in your now precarious position with the department. Carter made it pretty clear he wants you far away from this case now."

Toni reached into her back pocket and plucked out two cards. "I don't give this card to anyone, but if you ever find yourself in the position to consider other employment, call me. We could definitely use your spunk." Then, turning her attention to Jimena, she said, "You, too. I hear you were the one to suggest faking your death. That's the kind of move we might execute. Deception is kind of our thing." She winked.

Hank held up his hands, brandishing them theatrically in the air. "What? No men allowed? How come you never made an employment offer to me? I'm wounded."

Toni waved him off. "You don't want to leave the FBI. You love it there."

"Okay, you're right. I do." Hank looked lovingly at Steve. "Plus, Steve would kill me if I left."

Steve smiled. "Yeah, I would."

Toni grabbed her chest. "God, Steve, you're hiding like a mouse in the corner. You scared the crap out of me. I almost forgot you were in the room."

"Yeah, I'm like that. Sometimes it works to my advantage. I'll probably be the better choice to get your nanobots where we want them."

"He isn't wrong," Hank answered.

Toni stood. "Okay, then. I'll be in touch soon after preparing the nanobots for ingestion or injection. Your choice. Give me twenty-four hours. Okay?"

Hank walked Toni to the door, hugging her again.

CHAPTER NINETEEN

The next morning, Em struggled to wake from a nightmare where her brother had captured Jimena, threatening to shoot her in the same three spots they'd planned during the fake death setup. She must have called out in her sleep because she felt a gentle shake on her arm.

"Em, wake up. You're having a nightmare." The sweet voice finally made it through her subconscious, and Em pried her eyes open.

Scrubbing her hand over her face, Em pushed out the first thought that came to mind. "Shit. It was so real. God, I hope Toni has information for us today."

"I had another thought, one you'll probably dismiss as the stupidest thing you've ever heard, but..." Jimena's face flushed to a dark red against her beautiful complexion.

"I'd never think any idea you have is stupid. The fake death almost worked. If Karl had not had so many moles, it would have." Em turned to face Jimena, cupping her chin and moving in for a chaste morning kiss.

"We've been playing a lot of defense lately. I feel like every encounter is a trap. What if we set our own trap?"

"How?" Em asked.

"Karl doesn't know we have a technical expert working for us. This means he doesn't know we compromised his primary assets. So far, Teddy has not been privy to the location of the safe houses, right? Because if he were, I'm convinced we would not be safe."

"True. That information is highly classified. It takes special clearance," Em answered.

"I'd bet my house Teddy has tried to break into whatever system holds that classified information." Jimena resettled her position on the bed by stuffing a pillow behind her back and sitting.

Em used her arms to push her body against the headboard and smiled at Jimena. "I would never take that bet. You're undoubtedly spot on about that. Honestly, I'm surprised he hasn't cracked it yet. Teddy might be a first-class douche, but he's very talented. He also fooled most of us, giving critical information at just the right time to make it seem like he's doing a stellar job."

"Karl seems like the kind of guy who wants to personally see you die." Jimena pushed away a lock of hair that had fallen across her brow. "He's probably having kittens right now, learning that we both survived. If he somehow receives intel on our location, he won't be able to resist an attack. I've been thinking a lot about why that guy didn't go to your room first. The only reason that makes any sense is that Karl wants to deal with you personally. The psychopath can't resist looking you in the eye before killing you. He wanted you to know it was all him behind this."

Em grinned. "I thought you didn't want me anywhere near the SWAT team."

"I don't, but we'll be the ones setting the trap this time. If everything goes as expected, Karl won't even make it inside before a team takes him down."

Em held her thumbs up. "I like this cocky side of you."

†

The *click, click, click* sound of Em's crutches made Jimena anxious. Not only was the sound irritating, but Jimena was confident that pacing on the wood floor was not helping to heal Em's leg.

"Em, hon, Toni will get here when she gets here." Jimena patted the seat next to her. "Come and sit. Steve made this lovely lunch that you barely touched."

Hank had just taken a large bite and mumbled around his food. "Yeah, it's delicious."

Three rapid knocks on the door had all four turning their heads toward the sound. Steve placed his finger on his mouth, pulled his gun from the holster, and with the stealth of a large cat, crossed the room and looked through the peephole. Jimena exhaled when he reholstered his weapon and opened the door.

Toni bounced into the room with a massive smile on her face. "Hey, gang. What a treasure trove of information. And this is before we tap their phones."

Hank set his plate on the coffee table and turned toward Toni, pointing at his food. "Lunch?"

"No thanks. I already ate. But it looks scrumptious."

"That's all Steve." Hank made a grand gesture toward Steve, who simply followed Toni into the living area, taking a seat off to the right, almost in the corner of the room.

Em had thankfully stopped her pacing and taken a seat next to Jimena. "Well, don't keep us in suspense."

"They've been playing a sophisticated shell game, but that did not stop me from removing every single layer. Besides a few warehouses and the two houses in that gated community in La Jolla, the Russian-based corporation also owns two other homes in the San Diego area." Toni laid a sheaf of papers on the table. "I also found a list of numbers that I suspect are burner phones. You aren't going to like how long the list is." Toni waved her hand in the air. "I bypassed going to the cell phone carriers to track down the owners of these phones. Instead, I've got my own method of finding these assholes." Pointing at the papers on the table, Toni said, "There's a lot of numbers there, but the important thing is that it should be relatively easy to track the phones to individuals in the police, Border Patrol, and FBI."

"That's incredible, Toni. Are you sure you don't want a job with the FBI?" Em asked.

Toni chuckled and shook her head. "Nope. I'm exactly where I want to be. Besides, the FBI disapproves of my methods. Every time I hack their system, they have a hissy fit and try to find my location. Not cool." Toni cringed. "Um, there is one more thing. Em, you're on that list. I presume that is because you were undercover. We're not going to learn you're some double agent, are we?"

"Are you serious?" Em glared at Toni.

Toni laughed. "Nah, I'm only screwing with you. I figured you wouldn't be so gung ho about my nanotech if you didn't want to catch these guys. Besides, we've been tracking your career, and that kind of duplicity does not fit."

"I don't think I like hearing that your shadowy organization has been tracking me. I'd like you to stay out of my personal business if you don't mind," Em sniped.

Toni shrugged. "I get it. I was once the recipient of extra scrutiny, and I didn't like it any more than you. But I eventually understood that some things are greater than my personal comfort or discomfort over unwanted attention."

Em didn't want to let this go, but Jimena grabbed her hand and squeezed. "All right, I'm going to table this discussion for now to float an idea Jimena had. After learning about all the different properties Karl could hole up in, this might be a better angle to pursue." Em turned to Jimena. "Go ahead and tell them."

†

Jimena had barely noticed when Steve left the safe house. She appreciated Hank trying to keep her and Em occupied and not thinking about when the attack from Karl would materialize. They'd decided to put in place the tracking and monitoring bots to give them an extra edge before Toni would hack into the FBI system again and write the code that would leave bread crumbs to the location of the safe houses. It would be sufficiently challenging to have Teddy believe he was a genius rather than sniffing out a potential trap.

"Ha." Hank slapped down his cards. "Three aces, suckers, pay up."

Em smirked and fanned out her cards. "Gee, Jimena, I don't know. Does a full house beat his three aces?"

"You cheated," Hank accused.

"Did not. Can I help it if I'm lucky?" Em touched her Saint Christopher medal.

"I never should have given you that necklace back. You have an unfair advantage." Pointing at Em's chest, he asked Jimena, "Where can I get one of those?"

Steve burst through the door and interrupted the teasing. He was uncharacteristically animated.

"Well, that was fun," Steve said. "I think I like this spy stuff. Maybe I should apply to the CIA. Can we call Toni now? I want to make sure the trackers are working."

Hank went to his bag and unzipped the small front pocket, pulling the card from within. Then he retrieved his phone from the pocket specially designed for cell phones. He held the card in the air. "See, I keep Toni's card in my zippered pocket. Then I never have to worry about inadvertently washing it with my pants. Can you say the same thing? I'll bet you've washed a few items you didn't want to over the years," Hank accused. "Plus, this satchel has a special pocket for cell phones."

"Just call, Mr. Metrosexual," Em ordered.

Hank punched in the number and, after listening for a few seconds, answered, "Okay. That's great. See you soon."

"She's on her way over with several tablets for us to use. Good job, Steve. She said it worked. She already has both audio and visual on Teddy and Keith," Hank answered.

"What about the potential leaks in the local police?" Em asked.

"She has an update for us on that as well." Hank set his phone on the table.

Steve punched his fist in the air. "Yes!"

Jimena was excited for this to end. A satisfying end, she hoped. Neither she nor Em could risk another injury while they were still on the mend. But that didn't mean, like Em, she didn't want to be a part of taking down these sociopaths. Or was that a psychopath? She didn't actually know the difference between the two. She probably should have paid more attention in her psych class.

"Another hand of poker while we wait?" Jimena asked. "I need a chance to win back some of my money you card sharks took from me. Steve, you want in on this?"

"Nope, I'll hang out in this ridiculously comfortable recliner and read my book until Toni arrives."

"Getting to the steamy part, huh?" Hank joked.

Steve blushed but didn't respond to Hank's teasing.

"Deal the cards and leave Steve alone," Em ordered.

"Fine, but you're going down."

"Not on you, my friend, not on you." Em laughed.

"Ew, don't put that nasty visual in my head," Hank retorted.

†

Em snickered as she gathered all the chips. She wasn't worried when the knock on the door interrupted her gloating. She assumed it was Toni, and when she strolled in carrying a large sling pack, Em wondered if she should consider purchasing a small backpack. It seemed to be all the rage.

Toni set the pack on the table and pulled three tablets from inside. "I only brought three, so Hank and Steve, you'll need to share one, and Em and Jimena, you can share the other."

"Works for me," Em said.

"Us, too," Hank added.

"I developed a simple app you can use to make it easier for nontechnical people," Toni explained. "Let me show you.

Oops, before I forget, you'll need to set up Face ID first. Don't worry, you can set up two IDs."

"Why can't the FBI give us fun gadgets like this?" Em asked.

"They offered you a tablet last year. I have one," Hank answered.

Steve lifted his tablet in the air. "So do I."

"If you had a nice bag like mine, you'd be able to carry yours. Don't you remember telling Carter that a smartphone was easier to carry, so you'd pass on the tablet?"

"Oh yeah, I vaguely remember telling him that." Em ran her hand through her hair.

"Oh, these aren't just any old tablet. I've made a few modifications to all of them. The original tablets didn't have enough power for my liking. I'm not saying the latest version is shit, but mine is better. I simply enhanced the picture, speed, and audio." Toni grinned as she handed Em one tablet, Hank a second one, and then placed the third in her lap.

Jimena scooted a few inches closer to Em, looking over her shoulder as she powered up the device. "Do you know how to set up Face ID?" Jimena asked.

"If it's the same as a smartphone, yes," Em answered.

After navigating to the settings, Em found the Face ID and passcode link and began the process. Once completed, she handed the tablet to Jimena for her to set up her Face ID. All four finished setting up their security link, and then Toni directed them to a small eyeball icon.

"The app is super easy. The menu bar at the top allows you to toggle between subjects. Target one is Teddy. Target two is Keith. It's a long shot, but I set up a third target that may be Karl or one of his associates."

"How are you possibly going to get a nanobot into Karl?"

"As I said before, it's a long shot, but I have an injectable that someone can transfer to a third target via this." Toni held up a small device that almost looked like a pen.

Em was more than a little skeptical as she looked at the compact device. "How in the world will that help us? By the time he's close enough to inject, he'll be practically on top of us. And if we aren't prepared for whatever sneak attack he tries, we haven't done our jobs very well, have we?"

"Since we plan on giving him the location of all four safe houses in the area, we have a seventy-five percent chance of injecting him before he arrives here. Hopefully, he won't guess the one you're staying in right off the bat. How about if you leave my team to handle the coverage on the other three locations?" Toni asked. "They know how to use this device, which, for the record, has a range of five hundred feet now." Toni puffed out her chest. "I've made the tips so that the target barely feels it when they land. It might feel like a mosquito bite, and the person would have difficulty finding it in the dark."

Jimena nodded. "Clever."

"Okay, this looks easy." Em pressed the Target One box at the top and gasped as she saw a computer screen and heard Teddy tapping on the keyboard.

"Wow! That is super cool," Jimena exclaimed.

As if a cameraman panned to the right, the view changed to the doorway leading into Teddy's office, then returned to the computer screen. Em heard Carter's voice as he entered the room. Several windows were quickly closed, and now Em could see Carter walking closer.

"Were you able to track down the money trail? I want to know who owns the house next to the governor's mother's home? I needed that information, like yesterday," Carter boomed.

"I'm working on it, sir. Is Em okay?" Teddy asked.

"She's fine. They're both at one of the safe houses."

"Oh, that's good. Considering all the added security around the location of our safe houses, they should be secure," Teddy answered. "Although, I should make sure this terror cell can't hack into our system and find that information. It's also my job to make everything failsafe."

"Just follow that money trail. We've already taken all the necessary precautions. Right now, my computer is the only system with that highly classified information. It's more solid than the White House. Call me as soon as you have that intel. I want to know what rathole that bastard is hiding in."

"There are a lot of shell organizations to track down. Unfortunately, it isn't easy to find, sir."

"Just get me that information. I don't care how many systems you need to crack to get it for me." The heavy thud of Carter's feet echoed through the tablet, along with a mumbled *asshole* from Teddy, too low for anyone but the team to overhear.

Toni laughed. "Are you sure your boss isn't involved with this new plan? That should help speed things up because I didn't want to make things too obvious or easy to find. I couldn't have played that better myself. Watch, I'd bet my entire lab that Teddy digs into Carter's computer now. After locating the code I left, he will miraculously find a way into Carter's secure drive."

Em cringed. She knew she would need to deal with Carter after they captured Karl. In addition, they'd have to find new safe houses after all of this was over, which would be time-consuming and expensive. Em decided to change the focus. "Hank says you have more information on the local police and who might have fed Karl that intel."

"Oh yeah, I forgot. The good news is that there aren't any more burner phones linked to Border Patrol or the FBI. There were three phones attached to individuals in the local police department. They're all older officers."

"Let me guess. Frank Allen, Brendon Fuller, and John Goodman," Em interjected.

Toni wrinkled her nose. "Yeah, how did you know?"

"All three are old pals of my father. It didn't take too much deductive reasoning to figure that out, but I'm glad you could confirm my suspicions," Em answered. "I should phone Carter to get him started on surveillance. After catching Karl, I'd rather not have them still working for the police department. It would be nice to perform a clean sweep."

"Then you better also tell him about the other surprises I found. That long list also includes a few politicians. I know you have to be overly cautious with those names. You'll need to catch them red-handed and have all your ducks in a row before charging them with domestic terrorism. This is going to get ugly. I doubt you want to have my team resolve this because you might not like how we choose to sweep things up." Toni shrugged.

"Nope. I probably won't if you suggest we take them out Godfather style," Em answered. "I still believe in our justice system."

"Too bad, but this is your call. We're only offering assistance."

"It's not that we don't appreciate your help, Toni, but we don't want to become monsters like them, justifying our actions based on our personal perspective about justice," Hank answered. "Cold-blooded vigilante murder makes us no better than them."

"I get it. Normally, I'd be right there with you, but I've seen so much that sometimes it's awfully tempting to take the bad guys out and save the taxpayers a boatload of money. However, I suppose that even the organization I work for has standards, and a few crooked politicians don't necessarily match the moral code we've put in place, either." Toni grinned. "We're always having that debate, and not all of us agree."

†

Jimena was confident that nothing would happen during the day. Watching the surveillance screen hour after hour was getting boring until Teddy finally cracked the code to the location of the safe houses. Finally, the plan was moving along, although they did not have any indication which safe house Karl would check out first. There were so many channels to monitor that it would be easy to miss something. They had visual and audio on Teddy and Keith, but only audio on the burner phones. So far, they had not learned of any specific plans, which worried Jimena. By sheer dumb luck, the house next to where they were staying was a rental, and the FBI quickly made arrangements to position several agents in the home as both backup and additional surveillance.

Playing poker and ribbing one another had also lost its luster as the anxiety and impending attack weighed on everyone's mind. Toni had offered to send a crew to put in place an invisible fence system that would alert the inhabitants inside the house anytime something more significant than a midsized dog entered the property. But Em felt confident Karl would choose to make his move in the middle of the night while they were presumably sleeping. She thought for sure he would hit the safe house immediately, which would not give them enough time to set up the notification system, particularly if he chose the specific location they inhabited.

The four of them took turns monitoring Teddy and Keith, leaving chatter on the burner phones to Toni, who promised to call if she learned anything important. Jimena and Em were taking a nap, needing to be fully awake at night, when Jimena heard a light knock on their door. Hank poked his head inside.

"Hey, sorry to bother you guys, but I thought you should know that Karl is putting pressure on Teddy to narrow down the safe house choices. Apparently, he doesn't like the idea of playing Russian roulette. I almost detect a little bit of nervousness, like he is concerned this might be a trap."

Em sat up and rubbed her eyes. "Karl is a lot of things, but stupid is not one of them. Damn. He probably wonders why Teddy could suddenly get the location of all the safe houses. He, like me, doesn't believe in coincidences."

"Should we get Toni to hide the intel he's looking for inside the computer for Teddy to find?" Hank asked.

Em shook her head. "No, if he's already nervous, that might be the tipping point. We could always go to Plan B and send teams to all the properties owned by that shell company that Toni uncovered. That would still be a surprise that he isn't expecting, especially since we haven't descended on them yet. He might have a false sense of security right now."

"I think we should give this a few more days. Let's see how it plays out and what additional communications we can intercept from the phone taps," Jimena offered.

"I agree," Hank added. "It will also give both of you extra healing time. Nothing wrong with that. I was worried about your limited mobility. Plus, hiding in a closet all night can't be a lot of fun with your bum leg."

"It's not, but at least it's cozy and intimate with Jimena," Em joked. "Although, I never thought I would agree to go back into any closet. I thought those days were over."

"All right. I'll let Toni know we're fine with waiting," Hank answered. "Perhaps we can take her up on her offer to install an early warning system. Can't hurt, right?"

Em nodded. "No, it sure can't."

CHAPTER TWENTY

Em prided herself on remaining Zen in almost every situation. However, the waiting game was getting to her, and she snapped at Jimena. Sweet, loving Jimena, who was only trying to help. Unfortunately, Jimena's offer to clean her wound and put on a new bandage only brought her feelings of inadequacy to the surface. Em was convinced the only reason Jimena had come up with this hare-brained plan was that there was no way Carter would allow Em to join any raid on the target properties.

Em wasn't the only one on edge. Jimena was uncharacteristically quiet, while Hank became more obnoxious. The only person who seemed to take everything in stride was Steve. He remained calm and introspective, preferring to sit and read most of the time.

Ten days had passed with little to no additional information. As it turned out, that was plenty of time to install the early warning system. Although relying on Toni's tech did not change Em's preference to remain tucked away in the closet while two mannequins occupied the bed.

Em was about to take a big chance by venturing outside. Cabin fever was getting to her. If only she could go for a run, but although she had lost the crutches days ago, her leg still screamed at her when she did too much. Em headed for the sliding glass door in the back of the house.

Hank looked up from the tablet. "Where do you think you're going?"

"I have to get some fresh air. Right now, I'm wound too tight. I'm liable to shoot you in agitation if you don't let me have five minutes," Em snapped.

Hank shook his head. "Your funeral. I know not to stop you when you get like this."

Jimena approached slowly and touched her arm. "Babe, I honestly wish you wouldn't. The waiting hasn't been a picnic for any of us, but taking unnecessary chances endangers all of us."

Em sighed and slammed her fist against the wall. "What the hell is Karl waiting for? Why isn't he making a move?"

Hank's phone rang and broke the tension temporarily.

"Hello." Hank paused. "Oh, hey, Toni, can I put you on speaker?" Punching a button, Hank held out his phone as Jimena and Em gathered close to hear what Toni had to say.

"So, I have some good and bad news," Toni said.

"Go on," Em prompted.

"Karl and several men entered two of the safe houses last night. Of course, they were both empty, but they were in and out so quickly that neither team could hit Karl with a dart to inject him. We still don't have ears or eyes on Karl."

"If your bad news is that you couldn't put nanobots in Karl, that's okay. At least he's making a move, and we can expect him to hit this house tonight. We'll be ready," Em said with confidence. "Did you pick up any intel on why he only chose to check out two of the four houses? It seems odd that if Karl and his cronies were in and out of the other two houses, they would surely have had time to check the others."

What is he up to?

"Something smells off about this whole thing. First, Karl waits ten days to make his move, then he only makes his way to two of the four houses. It's like he's purposely toying with us," Jimena said.

"I haven't given you the other piece of good news," Toni interrupted.

"Sorry, continue, please," Jimena said.

"While we weren't able to inject him with nanobots, we placed a tracking device on his vehicle. We know exactly where he is. Which, coincidentally, lines up perfectly with the call we intercepted from that older woman. After cleaning up the recording, we could decipher the address that she provided. Your initial instincts were correct. Karl hasn't even left that gated community. They simply moved to the other property in La Jolla."

"I don't believe in coincidences, but I also trust that coincidences sometimes are the precursor to insidious traps," Em noted. "Something tells me Karl is expecting us to descend on his new place in La Jolla, and we haven't been cooperating like he expected. Are you sure that recorded call you salvaged wasn't a plant, like the code you left for Teddy to find?"

"It's possible. Teddy has much better skills than I initially gave him credit for," Toni answered.

"What do you propose we do?" Hank asked.

"I say we wait him out," Em declared. "Karl never was very good at chicken. He always swerved first. Plus, his ego will drive him because he thinks he has the upper hand. Let him believe that. Patience was never something he had an abundance of. No doubt he's stewing right now, wondering why we haven't swarmed his new mansion. Ego and irritation will drive him to come to us."

"I know another person's ego that might muck things up," Hank interjected.

"Who?" Jimena asked.

"Carter. He's growing impatient. He's got another tech guy working on unraveling the money trail. The guy's close. If they learn about the other house in La Jolla, he's likely to send in a team." Hank shrugged. "You didn't think he would just sit on his hands, did you?"

"I guess we will have to see how it all plays out and hope everything lands in our favor. Is Carter pulling you in for this impending mission?" Em asked.

Hank nodded. "Yeah, and all the agents in the rental property next door, plus Steve. He thinks the safe house is secure enough that you don't need those additional agents, Steve or me, as your personal bodyguards."

"Well, he isn't wrong about that. Jimena and I can take care of ourselves. Although it has been nice fleecing you out of your spending money in poker." Em grinned. "By the way, when were you going to tell me that?"

"Well, not this morning when you were all pissy and wanting to get some fresh air," Hank answered. "Steve and I are supposed to drop by the office today to get an update."

"Okay, well, I'm out. I'll let you guys work out your shit on your own," Toni interrupted.

"Thanks, Toni." Hank pushed the button to end the call.

"We're ready, right?" Em turned to Jimena.

"We are. And honestly, if your team beats us to the punch, I'm okay with that. I know Em wanted to be the one to arrest her brother. I'll admit, I wanted to be there, too, but whatever gets the job done. Em?"

Em sighed. "I guess I'll have to be fine with this. The ultimate goal is to make sure Karl rots in jail. I suppose with Steve and Hank leaving the other bedroom empty, we could use that to our advantage. Another twist that Karl won't anticipate." Em grinned.

†

Two more days passed, and Jimena noticed how increasingly agitated Em became with each passing day. Hank finally had called late in the evening to let Em and Jimena know that Carter was sending teams to all properties that Teddy, not his other tech guru, had provided to Carter. Em had told him to watch his back because she suspected they had provided the information for a very specific reason. He agreed, understanding they were all probably walking into a shit show.

Later that evening, Jimena and Em went through their nightly ritual by setting the scene in their bedroom. With all the blinds drawn in the pitch-black dark, the bed appeared to have two people spooning one another underneath the fluffy cream comforter. Grabbing the extra pillows from the other bedroom, they settled into the cramped closet, waiting for Karl and his men to descend on the house.

Slipping in the earbuds that Toni had provided linking the notification system she'd installed, Em settled against the closet wall, one pillow under her still-healing leg and the other behind her head. Jimena curled her body against Em's shoulder as Em wrapped her arm around her girlfriend. *Girlfriend.* That thought brought a big smile to her face. Yeah, she thought she could legitimately call Jimena her girlfriend. Despite the drama of the past few weeks, Jimena and Em had managed to reconnect. They were as strong as when they declared their love as teenagers. Maybe stronger.

"What are you smiling about?" Jimena whispered.

"I just thought that we're together, right? I mean, I know that calling you my girlfriend seems a bit juvenile, but we missed a lot of the wonders of young love, so it sort of feels good thinking that."

"Girlfriend, partner, lover, whatever you want to call me. Except sugar lips or some other ridiculous pet name might not work, but yes, we are together. You're stuck with me now."

"Good." Em leaned in to kiss Jimena. "I promise that we're taking a long-overdue vacation once this is all over. Anywhere you want to go, I'll take you."

Jimena captured Em's lips again, turning the kiss into something less chaste. But, before the kiss turned into something more, Em felt Jimena pull away. "I look forward to that. Since we have sun all the time, maybe we could go somewhere with snow?"

"You got it." Em bopped Jimena lightly on the nose with her index finger. "I love you."

"Right back at you."

The two women settled into each other's embrace and waited. Em could feel it in her gut that tonight would be the night. Either Hank and Steve's team would prevail, or they would. Em was finally okay with either option.

CHAPTER TWENTY-ONE

Karl Junior could trace back the exact day when his hatred for his sister had solidified, changing his whole life's trajectory. It all led to this moment. He would finally get his revenge. Fucking bitch had squirmed out of his grasp, along with her childhood lover, but that all ended tonight. Ever since Em had caused the wheels of abuse to intensify with her perverted ways, Karl Junior's life had also dramatically changed. Then she disappeared nearly fifteen years ago, and Karl Junior had become his father's whipping boy. Em was no longer there to take the brunt of their father's wrath.

Karl had gotten up before dawn because he was thirsty and heard the squeak coming from his sister's bedroom. He

*knew she was up to something, so he peeked his head into
her room. He was just in time to see her running away from
the window she'd crawled through. She'd stuffed her bed
with extra blankets and pillows to make it look like she was
still sleeping. He hurried out the back door to follow her.
Catching his sister doing something wrong and then telling
their father would earn Karl praise. Something he always
sought from his father. Running home, he'd spilled
everything he knew about his sister's clandestine affair. But
the result was not at all what he had expected.*

The next fifteen years had been almost unbearable with
his father. He'd played the dutiful son and wheedled his way
into his father's group of friends. His cold, calculated style
had gained him the credibility he'd needed to take over
leadership of the group after his father's untimely demise.
The stupid sheep who followed him hadn't even clued into
the fact that Karl Junior arranged the explosion that had
killed his father.

While the FBI was chasing their tails, trying to raid all
the properties owned by their benefactor, Karl was
personally leading the team to take out his sister and her
lover. The tiny sliver of the moon barely provided any light
as Smitty, Karl, and the other three men crept into the
backyard. Using the tool Smitty had brought to cut a small
hole in the window, Karl reached in and undid the lock. He
wasn't worried about Em or Jimena hearing a squeak as the
window lifted. His only regret was that he wouldn't see the
light in her eyes go out when he emptied his gun into the

closet. Em was always predictable. He counted on that. In his excitement, Karl failed to register that only Smitty had followed him into the house. The other three men were not beside him as he checked the first room, found it empty, then went to the next bedroom. When Karl noticed the two lumps in the bed, he immediately aimed his AK-47 at the closet door, peppering it with thirty rounds until Karl had exhausted the magazine, leaving the door resembling a large piece of Swiss cheese. With absolute glee, he flung open the closet door.

†

Before Em heard the beep indicating something significant had breached the perimeter, Hank had used the comms to let Jimena and Em know that every one of their teams had come up empty. Em could hear the stress in his voice. Hank was upset. He believed that going after Karl rather than letting Karl come to them with an entire team left Jimena and Em utterly vulnerable to attack. Feeling guilty, he told them he was bringing his team, and they'd be on their way. She should hang tight.

Em knew in her heart that this would all be over by the time Hank arrived with the backup team. One way or another.

After the beep, Jimena had nodded, and Em carefully pried the closet door open a couple of inches. Not seeing anyone in the room, they were about to push open the door and become the predators stalking their unsuspecting prey

248

when the explosion of gunfire startled them. After the noise abated, Em placed her finger over her mouth and gestured for Jimena to follow her.

Spotting Smitty, who stood with his mouth open outside of the other bedroom, Em quickly disabled him and shoved his gun into the back of her pants. Jimena dragged him to the side and placed a gun against his temple.

It sounded like a wounded animal to Em as she listened to her brother scream, almost as if he were in agony before letting loose a string of curse words. The litany of things he vowed to do when he caught "that fucking bitch" were the ravings of a pure lunatic.

Karl slammed another magazine into his AK-47 and turned to find the object of his loud rant. Em pointed a gun at his head. Although it was still dark inside the house, Em had adjusted to the low light and saw the ominous sneer on Karl's face.

"Don't do it, Brother. I'll drop you quicker than you can lift that penis weapon. I assure you, I never miss," Em said through gritted teeth. Em maintained her awareness of anyone else bursting onto the scene because she suspected Karl had more men than this. She had to trust that Jimena would literally watch her back. Her focus had to be on Karl because, with one quick movement, he'd repeat what he'd done earlier. Only this time, she'd become the Swiss cheese versus the closet door.

The movement was almost infinitesimal, but it was enough. Em did not hesitate as she fired, hitting Karl square in the forehead as the assault weapon only grazed one arm.

Several rounds fired wildly into the room as Karl crumbled to the ground. Em didn't have to check Karl's pulse to determine if he was alive or dead. His dead eyes and the neat hole in the center of his forehead told the entire story. Em didn't love her brother. Hell, she didn't even like him, but that did not stop her from leaning over his body and closing his eyes.

Em pressed the comm button to notify Hank and his team after seeing that Jimena had secured Smitty with the zip ties she had in the pocket of her sweats. Her body swiveled when she sensed that someone else had entered the house. Raising her gun, she met the steely gray eyes of a tall woman who held her hands in the air. Another woman followed closely behind, also putting her arms in the air.

"We're colleagues of Toni," the woman informed Em. "We've neutralized three men, and they're all outside, ready for you to transport them. We've swept the area. No one else is lurking about."

"Um, okay," Em answered. "Thank you," she added as an afterthought.

"We're going to go now," the other woman declared. "While I wouldn't mind seeing Hank again, I don't think the rest of the FBI will be pleased to know I was involved."

"You're Sophie?" Em asked.

The woman nodded once.

"Okay. We'll think up something. Hank and the team are on their way. Thanks again."

Almost as if they were ninjas, the two women disappeared into the inky black night before Em heard the sirens coming close. When Em went outside to meet Hank's team, she saw three men propped against the side of the house. All three appeared unconscious, secured, dressed, and ready to take into custody, just as the stoic woman had said.

†

Em was so quiet it was spooky. Jimena wondered if killing her brother weighed heavily on her. She knew this wasn't the first time Em had taken a life. Jimena wondered if being forced to shoot her own brother brought back memories of the war and Em's part in ending the life of enemy combatants who were so close she could see the whites of their eyes.

"You okay?" Jimena asked.

Em nodded and turned toward a black SUV that had arrived on the scene. Hank jumped out of the vehicle. He scanned the area before approaching Jimena and Em, who stood rigid on the front lawn.

"I guess you didn't need us after all," Hank noted wryly. He jerked his head toward the three men trussed up and ready to go. "Aw, that's so nice of you to think of presents for us. And they're wrapped so nicely."

Steve and one other man took their time climbing from the SUV and then made a beeline to the men propped against the house.

"I wouldn't exactly say that. If not for the help of two terrifying women that Toni sent, this could have ended very differently," Jimena whispered so that only Hank could hear. "You can thank Toni and her team for the gifts."

"Karl?" Hank asked.

"Dead," Em responded without emotion. "I'll let Carter know, and he can get the ball rolling for the shooting review incident team. He gave me no other option."

"I'm sure the thirty-plus spent rounds will be more than enough evidence to rule this a necessary use of deadly force," Jimena added defensively.

Hank held his hands in the air. "Hey, I am not questioning whether this was a clean shoot. The review team won't either."

"So, you didn't find my mother?" Em asked.

"No, sorry." Hank looked away, then returned his sympathetic gaze to Em. "She wasn't at any of the locations we raided tonight. Don't worry about calling Carter. I'll take care of that. Is there anyone else besides Karl inside?"

"Yeah, Smitty. Jimena took care of him. He's wrapped up nicely as well." Em handed Hank her gun. "Here's my weapon."

As Em handed her gun to Hank, Jimena noticed the blood on her upper arm. "Babe, you're hurt. Let me take a look?"

"Just a flesh wound. The stray bullet barely grazed my arm. I'll be fine," Em answered.

Jimena ignored Em and gently pushed up the sleeve to inspect the wound. "It doesn't look like a bullet lodged in your arm, but it isn't only a flesh wound. Let me get the first aid kit in the house, okay?"

"I said I'm fine," Em snapped.

Jimena and Hank shared a look, and Jimena took a step back, feeling the sting of Em's rebuke.

"God, I'm sorry, Jimena. It's no excuse, but I'm tired, and all I want to do is curl against your body and sleep for the next twenty-four hours. But I can't do that just yet." The strain in Em's voice worried Jimena. She looked at Hank, hoping he would rescue them from having to hang around for hours while they processed the scene. When Hank received the message loud and clear, Jimena sent a prayer to the heavens, thanking her God.

Hank touched Em's uninjured arm. "How about if we get your arm cleaned up a bit, then I'll take both of your statements? Steve and I can handle the rest. Do you have somewhere to go to get that rest you're jonesing for?"

"Yeah, my house," Jimena interjected. "I'll get the first aid kit. You wait here."

A nod was the only response Jimena received. Then, following Hank into the safe house, Jimena stepped around the bullet-ridden bedroom to get to the main bath, where she found the first aid kit. Jimena had a better one at home that she would pull out but, for now, she'd clean up the wound and redress it later. Em was still healing from her previous gunshot wound. If anyone needed a long rest, it was Em. Jimena had to admit that she was looking forward to curling next to Em and sleeping for a very long time. Neither one of them had gotten much sleep in the last week. They were long overdue.

CHAPTER TWENTY-TWO

The drive to Jimena's home was made in relative silence. Hank had asked Steve to take the women home after taking their statements. The silence gave Em time to think. It wasn't that she regretted killing her brother, but seeing him on the ground with those vacant eyes reminded her of her time in Afghanistan. She'd seen her fair share of dead bodies, but it never got any easier, especially when she knew she was directly responsible.

When they finally got inside, Em collapsed on Jimena's sofa. The fight had eventually left her body, and all she felt was extreme exhaustion. Em was sure she would see her brother's dead eyes in future nightmares. That was a given.

But, hopefully, she would stop having nightmares about her brother getting to Jimena.

Jimena had grabbed an afghan and lovingly placed it over Em's body while she searched for more gauze and antibiotic anointment. Em had to admit it felt nice having someone fawn over her. It had been years since anyone cared enough to minister to her wounds. She barely remembered when her mother had done that. When she was very young, she could recall that happening, but her father quickly stopped that as Em got older.

Em grabbed the remote and flipped to the news station. She wanted to know what the press was saying. Gaby was holding a press conference, and it sounded like she was dancing around some very pointed questions. One reporter had done her homework and already learned the dead body belonged to the brother of the FBI agent who had shot him. The pat answer that they could not release additional information during an active investigation did not stop the questions. Em pressed the remote and turned off the television. She couldn't watch anymore. Again, she'd placed Gaby in the hot seat.

They still had not found her mother, and something was niggling in the back of her head. Could her mother be more involved in all of this than she had initially suspected? Em dug into her cargo shorts and pulled the card Toni had handed her many days ago. She still didn't understand why she kept the card, but she had.

Punching in the number, Em heard Toni answer after the second ring. "Ready to join us?"

Em allowed the first genuine laugh to erupt from her mouth. "How in the world do you know who this is? And, no, not unless they kick my ass out of the FBI for the use of excessive force."

"I kind of hacked into the FBI database and learned this was your new cell phone number. What can we do for you, Em?"

"Well, first, I want to thank you for sending Sophie and that other supremely scary woman."

"Val, yeah, she's pretty intimidating but very efficient and deadly. You don't ever want to be on her bad side."

"Duly noted. Listen, we haven't found my mother yet. Something is not quite adding up for me. Any chance you can do some digging to see what you uncover?" Em asked.

"I can do that, but in return, I'd like for you to at least meet my wife. She can be very persuasive. Like scary persuasive, and she's been following your career. She is very interested in having you join our organization."

"Fine, I'll meet with her. Thanks for all your help. We could not have broken up the cell without you," Em answered.

"Great. Bring Jimena, too. We can meet for dinner. What kind of plans do you have over the next few days?" Toni asked.

"Sleep, sleep, and more sleep. Give us a few days, okay?"

"You got it. We're only in town for a few more days, though. Would day after tomorrow work?"

"Sure. Where do you want to meet?"

"You guys like sushi?" Toni asked. "We came across this great place the other day."

"Sushi?" Em glanced at Jimena, who crinkled her nose in displeasure. "Um, I'm getting the hell-no vibe from Jimena."

"How about if I cook for us?" Jimena interjected.

"Did I hear an offer of a home-cooked meal?" Toni asked.

"Yeah, you sure did. Jimena makes the best Mexican food you'll ever put your lips to."

"Sold," Toni answered.

"Have her come over around fiveish," Jimena said.

"Them," Em corrected.

Jimena arched her eyebrow. "Them? Is Toni nonbinary?"

"No, I don't think so. She hasn't said, but she has a wife," Em responded.

"Great, the more, the merrier," Jimena answered.

"Okay, Toni, do you need the address to Jimena's house?"

"Nope, GPS on your phone." Toni chuckled.

"You better not have put one of those nanobots in me. I'd rather not have you listening in on my private conversations or my intimate time with Jimena," Em teased.

"Don't worry. I would never do that. To you," Toni amended.

"I'll take you at your word. Let me know if you find anything out about my mother." Em ended the call and caressed Jimena's cheek. "Thank you. Now, how about that nice fluffy bed of yours? I'm ready to crash."

Jimena grabbed Em's hand and led her to the bedroom. "I am, too."

†

A day and a half later, Jimena laughed when she heard the almost musical knock on her door. She was in the middle of cutting her peppers, so Em rushed to answer the door. Continuing to prep the ingredients for her fajitas, Jimena listened while Toni introduced her wife. She wondered again who in the world this mysterious organization was after listening to the odd introduction.

The tall red-headed woman entered the kitchen with Toni and Em, smiling in greeting. The two women made a striking couple, and Jimena had difficulty not staring at them.

"So this is where the magic happens. I haven't had a proper Mexican meal in years. Thank you for cooking." The woman held out her hand. "I'm Char, Toni's wife, but you must call me Heather if we're ever in public together." She reached into her bag and pulled out a card.

Jimena accepted the card and glanced at the name, *Heather Stiles, Attorney at Law*. "Only the fajitas are a traditional dish. The salad is more Americanized. Nice to meet you. I'm Jimena."

"Yes, I know," Char answered.

"Um, I don't understand why I should address you as Heather? Do you work undercover, too?" Jimena asked.

"Something like that," Char answered. "Our organization is always on the hunt for new talent. We've had our eyes on Em for quite some time now, and forgive me, but only recently learned of your possible qualifications."

Jimena scowled. "Sounds like you've been spying on us. I'm not sure I like the sound of that."

Toni laughed. "Yeah, Sophie and I had the same reaction. We weren't very cooperative at first, either."

"I suppose I need to be a little more gracious. After all, you lent a hand at just the right moment. I'm not so sure we would have been able to handle all five men," Jimena admitted.

Char shrugged. "We only wanted to level the playing field. You may have been able to handle them independently, but why take the chance when we had the agents to spare? Unfortunately, we can't officially join forces with the FBI, but we're not opposed to providing assistance when the mission aligns with our own interests."

"And what interests are those?" Em asked.

"I'm glad you asked, Em," Char responded. "We've been in a long-term tussle with the Russians. Some might call it a war. Mostly, we've attacked their financial networks and broken up several human trafficking rings, but like cockroaches, they always re-emerge."

"But what we've been dealing with is domestic terrorism. I don't know a single thing about foreign affairs." Em leaned against the kitchen counter and popped a cherry tomato from the salad into her mouth.

"The two are not mutually exclusive," Char answered. "Recently, our focus has taken a different turn. The divisions in our country and the disinformation led to a cult-like admiration for a con man many have linked to the Russians. It's gone too far, and we don't have enough resources on our own to stop this runaway train. The terror cell you disbanded is only the tip of the iceberg. While we would certainly want you to join our team, Em, I understand how this might be a conflict for you."

Em wrinkled her nose. "Conflict? What are you talking about? I have zero conflict with stopping the misinformation and taking down domestic terror cells, no matter who is pulling the strings."

Char shared a look with Toni, who cringed. "You haven't told her yet?"

"I didn't get the chance," Toni answered.

"What the hell are you two talking about?" Em asked in irritation.

"Um, well, we also had a hunch about your mother. Once we pulled on that thread, everything started unraveling. Your mother is a Russian asset."

"What? You people are crazy. My mother is a weak woman who let her husband do whatever he wanted, including beat on his kids and wife when she 'stepped out of line.'" Em pushed away from the counter and glared at Toni.

"Where do you think you got your intelligence and undercover talents from? Your mother was pulling all the strings, including doing her best to involve you in their assignment. Unfortunately for your brother, he didn't want to listen to her advice and got antsy."

The furrow in Em's forehead deepened. "But her apology seemed so sincere. Why would she say that? It wasn't like anyone was around who needed to see her performance. We weren't expected to live."

"Perhaps a part of her was truly sorry. She is your biological mother. We confirmed that," Toni answered.

Em sat heavily on the stool. "Okay, wow! That was not at all what I was expecting."

Jimena didn't know what to think about this twist. The meek woman she'd known as Mrs. Schmidt was a Russian spy. Holy shit. Jimena stopped chopping the ingredients and approached Em, lightly stroking her arm. "Sorry."

"It's not like she was much of a mother to me. Maybe when I was a toddler, but the maternal instinct seemed to fall away the minute I started school. So there wouldn't be a conflict if I joined this mysterious organization," Em revealed.

"The one advantage we have over the FBI is that we aren't constrained to follow any specific regulations," Char stated. "This gives us a modicum of freedom to handle situations in the most efficient means necessary."

"I had enough killing in Afghanistan. So I think I'll pass."

"No, no, you've misunderstood me. Execution is the last resort. Although, I will admit a few of our agents try to suggest that more frequently than I am comfortable with," Char answered.

"I'm very flattered, and honestly, it is tempting, but I've found a place in the FBI that suits me." Em grabbed Jimena's hand. "Besides, I was going to propose that Jimena join the FBI since we made a great team with this assignment."

"While this isn't my preference, our organization is evolving. We no longer require our agents to live on the compound, and we've recently made the compound family-friendly. I believe we could create a different set-up for those who wish to remain employed by the government. You may find it helpful to have our organization lend support occasionally, much like we did for this assignment. What would you think about working for both the FBI and our covert organization? The only thing I ask is that you not share your connection to us or anything about the organization with anyone in the FBI."

"What about Hank?" Jimena asked.

Char smiled. "Hank is already on board. We recently asked, and he's agreed to work with us."

"Why that little sneak," Em said, but there was humor in her voice. "Steve?"

Toni grinned. "Him too. We've diversified. We don't have too many men in the organization, but Steve and Hank fit right in. So, what do you think?"

"I don't know about Em, but I'm intrigued," Jimena said.

When Em's work phone rang, she held up her finger. "Hang on, let me answer this first." Em pressed the button and answered, "Schmidt."

When Em answered her phone and heard the voice of the last person she thought would dial her work number, she frowned and then glanced at the group.

"Hello, Emma," her mother said.

Placing her finger on her mouth, Em pressed the button to put the call on speakerphone. "Mother. Calling to find out how I'm doing?"

"I'm going to say this only once. Stop looking for me. You have no idea what you've stumbled upon. I suppose I am glad you are alive, but if you wish to remain that way, you'll take your minor victory and move on. You may have won this round, but the war is far from over. I'd hate for you to be a casualty."

Toni twirled her finger in the air and pulled a tablet from the sling bag she'd set on the floor. Then, she mouthed, 'keep her talking.'

"Now, Mother, you know I can't do that. But, if you turn state's evidence, I think I can get them to cut you a deal."

Her mother's laughter sounded maniacal through the tiny speaker on the phone. "You don't even realize you hold none of the cards. You can tell Toni that whatever she thinks she can accomplish through her fancy gadgets, this phone is completely untraceable. I could talk with you for over an hour, and you'll never find my location. However, I'm bored now. Good luck, Emma. I always knew you would grow to be an intelligent, competent woman. You can thank me for that. If only you hadn't left at eighteen to join the Army. I was planning to bring you into the fold, but alas, that ship has passed. Goodbye, Emma."

"Got it!" Toni raised her fist in the air. "Good job, Em."

"But I thought she said her phone was untraceable," Em said.

"Did you send a team to the location?" Char asked.

Toni nodded. "Yup, sure did!"

"You did something to my phone, didn't you?"

Toni's face contorted in guilt. "Sorry, but we've been trying to get your mother for a long time. We didn't mean to keep you in the dark because we honestly wanted to recruit you, but we had to make sure you weren't some kind of double agent yourself."

"So you've been using me this whole time?" Em huffed.

"Not exactly, but we also weren't going to let a golden opportunity pass," Char answered. "Perhaps our methods haven't allowed us to put our best foot forward. Subterfuge is our modus operandi most days. It's hard to break old habits. Nevertheless, our offer is still sincere." Char swiveled to catch Jimena's eye. "For both of you."

Em smiled. "Well, I suppose an undercover agent would be the pot calling the kettle black if I complained too loudly about your methods. I don't suppose you'll let me in on my mother's location."

"We prefer to have our team handle it at this point. But if you join us, we can arrange for a transfer where you, Hank, and Steve get credit for her capture. Plus, we'll give you all the intel we've collected to ensure she stays locked up for a very long time." The corners of Char's lips turned up in a sly smile.

"Can I think about your offer? Maybe talk to Jimena, who seems sold already." Em glanced at her lover, who smiled back at her.

CHAPTER TWENTY-THREE

Em couldn't fault Toni for continuing to check her tablet throughout dinner. She wanted an update as badly as Toni felt the need to stay connected. On the other hand, Char seemed relaxed and at ease, only periodically glancing at her wife. She had a glow about her, and suddenly it dawned on Em why that might be. Char had politely refused any wine or margaritas at dinner.

"You're pregnant," Em blurted.

Em didn't think Char could transform into a more beautiful woman than she already was, but the smile that blossomed on her face only added to her radiance.

"I am. How did you know?" Char asked.

"Lucky guess. You turned down wine, but it seemed like you did that reluctantly. I pay attention to minor details, I guess," Em answered. Then, out of the corner of her eye, Em saw Toni press a few buttons on the tablet, then pop in a set of earbuds. "Something happening?"

Toni held up one finger and pressed her left earbud. Nodding, she began to speak. "Got it. Okay, I'll let Char know. Hang tight, and as soon as I get more information, I'll let you know. Soph knows how to work the app, so she can probably give you a location as well. As long as the dart landed on the target and not some random woman. Okay, okay, don't get your knickers in a twist."

"What's going on?" Jimena asked.

"That's what I'd like to know," Em added.

Toni pressed her left earbud again and explained, "Val says the place was crawling with security. It might have been a trap. Hard to know at this point. Our team didn't have any problems disabling the security team, but a man and a woman escaped through the tunnels. Val insists that Soph landed a dart into the woman she believes was your mother. If that's the case, we'll not only have a way to track her over the next twenty-four hours, but we'll see and hear everything in her line of vision and immediate vicinity." Toni began using her index finger to activate her app. "Target three should come online soon." Toni turned her tablet toward Em so she could see.

The small screen popped into view, showing the inside of a vehicle. Before Bridget started speaking, Em caught a clear view of a handsome man with a severe jawline and steel-gray eyes. She felt like she was looking at the male version of herself. Even his blond hair was the same shade as hers.

"I told you they would come," Em's mother said. "I'm disappointed Emma didn't join the team. We could have had a family reunion."

"Who's the man she's talking to?" Em whispered.

Toni chuckled. "They can't hear us, Em. You can talk normally. That guy is a high-ranking Russian oligarch. Ssh, this might be important."

"What now?" the man asked.

"I'll admit I've underestimated our daughter and her newfound friends' skills. The blasted organization is more slippery than ever, but I hoped we could rid ourselves of both problems. You said the security team was the best in the business. They couldn't even stop a small team of mostly women. We need higher-quality warriors."

"Are you still convinced we can turn her?"

"I am. Emma will fall in line once she understands everything, including how she fits into all this. We may have to exercise the new indoctrination techniques developed by our scientists, but so far, it's worked well given enough time."

Em's head reeled. Everything she knew about her childhood and family was a lie. Her father wasn't actually her father. Not that she cared that the bastard she knew growing up was not her biological father. But this man might be far worse. Could genetics make her an evil person like her mother and father?

Jimena reached over and grabbed her hand. "You are nothing like either of them. I know this is a shock, but our choices define us. Genetics only go so far."

Toni pushed the button on her right ear, and the sound on the tablet went mute.

"I want to join your organization, but I have one condition," Em stated

"Can we talk about this later? I'm getting pure platinum here, and I can't hear what they're saying if you continue to jabber," Toni huffed.

"No, we can't. I want your solemn promise that you'll let me join the team to track my parents and take them into custody."

"You have my word," Char answered with a massive smile. "I'll even go with."

"Oh, hell no, not with that baby growing," Toni barked.

"They are the size of a peanut right now. You know I can take care of myself," Char argued.

Toni placed her finger on her lips. "They have a hidden compound. The good news is that it isn't crawling with the same amount of security as their previous place. The bad news is the location seems to have booby traps like ours. Unfortunately, we won't have a better chance than this." Toni raised her eyes to Char.

"Right, then. Let's go," Char ordered.

"I'm coming with," Jimena declared.

"I assumed you would say that." Char grinned.

†

The four women crammed into the sleek sports car, and Jimena thanked the universe that she was small. Poor Em's long legs nearly reached her chest because she was so crowded in the back seat. Since Toni and Char were on the tall side, someone had already adjusted both front seats to ensure the front passengers had a comfortable ride, leaving the back seats uncomfortable for passengers.

"If I'd known we would ride in an expensive clown car, I would have suggested taking my beater," Em grumbled.

Toni turned her head to face Jimena and Em in the back. "I can move the seat up if you need me to," she offered.

"No, that's okay, then you'll just have your knees stuffed into your mouth," Em answered.

Toni chuckled, then turned around and addressed Char. "Take the next left and follow the road for maybe three miles."

They'd been driving for nearly two hours. It was always interesting to see how the terrain in California rapidly transmuted into exactly the opposite of the beautiful beaches and iconic palm trees. The landscape of the desert had a beauty all of its own, but not many preferred the bleakness of the desert over the abundance of vegetation bunched up against the ocean.

"Not much out here," Char noted.

"Yeah, it's perfect. Almost better than our old cabin in the woods. Not many places to hide a vehicle or approach without being seen. I'll bet even Val would have difficulty.

We need a plan because out here, they'll spot us a mile away," Toni groused.

"I guess we'll be on foot," Char answered. "How long until Sophie, Val, and Ronda arrive?"

Toni appeared to scrutinize her tablet. "Shit, we lost audio and video, but it looks like they have a similar setup to ours. They must love tunnels or underground compounds. Smart. However, wherever they've gone, the signal is blocked, but they're close." Lifting her head, she looked around the desert and pointed to the west. "There. Approaching to the right. Better pull over. We shouldn't chance coming too close to the coordinates if they have cameras."

A nondescript car with tinted windows pulled up next to Char and Toni's sports car. The window slowly whirred down, and the serious woman addressed Char. "Not much cover out there." She pointed to the vast desert. "Wait until complete darkness and approach on foot?"

Char nodded.

The back window went down, and a new woman smirked at Char. "Fuck, Char, could you have picked a more obvious vehicle?"

"We weren't expecting to go on a mission tonight. Thanks for coming, Ronda. Toni heard the place might have explosives protecting the boundaries. Between you and Em, we should be able to disarm them," Char responded.

"Why don't you sit this one out? We can handle it," Ronda suggested.

"Oh, for shit's sake. Not you, too. I'm not even three months pregnant yet. I think I can handle a short hike in the desert," Char huffed.

"Toni already suggested that, huh?" Ronda grinned.

"You're damn right I did, and I got the same snippy response." Toni glared.

Ronda emerged from the back seat, stretched, took a short walk, and squatted on the dirt road that forked to the right. "Tire tracks heading east." She pulled binoculars from her backpack and lifted them toward the tracks. "There are a few large rocks, a lot of scrub brush, and a few larger cacti that will work to mask our approach."

Jimena tentatively asked Ronda, "Do you mind if I take a look?"

Ronda handed Jimena her binoculars and said, "Knock yourself out, Jimena."

Jimena coughed. "You know my name?"

"Whoops. Sorry, Char, I thought you were going to talk them into joining. Have you not had that discussion yet?"

Char shook her head. "I did, but we're trying not to scare them away. I'm sure it feels uncomfortable learning that we know a hell of a lot more about them than they do about us."

Ronda stuck out her hand for Jimena. "Ronda, munitions expert."

Jimena shook the offered hand.

Ronda turned her focus on Em. "I hear you're as good as me with explosives. It's nice to finally meet you, Em."

Em nodded. "Not my favorite part of my time in Afghanistan, but I know my stuff."

Char pointed at the other two women. "You haven't officially met Val and Sophie. Jimena and Em have graciously agreed to join us, but like Hank and Steve, they also want to retain their current positions in the FBI and Border Patrol unless the FBI follows through with a job for Jimena."

Sophie grinned. "Good, more people to trust in the FBI, then. Besides you, Hank, and Steve, I'd lost all respect for the FBI. Too many traitors to root out."

Jimena turned her attention to the vast desert, bringing the binoculars up to scan the area. "I've spent a fair amount of time in this desert, and that rock is not native to the area." She pointed to the large rock formation. "The color is close but off just enough that I can tell it doesn't belong there."

Val squinted toward where Jimena pointed. She held out her hand for the binoculars. "She's right."

"It's too close to be a front for their underground compound. Besides, I didn't see the rock before the audio and visual signals went dark and silent. Instead, I saw a ranch house. Can I take a quick look?" Toni asked.

Val handed Toni the binoculars without saying a word, her expression grim. After Toni scanned the area. "Got it. The ranch house is maybe half to three-quarters of a mile from that large rock. That tracks with what my tablet indicates was the last location before we lost the signal."

"So, best guess on what that rock is there for?" Char asked.

"Cameras," Toni answered.

"Can you disable them?" Char asked.

"Maybe, but we'll need to get a little closer." Toni leaned into the car and pulled her large pack from the front seat. Setting a tiny device that looked like a small rodent on the ground, Toni began typing on her tablet. The tiny mouselike robot scurried along the cracked and dry earth in the direction of the rock. "I'm probing for heat signatures in case I'm wrong and there's another entrance via the rock. I'll have Minnie crawl over the rock to release the bot I'll need that will enable me to hack the cameras, if that's what's there."

Jimena's head was spinning at all the futuristic technology this strange organization she had agreed to join had at its disposal. It must have shown on her face because Sophie grinned at her and said, "You'll get used to it."

"How long before we can move out?" Char asked.

Toni glanced up from her tablet for a millisecond and answered, "Half an hour give or take." She returned to her tablet.

"That should work out well. I'd like the sky to darken a tad before we proceed, even if dweeb central determines the rock is a hidden camera. It would be nice if we didn't have to crawl on our stomachs the whole way to avoid detection," Val deadpanned.

"Be nice, Val. Dweeb central has saved our asses on numerous occasions. Don't forget what my beautiful wife contributes." Char leaned in to kiss Toni's temple while she worked.

"Don't call me dweeb central, or I won't inactivate those cameras, forcing you to suck in the desert while you crawl along its floor like a slimy little snake," Toni responded without looking up or stopping what she was doing.

"Do they always rib each other like this?" Em asked.

"Yes, but don't let either Val or Toni fool you. They've grown very fond of one another. Believe it or not, Val has mellowed quite a bit since the birth of her daughter."

"Val has a kid?" Em failed to mask the shock on her face.

"I told you we're a family-friendly organization now. Toni is a wonderful aunt, so I know she'll be a fantastic mother." Char rubbed her belly, which was still very flat. "Val doesn't trust too many people with her daughter, and Toni happens to be one of those she'll let babysit her precious little girl."

"You two done chit-chatting about Toni and me?" Val asked. "I think I'll scout ahead because I don't mind crawling around like a snake. You know, not all snakes are bad."

"Oh Val, have you been watching the science channel again?" Toni lifted her head long enough to smirk at Val.

"Pepper likes it," Val defended.

"Pepper is barely old enough to understand you're her mother," Toni challenged after letting out a hearty laugh.

"Not true. Pepper is very advanced beyond her age. Takes after her other mother." Val smiled proudly. "I want to check out that rock."

"My little mouse is almost there. Can't you wait one damn second?" Toni asked.

"No, I can't. I'm restless after that long drive. Pepper is better company than Ronda or Sophie, and she smells better."

"You're a titnob," Ronda responded while Sophie rolled her eyes.

"Well, just don't eat my little mouse, you evil serpent." Toni laughed again. "Awesome. Minnie made it to the rock. She's attached herself to the side." Toni began furiously typing on her tablet. "Gotcha. All right, the system is not as hard as I thought. I'm already in. Give me ten minutes, and I'll have that camera on a loop masking our approach. No need for Val to slither on the ground. It's definitely a camera system."

"Then we wait," Char commanded.

Jimena's head swam with thoughts of how Em and she could fit into this eclectic group of women. What could they possibly contribute? Ronda was their munitions expert. Toni had tech support nailed down. Char seemed to be a decisive leader. Sophie looked like she could handle herself in a fistfight or gunfight. And Val was a woman she'd never dream of taking on. Ever. She was downright petrifying. The only glimpse of humanity Jimena detected was when Val talked about her daughter.

Em touched Jimena's arm and whispered, "Are you okay? Did you want to hang with Toni and help her monitor everything for us?"

Jimena shook her head. "No, I'm good. I don't think I'd be any help to her, but one more body descending on their base of operations can't hurt. Right?"

"No, it definitely cannot," Char interjected, and then smiled at Jimena.

†

Em noticed the temperature had dropped rapidly. She grabbed her hoodie from the car and flipped the hood over her head, shivering in the cover of darkness. As soon as she moved along the desert floor, Em mimicked how Val progressed through the terrain, low to the ground. The woman was so graceful and smooth that she looked as though she belonged in the desert. Just another one of the creatures that might come out at night. Her colleagues were almost as efficient, and Em felt like a lumbering giant. Her injured leg certainly did not help Em travel the desert with the same level of stealth as her colleagues. Even Jimena moved quickly, quietly, and with the same grace as the others. But at least they were making progress to their ultimate goal.

Val gestured to the group to follow in her footsteps and not deviate. Every few minutes, she would raise her hand for the group to stop while she placed a small metal device on the ground, often changing her path as they zig-zagged through the brush and cacti. Em heard a faint beep every time Val changed direction.

Their trek to the ranch house seemed to take forever, but when Em glanced at her watch, she noted they'd only been at this just shy of thirty minutes. The slog to the target required far more caution than any mission she'd participated in during her tour of duty in the Army.

The team was finally within striking distance of the ranch house, and Val lifted her hand for the group to stop. Setting the metal object to the ground, the light beeping sound appeared to form a constant staccato. Val made a sweeping motion with her hand and pointed to Ronda. Ronda, in turn, gestured between Em and herself.

At first, Em didn't understand what they expected of her until she moved closer and noticed the line of explosives hidden amongst the brush. She realized that if any mass of significance crossed this perimeter, they'd all be blown to bits.

Finding the wires closest to herself, Em disarmed one explosive. Ronda nodded enthusiastically as she disarmed the one closest to where she had inched forward. The two women worked quickly and quietly until they developed a clear path. Ronda then gestured for Val to retake the lead.

Val's methodical approach amazed Em, since she had appeared agitated to be standing still earlier in the evening. Em had erroneously assumed Val was not a patient person, but her slow approach demonstrated much more than patience. These women were the best of the best.

Val signaled for the team to wait while she used her device on the ranch's perimeter. Then, after ensuring there were no additional booby traps in close proximity to the outside walls of the ranch, she motioned for the team to spread out and cautiously enter the structure.

Em hoped that if cameras were inside the ranch house, Toni had managed to either disable them or put them on a continuous loop. Each team member entered via a different location. Some crawled through windows. Others picked the locks on doors.

Em drew in a large breath of relief when they didn't find anyone inside. Even so, disappointment hit her square in the face at finding the structure empty.

Char touched her right earbud and whispered, "Toni, we need a little help on which door leads to the basement or the lower level where I presume they are hiding out." Pointing to a painting of the desert, Val lifted the piece of art, exposing a small panel.

Val lifted her thumb in the air, then waved her hand over her face.

Char nodded and clicked her right earbud again. "Facial and thumbprint recognition access." Pausing and listening, she answered. "Got it." Char beckoned the rest of the team over for them to regroup.

"Can Toni get us through the door?" Val asked.

"She's going to try, but we may have to go to Plan B, which means we'll be entering hot. Ronda can attach the small explosive and blow open the door."

"Nothing like announcing our arrival with a bang," Val grumbled. "I hate going in hot. I much prefer a sneak attack."

"Becoming a mom has made you soft," Ronda quipped. "It's not like we've never done this before."

"Shut it, Ronda, or I'll make you take the lead," Val answered.

Char held up her hand. "Stop squabbling. I can't hear Toni with you two jabbering away."

The group quieted as Val and Ronda glared at one another while Sophie stood to the side with her arms across her chest. Em didn't know what they expected of her. Would Ronda ask for her help with the explosive? She had an awful feeling about all of this.

Char nodded again. "Toni says it will take her too much time to hack the door. They've put too many layers of protection around the system. Unless we're willing to wait another couple of hours for her to break the codes, she recommends Plan B. However, she suggests that Sophie pull out the prototype she gave her to detect heat signatures. Once we've blown open the door, we need to activate the device. We'll at least know how many people we're up against and their location. One piece of good news is that Toni can shut off their lights. That will give us an advantage. We have enough night vision contacts to outfit us all."

Sophie slipped off her pack and dug inside, removing a small gadget no larger than a cell phone. Then, holding the device in her hands, she announced, "I'm ready whenever the rest of you are."

Char unzipped the front pocket of her pack and retrieved six contact lens cases. She handed each person on the team a case. "Pop those into your eyes and follow Val. Soph, as soon as you know how many and the location, call it out for the rest of us. Em, Jimena, if you want to stay above ground and wait for us, none of us would think less of you."

"No way. I didn't come on this little road trip to be side-lined," Em stated.

"Me neither," Jimena added.

Em popped in the contacts. She looked around the room in amazement, noticing everyone's face in precise sharpness. She felt like the space had suddenly turned into a seventy-five-inch high-definition television screen. "Holy shit, these are incredible!" The contacts were nothing like the almost prehistoric version of night-vision goggles that the Army used.

Ronda grinned. "I know, pretty sweet, huh?"

"Do you need any help with the explosives?" Em asked.

"Nah, I got this one," Ronda answered before digging into her pack and pulling out a small brick of explosive matter. Carefully attaching the C-4 next to the trim line, indicating the edge of a door and the locking mechanism, Sophie gestured for the group to step back. Then, lifting her hand in the air and holding up her four fingers, she methodically curled down each finger until only her fist remained. The medium-sized explosion created a bright flare before the steel door popped open.

Em barely saw Val enter before Soph called out, "Two at the bottom of the stairs, fifty yards to the right. Three on the move in what looks like a corridor on the left."

Em continued to follow Char down the stairs and hadn't reached the bottom when she heard two quick pops.

"Two behind you, Val, look out," Sophie yelled.

Em hadn't yet reached the corridor to the left where Val began her sweep toward the three Sophie had pegged in her earlier declaration. This was fortunate for Val because Em had a clear shot of whoever had raised their gun preparing to shoot Val. Almost as if she was in slow motion, she took the person out simultaneously to Val, who pivoted and dropped the second man.

Jimena yelled, "Duck!" and fired off a shot at one of the three men charging. Em wasn't sure who had taken out the other two, but when she continued down the corridor, all three men were slumped on the ground, not moving.

"Fucking A, they're like cockroaches, we take down two, and three more show up," Ronda exclaimed. "Soph, how many more?"

"Five. But none of the targets are moving. They're gathered in one area. I'm looking to see if there are any more, but it looks like that's it," Sophie answered.

"Excellent. We've evened the odds now," Char noted. "Val, it's preferable to take Em's parents alive versus in a body bag. They may have information we need."

"Understood. Switching to darts. Soph, which way?" Val asked.

"Keep following the corridor for another fifty feet, then hopefully, there is a new corridor on the right," Sophie answered. "Fuck, sorry, sorry," Sophie announced. "Three more are approaching fast down a corridor on the left."

Val was like an acrobat, exercising a controlled fall to the floor while pivoting and catching two of the three, dropping them quickly. Em watched in horror as the third man moved out of the line of fire with barely enough time to avoid Val's attack, but not before his shot went wide but ricocheted off the metal wall, nicking Char.

Val was like a wild animal when she glanced at where Char had fallen, and an inhuman scream erupted from her mouth before she put three bullets into the person who had shot Char.

Char pressed her hand over her right shoulder and gestured for the group to continue with her right hand. "I'm fine. Go, go, before they scatter."

Em continued to follow Val, but before she went too far down the corridor, she looked over her shoulder and saw Jimena squatting next to Char, taking over and pressing a cloth against the wound.

†

"Paranoid assholes," Val muttered.

"What now?" Sophie asked.

"Another door with facial and thumbprint recognition," Val answered.

Em could barely make out Ronda's strained expression as she explained, "Too dangerous to set a charge in this cramped corridor. Ideas?"

"Yeah, get the nerd to open the door for us," Val grumbled.

"Well, considering we've lost radio contact ever since descending into the bowels of hell, let's hope Toni found the code and the second barrier," Ronda mumbled.

As if Toni was actually listening in on the conversation, Em heard a quiet snick, and the door popped open. Val held up her hand and whispered, "Wait. It could be a trap. Let me lay some fire down first."

"Three ten feet directly in front of you, Val," Sophie called out.

Val burst through the door with Ronda and Sophie following closely behind. By the time Em made it through the door, the pandemonium of gunfire and rapid movement inside the large room had ceased. Val pushed the three guards directly in front of her to the side. Em scanned the room, looking for her parents. A movement to her right caught her attention, but not before her mother did something that caused sirens and lights to activate, creating temporary confusion.

Through the strobe lights, Em watched both individuals crumple to the ground. The sirens were deafening in the room. Em wanted to clap her hands over her ears and shut her eyes to block the irritating lights and sounds that she felt sure would cause a horrendous migraine.

"What the fuck is this?" Ronda waved her hands dramatically in the air.

"Nothing good, that's what," Val answered. "We need to get out of here. Now," Val ordered as she grabbed Em's mother and threw her over her shoulder. "Go, go, go, back the way we came."

"What about him?" Ronda pointed to Em's father.

"Leave him. He's too large to carry," Val answered.

Em started running through the corridor and was the first to approach Jimena and Char. "Jimena, we have to help Char. Hurry, we need to get out of here."

Em had tried to modulate her voice so it didn't sound panicked, but she knew she hadn't accomplished her goal after seeing Jimena's eyes widen. However, Jimena immediately grabbed Char's good arm and threw it over her shoulder. If it weren't so dire, Em would have laughed at how comical it looked with Jimena assisting Char, considering their dramatic height difference. Em decided that despite her throbbing leg, she would be the better choice to help Char move quickly through the tunnels.

Approaching the struggling women, Em barked, "You go ahead, Jimena, I've got Char." Em sighed in relief when Jimena didn't argue with her. Sophie, Ronda, and even Val passed Em and Char as they moved slowly through the dark corridor. Em could still hear the sirens and hoped that whatever the noise was announcing would not activate until they were clear from the ranch.

Finally, Em and Char reached the stairs to the upper portion of the complex. Em could barely make out the rest of the team as they ran away from the ranch house into the desert. Just as she felt Char losing steam, Val materialized in front of Em after doubling back and said, "I got her, go, go, go."

Em hesitated a second until she felt a push. She stumbled toward the rest of the team and didn't look back until she heard the explosion and felt the heat against her back. When she finally reached Sophie, Ronda, and Jimena, she turned her focus toward the burning structure, never so relieved in her life to see Char and Val stumbling away from the wreckage. Her mother lay unconscious on the ground next to the group of women.

"Jesus Christ, what is it about booby-trapping houses with explosives?" Em groused.

Ignoring Em's grumblings, Val asked. "Soph, can you get Toni on the comms?"

"Yeah, already called for the medical team," Sophie answered.

"What about a hospital close by? I'm not sure we have the time to wait," Jimena said.

"No, no hospital. Gunshot wounds have to be reported to the authorities. We can't risk that. I just need to keep pressure on the wound," Char insisted.

"How long until medical gets here?" Val asked.

"Fifteen or twenty minutes," Sophie answered. "Toni is panicked right now. Char, you better talk her off the ledge."

Char's quivering hand reached to her ear. "Toni, listen to me. Take three deep breaths, babe. We still need you to monitor the situation. If the explosion attracts any unwanted attention, you will have to find us a way out that leaves a wide berth. Honestly, I'm fine."

Val interrupted, "Tell Toni to grab the first aid kit from the SUV and follow the tire tracks, then through the area that Ronda and Em deactivated." She glanced at Ronda. "Coordinates?"

"I got it. I'll send coordinates to Toni," Ronda responded.

"How long before you think the authorities will arrive?" Sophie asked.

Val looked to the sky as if the clouds may have the answer, then shrugged. "This is a pretty remote location. I'd guess at least forty-five minutes. Could be a maximum of two hours."

Looking increasingly pale, Char wheezed, "We'll need to figure a way to do some cleanup and come up with a cover story about how Em and Jimena captured Bridget. None of us can be here when they discover this location." Char touched her ear. "Toni, we need you to redirect the authorities. Hold them off until we can get a team to clean the site." After pausing and listening to what Toni was saying, Char snapped, "That is not the priority. Forget the first aid kit until you send the local authorities on a wild goose chase anywhere but here. I told you I'll live…the baby, too. I promise."

Em watched as Char seemed to lose strength. Recognizing Char's poor health, Jimena scrambled to lend a hand again, taking over the compress and letting Char lean against her body. A few minutes later, the sports car roared on the scene, and Toni jumped from the vehicle with a large bag in her hand. She hurried to her wife's side, ripping the bag open, and began to administer temporary aid. Em couldn't hear the words Toni mumbled to Char, but the love was readily apparent.

Fifteen minutes later, Em heard the telltale sign of a helicopter approaching. The arid dirt swirled in an impressive dust tornado as the copter touched down fifty yards away. Sophie, Ronda, Toni, and Val looked visibly relieved when a short woman with close-cropped hair emerged from the helicopter along with two other medics and began to bark orders.

The woman inserted an IV, and like a well-oiled machine, the other team members secured Char to the gurney. Em had heard of first responders who could perform an in-field blood transfusion, but she'd never seen it happen before, not even on the battlefield. Em knew from her experience in combat that Char needed a transfusion to save her life. That was the first thing Em had noticed—the massive loss of blood. Whoever these women were, she was positive they would ensure Char survived.

As Toni ran along with the gurney, Em heard Char tell her to stay and make sure she redirected those authorities. Toni began to cry, her indecision written all over her face, until Char pleaded with her.

The medic team leader barked, "Toni, we need to go now. You'll just be in the way. Please don't stress Char anymore than she can deal with in her condition. Let us take care of her."

Toni nodded, and Em could almost feel her anguish. If it had been Jimena, she would have wanted to go in the helicopter with her as well.

CHAPTER TWENTY-FOUR

Sophie touched Toni on the shoulder and said, in the most calming voice Jimena had heard come out of Sophie, "Toni, I know you're worried, but we need to get your head in the game. Cindy has this. Trust her like we trust you to take care of all the tech stuff that none of us are capable of."

"We need to get out of here and let the clean-up crew take care of everything. How many minutes out are they?" Ronda asked.

"Ten minutes tops. I put them on standby and kept updating them on our location," Toni answered, her head bowed in defeat.

"Let's go, then. I'll drive," Em offered.

Without looking up from her tablet, Toni continued to type. "I should probably drive, but I need a few more minutes to redirect the local authorities. Char rarely lets anyone drive her baby. She barely lets me drive her."

Again, Sophie carefully approached Toni. "Let Em drive, Toni. I'm sure Char will understand."

"Okay. So far, nothing on the scanners about the explosion, but I still need to do something to hijack any transmissions that will alert them to the scene," Toni answered.

†

Jimena watched Val run through the desert, assuming the trek to the SUV would go a lot quicker without her concerning herself with falling into a trap. Ten minutes later, the SUV crested over the slight rise of a small hill roaring toward their location with a fleet of vehicles following.

"Clean-up crew is here. I'll stay and help. The rest of you need to head back. Take Toni directly to our temporary compound in San Diego. For now, we can transport Bridget to the compound and then figure out a story to tell the FBI." Val reached into her pants and pulled out several syringes. Handing them to Sophie, she directed, "She should be out for at least two hours, so I recommend jabbing her before she wakes up. Ronda can drive the SUV. Em, follow her."

The somber crew climbed into the two vehicles. Minimal conversation broke the silence inside the vehicle as Ronda pushed the speed limit to make it back to San Diego in record time. Em had absolutely no problem punching it to follow Ronda. She would risk a speeding ticket if it meant the strained and sad look on Toni's face dissipated.

Jimena had tried to engage Toni, but that went nowhere after Toni grunted her response, limiting it to one or two words. Jimena wanted to wrap her arms around Toni and tell her everything would be okay. Unfortunately, she couldn't make that promise, but she could pray for Char and hope God was listening. She'd come to appreciate how much help Toni had been in shutting down this terror cell. It tugged at Jimena's heartstrings to see her so despondent.

Em continued glancing at Toni but hadn't said much, turning up the radio instead to fill the void of silence. She caught Jimena's eyes in the rearview mirror. Jimena offered a sad smile, not knowing what else to do.

When they reached the outskirts of San Diego, the SUV took the exit to a nondescript housing community and pulled into the driveway of one of the larger houses in the neighborhood. Jimena wasn't expecting to see something so ordinary as this temporary base of operations.

"Uh, this looks very conventional," Jimena blurted.

"Hide in plain sight. We didn't have much time to establish something similar to the main complex. This is only a rental because we didn't expect to remain in California very long. Still, we've outfitted the house to accommodate our needs, including a state-of-the-art room for medical emergencies. Obviously, it doesn't have a surgical suite, but Cindy is very adaptable. Thank you for driving," Toni said quietly as she climbed from the car and jogged inside the house.

The SUV had pulled into the garage. Jimena assumed it was because they needed to carry Bridget from the vehicle and away from prying eyes.

†

When Em walked inside the house, her surprise at what she found equaled the immense transition of the place to a combination state-of-the-art medical facility and some kind of technology lab. She felt her eyes nearly bug out as she walked from room to room, inspecting the deceptively large space inside. The only areas that seemed to retain their previous functions were a couple of small bedrooms, a midsized living room, and a large kitchen.

Toni had already made a beeline to the small medical facility where the commanding woman who had arrived at the scene fiddled with the lines and tubes sprouting from Char's body like vines in overgrown ivy. Char's eyes were closed, but a marginally healthier glow had replaced the paleness Em had seen before.

Jimena expressed the exact sentiment that Em held when she blurted, "Wow! How in the world did you convert this home into this?" She waved her hand at the facility.

"We've been in California longer than you think. Bridget and Mikhail have been on our radar for quite some time. So when the opportunity presented itself for us to work together, we jumped on it," Sophie explained.

Em assumed Sophie or Ronda had carried Bridget into the living room and settled the still sleeping woman onto the couch. Ronda looked relaxed, sitting on the adjacent recliner and stretching her legs as she pivoted her focus to the group.

"Why don't you take a seat, and we can discuss where to go from here," Sophie suggested.

After Em and Jimena had settled into two chairs a small distance from the couch, Ronda and Sophie settled next to Em's mother. Sophie took the lead, opening the discussion.

"Obviously, we can't simply march up to the FBI office and dump your mother on their doorstep," Sophie deadpanned. "I called Hank and Steve, and they should arrive any minute. Perhaps they can weigh in on this."

"Why can't we keep her drugged until we deposit her at one of the houses owned by the shell corporation? Then we can arrange for an FBI raid and conveniently capture her?" Jimena suggested.

Sophie grabbed her chin. "That might work, although we'll have to get the timing just right. Maybe a raid in the middle of the night. We could attribute any residual grogginess to catching her off guard while sleeping."

"Won't that seem suspicious considering we've already raided all the places previously and come up empty?" Em asked.

"Could Toni create a fake paper trail showing a purchase of another house that wasn't included in the original raids?" Jimena suggested.

Em frowned. "How would we find a place quickly enough for that to work?"

293

Ronda grinned. "You don't think we all live here, do you? We have another place that is a bit more comfortable. That should be perfect. Once the clean-up crew returns, we can have them transform that place into one of Thomas Smith's corporate holdings. That should be easy enough."

Two quick knocks on the door preceded Hank and Steve as they strolled into the house as if they owned the place. Em thought they had clearly been at this location previously. However, she didn't want to hold a grudge for not knowing a single thing about their recent agreement to join the organization.

"Hey, hey, the gang's all here," Hank joked.

"Mister, you've got a lot of 'splaining to do," Em said.

Hank cringed. "Yeah, sorry about that, Em."

"You're forgiven, but buying all the beer for the next year," Em replied.

Steve simply waved his hand and took a seat.

"Okay. I suppose that's fair. So, what's the plan?" Hank asked.

Em updated Hank and Steve. "We were batting around the idea of engineering a raid in a new location that Toni will magically put in front of the new tech at the FBI. You can stage a raid where we'll find my mother and take her in."

Nodding, Hank answered, "Yeah, that would probably work." He glanced at the lump on the couch that was still fast asleep. "Timing will be critical. I assume you'll keep her drugged until we're ready to move on it?"

"That's the plan," Sophie confirmed.

"What about Mikhail? I assume the cleanup team has removed any evidence of his demise at the place you blitzed earlier? Of course, you know the FBI will keep looking for him."

Sophie frowned. "They will, but they have to know that sometimes the rat escapes the trap. Hopefully, they'll assume the Russians got him out."

Hank pursed his lips. "I don't think so. They'll wonder why he left Bridget behind."

"You got a better idea?" Ronda asked.

"Do you have access to his remains? Or at least a piece of him we can identify later?" Hank asked.

"Why?" Sophie leaned forward, seemingly more interested in what he had to say.

"I think a controlled explosion at a selected site that we'll make sure is free from actual casualties would work. We can stage a bombing gone wrong, like with Karl Senior." Hank grinned.

"Hmm. Not bad. Not bad at all, genius boy. I knew you were a keeper when Soph approached you," Ronda answered.

"Let's split into two teams. Steve and I will handle taking Bridget into custody because Em is supposed to be far away from her. Carter was pretty explicit about that. And, sorry, Jimena, but you're an extension of that order."

"I've no problem with that." Em grinned. "I already got my wish. But I do want to look her in the eye one last time before you take her in."

Hank shook his head. "Not a good idea, Em. Can't you just let it go? We've got her. That's the most important thing. Your fucked up family dynamic is not critical in the grand scheme of things."

Jimena touched Em's thigh. "He's right, Em. You don't want your mother unraveling this whole mission after everything we've been through. The last thing needed is for the FBI to poke its nose into this organization and cause problems for these wonderful women. We owe them everything. Without their aid, we never would have captured the head of the snake."

"You can ask Carter if he'll let you interrogate her after she's in custody," Steve suggested.

All eyes turned in his direction since Steve rarely said anything, but when he contributed, most agents listened. His contemplative style of thinking always provided sound advice.

Em nodded her agreement with the plan they would set in motion.

CHAPTER TWENTY-FIVE

Em and Jimena had returned to Jimena's home to await hearing from Hank and Steve, who had promised to call as soon as they had Bridget in custody. Em didn't exactly know what she would say to her mother. It wasn't like she had a particularly affectionate connection with the woman who had given birth to her. Still, there were fleeting moments of tenderness that she vaguely recalled when she was a toddler. She wondered if those moments were real or simply part of Bridget's cover and required for the role she had been assigned to play. Never having met Mikhail before, Em had zero feelings about his premature demise. Good riddance. Em felt an equal amount of hatred for both her biological father and the one she had believed was her father.

Taking out her frayed emotions and examining them in the harsh light, she realized that her most significant aggravation was the fact that her entire childhood was part of a big lie. She couldn't wrap her arms around the truth. If Em had ever bothered to research her genealogy, she would have learned years ago that she wasn't German at all but the product of two Russian spies. How fucked up was that? How had Em avoided both nature and nurture? She supposed free will truly was a thing, and she could escape her upbringing and biology. Thank goodness for that.

Jimena had been a rock, talking her through her jumbled emotions. No matter what happened, she knew she would never make the mistake of letting her go again. Jimena had convinced Em that staying awake practically all night wouldn't do her any good. By the time Hank and Steve engineered the capture and brought Bridget in for questioning, it would likely not happen until the following morning. That did not stop Em from tossing and turning all night long. Finally, Em gave up and quietly crawled from the comfort of Jimena's arms. Sitting at Jimena's kitchen counter, Em wrapped her fingers around the warmth of the coffee mug and let her mind wander.

When the call finally came, Em answered on the first ring. "Hey."

"I'm sorry, Em. Carter doesn't want you anywhere near this," Hank said.

"Has she said anything?" Em asked.

Em heard Hank's audible sigh through the tiny speaker on the phone. "She won't talk with anyone but you."

"I don't understand. I would think Carter would want me involved if I could glean more information from her, regardless of my connection."

"Carter is concerned this will just be a mind fuck. We won't get any useful information, and all this will do is fuck up our case. He's only looking out for you."

"That's bullshit," Em responded with an iciness that Hank didn't deserve.

"Hey, don't shoot the messenger."

Em took a deep breath, closing her eyes to regain her composure. Jimena shuffled into the kitchen and gestured for Em to put Hank on speaker.

"I'm coming down. If there is a chance we can gather additional information, it's worth every risk," Em responded.

"Carter is getting pressure from some unlikely places. The entire case against Bridget could blow up in all our faces. She has powerful allies."

"Please tell me you aren't going to let her go," Em responded with exasperation.

"We're working on it. Fortunately, we have our own power brokers wading into the complicated politics of the situation. There is a fight occurring way above either of our pay grades. Carter doesn't even have much to say about the ultimate outcome," Hank explained.

Em stood and began pacing. "Unbelievable. Six months of work down the drain."

"Not necessarily. Let me see what I can do on my end. I'll talk to Carter. If it means anything, I agree with you. Our best chance to get more information is to let her speak to you. Not to mention how pissed our mutual friends will be if they let Bridget go. Val is likely to take matters into her own hands. So, please, stay put, and I'll call you later. Sometimes, you have to know when to let things go."

"You know I can't do that. I'm tempted to tender my resignation and be done with the FBI once and for all," Em stated.

"Don't do that. Give me twenty-four hours. Go cuddle with your woman and accept the gift of time with her."

"Fine. You have twenty-four hours." Em pressed the button to end the call, more frustrated than any other time in her life.

Jimena stroked her arm and silently grabbed the coffeepot to refill her cup. "What can I do?"

Em shook her head. "Nothing. But I think we better call Sophie and give her an update. Maybe they have a suggestion on how to proceed."

"That sounds good. I'd like to know how Char is doing, anyway," Jimena answered.

"Yeah, me too."

†

Jimena had busied herself making a special meal for Em, trying very hard to let her work through whatever she needed to. The television hummed softly in the background with the murmured voices of the different CNN anchors as they shuffled through each breaking news story that wasn't actually breaking news but the same-old-same-old rehashed stories. But as the hours slowly dwindled, Jimena felt Em slipping from her again. Only this time, Em was the one letting her family get between them instead of them abruptly taking her away from Jimena. She had tried to engage Em, but even inane conversation was met with one or two-word answers. Jimena had finally reached her limit.

"If you're going to run away again, you might as well march your ass out my front door right now," Jimena said through gritted teeth.

"What?" Em's wide eyes finally turned to face Jimena. She had Em's attention now.

"I get that you're upset about what's going on, and you feel helpless, but I will not sit by and let you shut me out again." Jimena didn't look away as she met Em's panicked eyes. "Talk to me."

Em sighed. "I'm sorry. I don't know how to put into words what I'm feeling right now. This whole situation is testing my limits, and I suppose I need to admit that I have control issues. Besides the possibility of Bridget slipping from the authorities, I have questions, and none of them have anything to do with her involvement in the Russian government."

"You want to know if she ever cared about you," Jimena guessed.

Em nodded. "Stupid, I know."

Jimena grabbed Em's hand and held on tight. "Not stupid. She's your mother and not just by biology. She raised you. Although I use that term very lightly."

Tears formed in Em's eyes. "As much as I want to hate her, I can't seem to shake those small moments when she actually was a mother to me. Granted, as I grew older, those moments became few and far between. I keep thinking that if it had not been for your family, I would not be the person I am today. They were the ones to provide love and guidance through my formative years."

"What else did you want to ask Bridget?" Jimena prompted. Em was talking now, and Jimena was not about to close the spigot.

"How did I figure into their master plan? Did Karl Senior know I wasn't his, and that's why he was such a bastard to me, or was that just who he was? Is there any small part of me that inherited their evil?" Em took a breath and continued, "How could I have missed her deception?"

"How could you not?" Jimena countered. "The woman let Karl Senior beat her, for God's sake. I'd say she was a master manipulator, playing her part to perfection."

"I suppose it does all come down to that fundamental question, after all. I want to know if Bridget was always playing the part of a mother? Considering she was so good at fooling everyone, perhaps those fleeting moments were all an act. And now I can't even get anywhere near her to ask my questions. It's beyond frustrating."

"Hon, even if you could ask those questions, how will you know if she's being truthful? Sometimes, there are questions we'll never know the answers to. People have been pondering the meaning of life since the dawn of time, and I don't believe anyone has ever solved that mystery." Jimena offered Em a small smile. "At some point, you have to embrace the serenity prayer."

Jimena didn't know if it was divine intervention or that Em always was more aware of her surroundings, having the ability to pay attention to several things at once. Her eyes traveled to the television, and Jimena followed, tuning into the breaking news sound. They flashed a picture of Bridget and Mikhail on the screen, along with three sitting congressmen and one senator. At the same time, Em's phone rang, but she didn't move to answer it as her eyes remained glued to the TV.

Anderson Cooper announced a CNN exclusive, citing an anonymous source who had provided recordings of conversations between suspected Russian spies and the members of Congress. CNN was trying to verify the information.

The phone rang again, and after Em answered, she pushed the button to put the call on speaker.

"Turn on the news," Hank directed.

"It's on. I have you on speaker," Em answered.

"I think our buddies decided enough was enough. Somehow, they knew we were about to release Bridget. All hell is breaking loose here. If you want a few minutes with Bridget, now is the time to take advantage of this cluster fuck."

"I'm on my way." Em was already standing and ready to head out the door.

"I'm coming with," Jimena declared, leaving no room for argument.

†

It was just Em's luck that she ran into Carter almost the minute she entered the building. She'd wanted to sneak in and have a brief conversation with Bridget and be out before he even knew she was there.

"Where do you think you're going?" Carter growled.

"I need answers," Em replied as calmly as she could muster.

"Tough. Sometimes we don't always get what we want," Carter answered.

"She asked for me. We can turn off the cameras. I'm not going to interrogate her in my official capacity. This is personal. You owe me, Carter. The FBI owes me this," Em pleaded.

Carter sighed. "Fine. This whole thing is a cluster. I doubt you'll mess anything up any worse than it already is. Follow me. But Jimena can't go in there with you."

"I wasn't planning to," Jimena interjected. "Just point me to one of your waiting rooms or wherever. Stick me in another interrogation room if you need to."

Carter led them to the elevator, and the three of them stared ahead, not saying anything as they rode to the third floor of the building. Carter directed Jimena to his office, and then Em walked with him to the first interrogation room. Em watched him turn off the camera.

Centering herself, Em sucked in a large breath before opening the door and greeting her mother. "Hello, Bridget."

"Emma. Thank you for coming," Bridget responded politely. "I suspect you have questions."

"You're damn right I do, but you can save your breath on anything related to your Russian pals," Em gritted out.

"You must understand, they groomed us to serve our country. It does not differ from the calling you found with the Army," Bridget responded. "I did love you and sincerely did not wish you harm. You were my daughter, but there are far greater principles at play. All of us were always prepared to sacrifice for the republic. Unfortunately, those sacrifices extended to you. Had you not become involved, that cost would not have been necessary."

"So, it's my fault?"

"Yes," Bridget answered simply.

"Were you going to recruit me?"

Bridget nodded. "That was the initial plan. Growing up an American would have made you the perfect asset. You were bright, strong, and possessed exactly the skills needed. Unfortunately, you were also headstrong and unduly influenced by Jimena's family. It is my error that we never took them out when I had the chance before their influence was too great. I also should have eliminated Karl Senior before he could negatively influence our plans for you. Had Karl not been such a terrible father, things might have gone differently. A fatal error on our part."

"Did you order the hit on Jimena's father?"

Bridget shook her head. "No, that was all Karl Senior. He held a grudge that he couldn't let go of and sent two thugs to take out Jose. It made no difference to us either way.

You'd already been unduly influenced. Jose was never a primary target."

Em wanted to smack the indifferent expression off of Bridget's face. Em would have to think of a way to break this news to Jimena. At least Jimena would finally have closure, and a sort of justice had already occurred since Karl Senior was dead. But was that too easy? Maybe Jimena would have liked for him to face the consequences of his actions by spending the rest of his life in jail.

"Why would you admit all of this to me?" Em asked.

Bridget shrugged. "If I'm not mistaken, the cameras are off. They would never allow you to officially interrogate me. I thought the least I could do was provide you with the answers you seek. You are, after all, my daughter. I am not the monster you believe me to be. Simply a faithful comrade. Can you say that everything you have done for your country is without questionable morality? What is the saying, 'those who live in glass houses should not throw stones?' Americans are arrogant to believe that only their actions and beliefs are above reproach."

"Why rig your safe house to blow?" Em asked.

Another slight lift of her shoulders. "Death was preferable to whatever hole your government decides to throw me into."

"Bullshit. We know you have connections with our government. Unfortunately for you, someone caught your four puppets on tape. I don't think they'll be coming to your rescue. The media already has the audio. The game is over."

Initially, Bridget's eyes widened, then a tiny smile appeared on her face as she uttered two words. "Fake news."

"We'll see about that. Want to try again with why the house blew?" Em pushed.

Bridget smirked. "I suppose it doesn't make much of a difference now. We hadn't planned on the team's efficiency. The compound had an escape route, of course. I am somewhat surprised you drugged me versus elimination. I believe you may find that is a grave error you'll wish you had not made when I'm released."

"I wouldn't count on it. Americans aren't as sympathetic to the Russians as you might believe. Now that the genie is out of the bottle with the press uncovering those audiotapes, I think you'll find your connections aren't as helpful as you think. That hole they decide to put you in won't be pleasant. As you've said before, Americans don't always take the moral high ground."

Bridget's face lost its former arrogance, and Em left her with that final parting comment.

†

The interaction with her mother had both unsettled and mollified Em. She needed answers to her burning questions but worried that her mother might have been correct, and somehow she'd escape justice.

As she met Carter outside the interrogation room, she decided to make her opinions known. "This is one time I advocate for the Department of Homeland Security usurping

307

our authority. I hope they will decide to throw her in the deepest, darkest hole possible. I don't care if she is an American citizen. She shouldn't have any rights. For once, I hope our government lives up to its despicable reputation for brutality."

Carter grinned. "Surely you aren't advocating for enhanced interrogation."

"That's exactly what I'm hoping for. Unfortunately, Bridget thinks her powerful friends will engineer her release. I hope you don't let that happen."

"Funny you should suggest that. Things are happening way above my pay grade. I've already been notified that Homeland Security is taking over. I'm okay with that. Did you get the answers you need?" Carter asked.

"I did. Thank you."

Carter shrugged. "The minute they told me this was no longer our case to make, it failed to matter that your interrogation might screw things up. Besides, I didn't want to lose one of my best agents. You take care of yourself, Em. Go on a long vacation. That's an order. I don't want to see the whites of your eyes for at least another month."

"You know, I will take you up on that order." Em smiled and walked out of the office. She hoped she could convince Jimena to take that long vacation with her. They both deserved it.

†

Jimena must have been looking out of Carter's small office window because she greeted Em the minute Em exited the interrogation room.

"How did it go?" Jimena asked.

"About as I expected, but I have something I need to tell you. It's about Jose."

Jimena's brow knitted together in confusion. "My papa? What does he have to do with all of this?"

"I don't know how to say this…"

"Just spit it out, Em. I know whatever you have to tell me isn't your fault," Jimena soothed.

"Remember when I told you I might have a hunch about your papa's death?"

Jimena nodded.

"Turns out I was correct. When the FBI first recruited me, Karl Senior was already on their radar, but he hadn't gotten in too deep with the cell. That came a little later. However, they suspected him of a few hate crimes. When you told me about your papa, I suspected Karl Senior had something to do with it. He always carried a grudge, all the way back to when Jose would step in on my behalf. The fact that Jose was Mexican only angered him further. No doubt, he got a few of his friends to do the dirty deed."

Jimena found the first chair open in the waiting area and sat down heavily. "Wow. Okay, do you know who those friends are?"

Em shook her head. "My mother didn't provide those details. I don't think she knew."

"I want to find them," Jimena stated, with no room for compromise.

"I know you do. Since we now have friends with the kind of resources the FBI could only dream of, I say we start with them. I know they don't owe us anything. On the contrary, we are in debt to them, but somehow I believe they'll be amenable to offering assistance."

"Thank you for understanding."

"He was the only father figure I'll ever acknowledge. So I want to get justice for Jose just as much as you," Em stated.

Jimena nodded and stood. "Let's get out of here."

Em took Jimena's hand, not caring who might see them, and they left the FBI offices.

CHAPTER TWENTY-SIX

When Em floated the idea of a vacation, she remembered how they had talked about going somewhere with snow. But, after checking the weather in Alaska and other colder climates, Jimena had nixed that idea and suggested one of those all-inclusive resorts in Mexico. She'd confessed to always wanting to relax on the beach while sipping pina coladas or mojitos until she turned absolutely goofy. And she'd insisted knowing the language would help if they wanted to explore the area outside the resort. Unfortunately, while Em knew enough Spanish to get by, she was by no means proficient in the language.

Jimena still had family in Mexico that she hadn't seen in many years, so they decided on a resort that would be an easy driving distance from her aunts and uncles. They were excited to meet Em since Jimena's entire family had talked about her before Em had moved and lost contact with her second family.

The flight to Puerto Vallarta was less than three hours, and the drive to San Sebastian where Jimena's extended family lived was a little over an hour's drive and even more convenient. After searching online, they finally settled on an adult-only resort. Not that either of them disliked kids. On the contrary, Em had decided this was the right time to finally put a ring on it and not just a promise ring. Getting married was simply the first step. She wanted kids as much as Jimena, and Em certainly wasn't getting any younger. Envisioning herself coaching a soccer team did not include creaking knees or a full head of gray hair.

They had finally settled into their room at the resort after what felt like the royal treatment. The staff had presented Jimena and Em with glasses of champagne upon their arrival and wet towels to wipe their sweaty hands and faces. Jimena glanced at Em, giving her a strange look when Em's leg bounced with nervous energy as she waited for Jimena to change into her swimsuit.

"What the hell has you so jittery?" Jimena asked. "We're on vacation. No timetable to adhere to. It's not like the sun is going to suddenly disappear. We have three whole weeks of fun in the sun, good food, and lots of alcohol." Jimena grinned. "I promise, my aunts and uncles will be on their best behavior. I've already threatened them."

The ring box burned a hole in her pocket, but Em wanted to wait until the following day. Maybe it was cheesy to try and duplicate her adolescent declaration when she'd confessed her undying love and gave Jimena the promise ring at sunrise, but that was about as creative as Em could get. She only hoped it was romantic enough to receive an affirmative answer. Not that she expected Jimena to say no, but one never knew about these things. Moreover, she'd been absent for fifteen years, which didn't bode well for a definitive yes.

Em pushed down on her leg to stop it from bouncing. "Sorry, I guess I'm out of practice. I haven't managed to relax on vacation very often. The concept is somewhat foreign to me."

"We don't have to hit the beach yet. I can certainly think of several ways to relax you." Jimena waggled her eyebrows.

Em laughed. "We'll have plenty of time for that. All I need is another drink, and I'll ease into vacation mode. Preferably one with a tiny umbrella. I always wanted one of those," Em joked.

Jimena pulled the straps up on her one-piece, and Em couldn't take her eyes off Jimena. She hadn't expected to have such a visceral reaction to seeing Jimena look so sexy in her suit.

Jimena ran her hands down her body and smiled. "Like what you see?" She winked. "Okay, my sexy lover, let's get those tiny umbrellas."

†

313

The alarm on Em's smartphone blared loudly on the side stand, and Em reached over to shut it off. Jimena stirred next to her and grumbled, "Who sets their alarm on vacation?"

Em popped from the bed and began throwing on shorts and a T-shirt. "Come on, we have to hurry if we're going to catch the sunrise."

"But I don't want to catch the sunrise," Jimena groused. "You seen one, you've seen them all."

"Not in Mexico, I haven't."

"Well, I have." Jimena turned and pulled a sheet over her head in protest.

"Please. It's important to me," Em pleaded.

Jimena tossed the covers aside and moved slowly to the dresser to retrieve clothes. "Oh, all right, but I'm not doing this every morning. You can get up with the birds and chirp with them from here on out. I'm staying in this nice comfy bed. And you can bring back coffee if you feel compelled to rise at O Dark Hundred."

Em laughed and grabbed Jimena's hand, dragging her to the door after donning her own shorts and T-shirt. Em had scoped the perfect spot for the proposal and led Jimena to the beach. The reds, oranges, and golds were starting to streak across the bright blue sky as Jimena and Em settled onto the loungers arranged in neat rows on the beach. The leaves on a large palm tree gently swayed in the light breeze.

Delicate strands of Jimena's dark hair that had escaped the confines of her hastily arranged ponytail fluttered around her face. Em had never seen her look more beautiful than in this morning light. She absently brushed them aside and turned to look at Em when she moved from the lounger and put one knee in the sand.

"What are you doing?" Jimena asked.

"What do you think I'm doing?" Em pulled the ring from her pocket. "I know I'm probably ten years tardy on this question, but better late than never. I gave you that promise ring over fifteen years ago, and now I'd like to make it official." Em opened the ring box and thrust it forward for Jimena to see. "I told your brother I wasn't going anywhere and that once Karl Junior was in jail, we would start our life as a proper lesbian couple. To me, that means marriage and eventually a couple of kids. The number is negotiable." Em grinned. "I'm not getting any younger, and I'd like to start that process sooner rather than later."

"Are you trying to ask me to marry you? Because if you are, I think that is about the longest proposal I've ever heard?"

Em chuckled. "Everyone's a critic. Well?" She raised her eyebrow.

"If you want an answer, you need to use your words and ask the question," Jimena teased.

"Will you please put me out of my misery and agree to marry me?"

"About time. Of course, I will." Jimena pulled the necklace with the promise ring from beneath her T-shirt. "I'm not getting rid of this, though. It will remain around my neck for as long as I live."

"Does that mean you don't want this ring?"

"Now, I didn't say that." Jimena held her hand out. "Gimme."

Em grabbed her hand and turned it over, gently pushing the ring on her finger. "I love you, Jimena. Always have. Always will." Placing a kiss on her lips, she sealed the deal.

"Same. How do you feel about large weddings?"

"Anything to make you smile. Invite the whole damn world for all I care, as long as you walk down that aisle. But I draw the line at wearing a dress."

Jimena smiled. "Dress, tux, tank top, or shorts. That is the least important thing to me. I can't wait for us to tell my family. I only wish Mama and Papa were alive to see this. You might not believe it, but I can feel them looking down on us and smiling brightly. The full sun won't be the only reason we need sunglasses. I couldn't love anyone more than I love you."

When Em's phone buzzed in her pocket, she wrinkled her nose, and her automated response compelled her to glance at who was calling. She almost didn't answer when the number was one she didn't recognize, but her heavily ingrained sense of duty prompted her to hit the button.

"Hello."

"Hey, Em, sorry to disturb your vacation. Is Jimena there with you right now?" Toni asked.

"She is."

"Can you put the call on speaker?"

Em pressed the button to put the call on speaker. "We're listening."

"Somehow, they highjacked the vehicle transferring your mother to an undisclosed location. She's in the wind right now. We thought you should know. But don't worry, we have a way of tracking her. Unless you're opposed, we've determined it's time to eliminate the problem once and for all. We aren't planning on returning her to Homeland Security or anyone else."

"Do what you have to do," Em responded.

"Okay, thanks. We'll be in touch," Toni answered.

"Hey, how is Char doing?" Em asked.

"Good. Thanks for asking. Char will make a full recovery."

"And the baby?" Jimena chimed in.

"She's good, too. Whoops, I mean, they're fine. Char has been training me to use gender neutral terminology."

Em could almost see Toni shrugging with that declaration.

"How would you all feel about coming out of hiding to attend a wedding?" Jimena asked.

"No shit, really?" Toni exclaimed. "Good for you, Em. I assume you did the asking."

"I did."

"Tell us the time and place, and we'll all be there. Now, enjoy the rest of your time off. We want both of you refreshed when we send you on your first assignment. Have several drinks for me. Later."

The call ended, and Em noticed a frown on Jimena's face.

"What's wrong?" Em asked.

"You know what Toni meant by a permanent solution, right? So, you're okay with that?"

"I am. Bridget was never a mother to me. Do you think less of me now?"

"Nope. I still love you like crazy. I understand. I had a front-row seat to all the trauma you endured. Nothing in life is entirely black or white. Shades of gray exist for a reason. That includes morality and ethics."

"Thank you. Now, where were we before we were so rudely interrupted?"

"Planning our epic wedding," Jimena answered.

Em grabbed Jimena's hand, lifted her to her feet, and kissed her with such fervor she could almost feel Jimena swoon in her arms.

ABOUT THE AUTHOR

Annette is an award-winning author, published by Affinity Rainbow Publications, who lives in the beautiful Pacific Northwest with her wife and their four furry kids. With twenty-eight published novels, three Lesfic Bard Awards, and one Goldie Award for her fourth novel, *Locked Inside*, she finally feels like a real author. Annette is as much a reader as a writer and is always looking for the next sapphic novel to queue up. She came up with the One Fan at a Time tagline, because it rolled off the tongue much better than One Reader at a Time. After pondering who she was at her core, she feels it was all about connecting to each reader on a personal level. Annette would be the first to admit she doesn't do well with the masses. If someone picks up her book and it touches them, she believes she has achieved what she wants with her writing by reaching each reader. It is who she is at her core. Drop her a line. She loves to hear from readers.

Email: annettemori0859@gmail.com.
Sign up for her mailing list: http://eepurl.com/cS7nr9
Check out her blog: Everyday Occurrences:
https://annettemori0859.wordpress.com/
Visit the Affinity Rainbow Publications website for her books and many other outstanding authors: www.affinityebooks.com

OTHER AFFINITY BOOKS

Changing Times by Jen Silver

Thirty years on from when we first met Dani Barker and Camila Callaghan in *Changing Perspectives*, they're enjoying marriage and semi-retirement in a luxury flat near London.

Dani's niece, Holly, runs their mixed media business, now gaining a foothold in the highly competitive online games market. Holly's older sibling, Luc, influences people to take action on climate issues with their website, Gaia One: One Earth, One Chance.

Romance has been in short supply for both Holly and Luc. Immersed in her work, Holly's dating life is non-existent. For Luc, family prejudices stand in the way of a relationship with the love of their life.

Can Holly and Luc succeed in making the changes necessary to achieve their own happy ever afters?

Midnight in Nashville by Ali Spooner
The Bentleys have successfully finished cutting their
first album, *Six Strings and a Dream.* When the Covid-19
epidemic hits, tours and live performances are cancelled as
the world goes into lockdown. With the closing of the
restaurant, employment for the band members has been
severely impacted. The group comes together to make life
work at Ma Bentley's Boarding House. They take advantage
of their down time and use of the studio to record more
songs. Cedra has challenged each of her bandmates to create
a song for their next album. Juliet's song, "Midnight in
Nashville," is chosen as the title track. Join the group as they
venture into new marketing avenues and create their first
music video for the title track.

Compound Interest by Annette Mori
The kick-ass women in The Organization are back and
they have their sights set on a few new recruits. Not
everyone is jumping for joy at the choices, considering
subterfuge is front and center in the games the new recruits
have been playing.

Dani is supposed to get her happily ever after, but she's
not sure what's real anymore including Candy's feelings for
her. When a new enemy takes Candy captive, Dani vows to
uncover the truth by insisting on going on the mission to save
her. Candy is not what she seems, and that presents a new set
of complications for Dani and her feelings.

The Organization continues to have challenges when those damn book magicians and book witches keep popping back in to warn them of new catastrophes on the horizon. She doesn't have time for their warnings, until their enemies intersect once again to keep them working together.

From award-winning author, Annette Mori, find out what happens in this final chapter of the combined *Asset Management/Book Addict* series.

Six Strings and a Dream by Ali Spooner
Cedra Tyler's dream of becoming a songwriter in Nashville was put on hold due to her mother's failing health. When the time came for Cedra to start her journey, she left her home in south Alabama with a heavy heart.

Arriving at Ma Bentley's boarding house, meeting her housemates, also fledgling musicians, she feels the warmth she was missing since leaving home.

Her housemates realize Cedra's talent as a song writer and begin to gel as a group. The pain and loss she had experienced added a layer of emotion and longing in her lyrics unusual for someone of her age.

They form a band, The Bentleys, named after Ma who is much more than a landlord to them all. Cedra falls for bandmate Juliet, and that inspires her creativity even more.

Will The Bentleys achieve their dream of making it big in Music City? Has Cedra found her forever in the arms of Juliet?

Trouble in Paradise-Trophy Wives Club book 4 – Ali Spooner & Annette Mori

The gang from the Trophy Wives Club is back. This time they're taking their fun to a new and exciting location. The club's future is looking bright, and as a thank you, Lindy rewards the crew with an all-expenses paid trip to paradise over the holidays. Soon after arriving on the island, an attractive stranger catches the eye of more than one person in their tight-knit group, but Lindy is especially intrigued. Could Angel Dubois, the owner of an all-woman financial planning company be the answer to Lindy's crushing feelings of loneliness? Along with fun in the sun, the gang navigates treacherous waters to ring in the New Year.

Georgetown Glen by Annette Mori

Lucy Manetti is positively euphoric over her recent purchase of an old ghost town. Unfortunately, she failed to consult with her wife, Bea, before buying the abandoned village. Predictably, Bea is not as enamored with transforming the ghost town into a sapphic retirement community, but Bea's love for her wife trumps her displeasure over Lucy's impulsiveness. The mature couple hires Fiona, an expert at restoring old houses, and Saville, a certified electrician, to bring the ghost town back to its glory days.

According to the adorable real estate agent who recommended the pair, Fiona and Saville have *history*. Lucy detects a spark between the two young women and decides, against the advice of her wife, to play matchmaker, bringing her beautiful niece into the mix. As the ragtag team begins their work on the old saloon, they discover a lot more than they bargained for, including ghosts, long-buried secrets, an abused golden retriever, and maybe even love.

Affinity
Rainbow Publications

eBooks, Print, Free eBooks

Visit our website for more publications available online.

https://affinityebooks.com/

Published by Affinity Rainbow Publications
A Division of Affinity eBook Press NZ LTD
Canterbury, New Zealand

Registered Company 2517228

www.ingramcontent.com/pod-product-compliance
Lightning Source LLC
Chambersburg PA
CBHW051528280626
47161CB00021B/424